LORD
VISHNU'S
Love Handles

A SPY NOVEL
(Sort Of)

WILL CLARKE

SIMON & SCHUSTER
New York   London   Toronto   Sydney

SIMON & SCHUSTER
Rockefeller Center
1230 Avenue of the Americas
New York, NY 10020

SIMON & SCHUSTER and colophon are registered
trademarks of Simon & Schuster, Inc.

For information about special discounts for bulk purchases,
please contact Simon & Schuster Special Sales at 1-800-456-6798
or business@simonandschuster.com

Designed by Jaime Putorti

Manufactured in the United States of America

10 9 8 7 6 5 4 3 2 1

Library of Congress Cataloging-in-Publication Data
Clarke, Will.
Lord Vishnu's love handles: a spy novel (sort of) / Will Clarke.
    p. cm.
1. Vishnu (Hindu deity)–Cult–Fiction. 2. Electronic commerce–Fiction. 3. Married people–Fiction. 4. Millionaires–Fiction. 5. Hindus–Fiction. I. Title.
PS3603.L38L67 2005
813'.6–dc22   2004065086
ISBN-13: 978-0-7432-7147-9
ISBN-10:   0-7432-7147-5

For my mom and dad,

Sybil and Dee Clarke

Reality is merely an illusion,
albeit a very persistent one.
ALBERT EINSTEIN (1879–1955)

It's kind of fun to do the impossible.
WALT DISNEY (1901–1966)

I am become Death, Shatterer of worlds.
ROBERT OPPENHEIMER (1904–1967),
CITING THE *BHAGAVAD GITA*, AFTER WITNESSING
THE WORLD'S FIRST NUCLEAR EXPLOSION

1

Dreams More Bitter Than Sweet

Shelby is a slut. She is also my wife. And that presents certain problems. Actually it presents major problems; I just don't like to think about them. Mainly because I have no real way of knowing that Shelby is a slut. I just have these dreams. And I can't exactly say to her over breakfast, "Honey, I had this dream last night that Reed Bindler was knocking your bottom out. And I think this needs to stop."

That would be crazy talk. And I've spent my life pushing crazy talk like that to the back of my mind so that I could lead a normal existence. So that I could have a happy life here in Dallas. With Shelby and our two-year-old son, Noah. We live in a big Mission-style house on Lakewood Boulevard. I've got a green Range Rover and a hyper Border Collie named Max.

It's a good life. And I don't think I should mess it up just because I have bad dreams about Shelby. That would be stupid.

However, to be perfectly honest, I do have this habit of just knowing things. And that scares me. What's wild is my knowledge has no logical basis. I didn't read it in a book or pick it up in conversation. Sometimes I just know. And I'm not talking about getting a weird feeling about lottery numbers or shit like that. I'm talking about full blown, I-know-this-for-a-fact, Jack. Like right now, I know that the phone is about to ring and it's going to be Shelby's mom. And I know that Noah is about to get a sore throat. I can taste it coming on. And sure enough, he gets one. And sure enough, the phone rings and it's my mother-in-law.

This knowing things was what got me into the Internet back before anyone knew it would go colossal. This knowing things has put a very nice roof over our heads. But it is also part of my problem. A therapist once told me I might be crazy. Well, he didn't say that exactly, but I knew what he meant. That's when I stopped talking about what I "know." And I stopped seeing that asshole. Now, I keep what goes on inside my head *in* my head. I just go to work building Web sites and I play golf at the club. I keep my mouth shut. I make money, which makes Shelby happy. And this, in turn, makes me happy.

Or at least, close to happy.

Okay, truth be told, I'm not all that happy. It's the dreams and all this knowing-things-that-I-shouldn't. It stalks me and beats me in the head. Like every time I think Shelby cheats on me. And I think she does this quite often. She fucks the pool guy. She screws her tennis pro. And she nails my best friend and business partner, Reed Bindler, every Wednesday night when she says she's at Bunco. I dream about all of this; and I am afraid that this is true. I know that Shelby loves me. But I keep having these dreams and they are burning me alive.

Now, hold on to your seat because this is where things get really wacko. I think I know why Shelby cheats. I saw it one night after I rolled off her sweaty body and into a dream where her genes, her actual DNA, spoke to me. I know this sounds absolutely crazy, but they told me of their plan. They told me that they were promiscuous genes, programmed by nature to fuck around. Nothing against me, they said. Shelby just has slutty DNA. And from a survival-of-the-fittest perspective, this is a very good thing. Something about a wide range of spawnings adding variety to her own genes and thus ensuring their replication.

This is how her genes told me it works: Shelby marries me, a cerebral provider. They *actually* called me that. A "cerebral provider"? I mean, is that a compliment or is that a put-down? Anyhow, Shelby gets all her food and shelter needs met by me in spades. And our coupling will produce children who share my genes and her genes. This is good for me because my genes tend to be the faithful sort. Matched up with Shelby's slut genes, my seed will spread all over the place. According to Shelby's DNA, our son, Noah, is likely to grow up to be a wealthy philanderer who will father tons of kids out of wedlock—who will in turn grow up and do the same. This will be very good for my genetic proliferation. Morally, though, it kind of sucks. But Shelby's DNA reminded me that evolution is amoral and so is Shelby's sex drive.

It's her way of hedging her evolutionary bets. If there's a war or something and we go back to a primitive society, her hearty offspring from those athletic fucks will survive, whereas my offspring might die because they're too brainy. Plus her genes get the best of both worlds. She can have genetically diverse offspring and still be married to the "cerebral provider" who will use his high IQ and income to raise her bastard kids.

Shelby would tell you this is all horseshit. She will tell you she's never once thought about genetics or evolutionary strategies. And she would be telling you the truth. But her genes have told me the real story. And it's really fucking me up.

So far, we've only had one kid. Noah. And he's mine. I can see it in his eyes; I can read it in his soul. Besides, Noah looks just like I did in baby pictures—all blue eyes, blond hair, and slobber. You see, my DNA has a little trick of its own. My sperm are a fierce sort and my body knows what Shelby's up to. So I fuck her every chance I get. At least once a day. That way my little guys attack and kill all the foreign sperm. So far this has kept her extramarital affairs from fertilizing any eggs. Which is good, considering Shelby refuses to go on the Pill; she says it makes her fat. Plus, her infidelity always peaks when she's ovulating. Or at least that's when my dreams about her infidelity always peak. So far I've been winning. But I'm not sure how much longer me and my little guys can keep up the fight.

Anyway, it really doesn't matter if I'm right about Shelby or not. Either way I'm fucked. Either my wife is cheating on me or I'm a nutcase who thinks DNA chitchats with him. So take your pick. That's why I'm not going to worry about it. I learned a long time ago if you go around digging for answers, you'll only find problems. It's best just to live your life: go to the grocery store, bicker with your wife over your checking account balance, watch TV, and read your kid to sleep. That's where reality is and that's where I try to keep my thoughts these days.

Let me back up here. There's a lot of stuff you need to know other than all this mental crap anyway. First of all, my name is Travis Anderson. I graduated from SMU. Right out of school I started my own Web development company with my fraternity brother, Reed Bindler.

I'm not a bad guy. I'll admit I've paid for a handjob or two at a titty bar. I've cheated a little bit on my taxes. And I lie constantly about my golf game. But then again, who doesn't? The hardest drug I've ever done is pot. And I go to church at Highland Park United Methodist almost every Sunday. I feel confident in saying that I'm the good guy in this story. I would never fuck around on Shelby. (You've got to be kidding if you count the handjobs. I could do that myself. And anything you can do yourself doesn't count.) I'm just your average guy who has had slightly above average luck with his finances.

But unlike Shelby, I didn't come from money. I grew up in a suburb that was planted smack-dab in the middle of a north Louisiana cotton field. We're talking tract houses with carports and station wagons. We weren't poor but we weren't rich, either. We were just white. My childhood was a blur of dirt clod wars, *The Dukes of Hazzard,* and Jiffy Pop. I just happened to test really well. So after high school, I went to SMU on scholarship. It's like my dad always said, "You lie down with dogs and you'll wake up with fleas." And sure enough, after four years of being around all that money, I was itching for cash.

That's when I had this dream about the Internet. I wish I could say that this big revelation was visited upon me from an angel on high. But that wasn't how it happened. I just dreamed about laptop computers; they were everywhere and everyone was using them. It was kind of like a Microscoft commercial. I mean, the Internet was already out there. It was pretty obvious what I should do. So I bought some books about HTML and I taught myself how to build Web sites. Now if I had thought big like maybe Jeff Bezos or Mark Cuban, I would have built my own e-commerce site. However, I didn't. I just built crappy little Web sites for crappy little companies. Now, instead of being a billionaire without any real worries, I'm a millionaire with about a million problems.

In fact, one of my biggest problems is my business partner, Reed. His dad financed my idea back when we graduated. Reed is worthless. He's been my best friend for over ten years now and I've never once heard him say anything that gives any evidence that he's capable of higher thought. He's conceited, mean-spirited, lazy, and completely unfunny. But he drives a silver Boxster and in Dallas that goes a long way.

Oh, yeah. Reed is also bald.

Or he would be bald if he didn't have some Asian's hair sewn to his head every week. Reed zips around uptown in his Porsche with his thick black hair blowing in the wind, acting like he invented sex. The other day I found myself keying his car. Ever since I started having dreams about him and Shelby, I have grown to hate Reed Bindler.

And he knows it, too. I mean, I don't think he knows I keyed his car, but he knows I can't stand him. We never talk to each other anymore. Even at work. I go into my office and he goes into his. We occasionally send each other emails. I hate to say it, but our little company isn't doing so well in this war zone.

But you know what? I don't care. I'm not the one who came from money and I'm not the one who needs it. I could go back to my tract house life. Maybe Shelby couldn't, but I could and I would like it. So I sit in my office and I play on the Internet. There's this site called PsychicCow.com. It's a game where you guess what color the cow's udders are going to be. I beat that cow all day long while I let Mr. Fancy Pants run our company. Let that mutherfucker run it right into the ground and then let's see if he can afford the Porsche and the fake hair. Let's see Reed Bindler with his bald head driving a Ford Taurus and selling insurance. Let's see how Shelby's DNA gets off on that.

I keep obsessing about Reed and Shelby. And I don't even know for sure if they are cheating. I told myself I really didn't want to know. But that's horseshit. I do want to know. I *have* to know. Reed Bindler is a fuck and if he and Shelby are screwing around behind my back, somebody's going to pay. I mean, if I'm right about Reed, then I'm probably right about the pool guy and the tennis pro. Then my dream about Shelby's DNA wouldn't be crazy at all; it would be prophetic.

Here's what I'm going to do. I'm going to send Shelby a book recommendation from Amazon.com. They have this *email-a-friend-about-this-book* thing. Except, instead of putting that it's from me, I'll change the name and return address to Reed's. Within seconds, Shelby will have some approximation of this message in her mailbox:

To: shelbycat@halowire.com
From: reed@andersonbindler.com

SUBJECT: Check out *Cheaters* at Amazon.

Shelby,
Thought you'd be interested in this item at
Amazon.com.
*Cheaters: 180 Telltale Signs Mates are Cheating and
How to Catch Them*
Enjoy!
Reed Bindler

Our Price: $11.17
Availability: Usually ships within 24 hours

2
Udder Madness

I think I'm getting a brain tumor. My head hurts. It has all day.
I think I played too much Psychic Cow. And to top it off,
Shelby's not really speaking to me. That makes me nervous.
Shelby picked up a honey-glazed pork tenderloin and roasted
vegetables from Eatzi's–this meals-to-go place. It smells good,
but I can't eat. I think I'm getting an ulcer. Shelby and I don't
talk while Noah plays with his food and sputters. The tension
between us is thick and soupy; it's giving me cancer.

"What's the matter?" I ask.

"Nothing," she says without looking me in the eye. "I'm
probably just tired."

"How about we go for a walk? Maybe get some fresh air?"

To my surprise, she takes me up on it. So I wipe off Noah
and put him in his baby jogger and the three of us head out.
Shelby breaks into her power walk and I push Noah. The June

sun hangs pink on the horizon and fireflies flash like micro-
scopic paparazzi. This would all be magic if I didn't hate her so
much. We're halfway down the block and Noah has already
fallen asleep.

I hum to myself and act like her silence doesn't bother me.

"So, who is she?" she says out of nowhere.

"What?"

"You heard me." Shelby stops walking.

"What are you talking about?" I quit pushing Noah.

"Don't lie, Travis."

She has obviously read the email. I want to laugh. I want to
spike a football and jump up and down. But I don't. I have to
play this cool. I mean, I was expecting her guilty silence and
complicity, but not this.

"Who is she?" She wipes the sweat from her forehead.

"Okay, back up. Way up. I don't know what you're talking
about."

"Don't do this, Travis." She shakes her head. "Don't lie."
She pulls a folded piece of paper out of her pocket and hands
it to me. "I got this today."

"What?" I unfold the paper and act like I'm reading this
email for the first time. "Oh, this is so not-funny."

Shelby bites her bottom lip and looks down at Noah asleep
in his stroller.

"Shelby. Honey. No. No." I chuckle a little. "This is a joke.
This is Reed's idea of a joke."

"I'm not an idiot, Travis."

"It's a joke. Reed's a sick fuck."

"Why would he do this?" She puts her hand on her hip.

"I don't know. Why does Reed do anything? I mean, why

does he date strippers? Why'd he get lipo?" I shrug. "This is Reed Bindler we're talking about."

"So you're telling me this is all some kind of prank."

"Yes." I look her in the eye. "Out of all my friends, he'd be the last one to narc on anyone. Especially for cheating."

She pauses for a second. She exhales. I can tell by her eyes that she's doing the math.

"Hmmm . . ." She rolls her eyes and then makes this sheep-ish face. "So you're not cheating?"

"No, I'm not."

She takes a deep breath. "Then Reed Bindler is an ass-hole!"

"Yeah, I'd say so." I put my arm around her and kiss her head. She smells sweet and warm—like a cake right out of the oven. She pushes me off her.

"No, I'm serious. I'm pissed. I can't believe he thinks that's funny."

"So what do you want me to do about it?"

"I never liked him. And you know what? He will never step foot in my house again. You got that?"

"Look, I'll talk to him." I start walking and pushing Noah again. "Come on, it's getting dark, and Noah's sacked out."

"What are you going to do?" She jogs to catch up.

"Beat his ass." I smirk.

"Trav, you're thirty-three. You're not beating anyone's ass."

"Well, I'll figure something out."

We get back into a comfortable stride and for the first time all day I can feel my neck and shoulders relax. I can breathe. The tension between us is gone. The betrayal is washed away; we hold hands.

"So Reed got liposuction?" She cracks a mean smile.

"Yeah, two years ago. You knew that."

"No, I didn't." She wipes the sweat from her upper lip with her T-shirt. "The guy got liposuction? Where?"

"His stomach. I think maybe his ass."

"Gross! That is just so . . . I don't know what that is . . ." She shakes her head and kind of cringes.

Okay, I feel like shit. But it feels better than thinking that Shelby's cheating. I mean here I am pushing my boy in his stroller and holding my wife's hand. And her hand is a hand that's faithful and true. I kiss that hand and all is right in my world.

"You're sweet." She winks at me.

No, actually, I'm a total bastard. If she only knew what I did. I'm a complete fucking liar. I don't deserve to hold her hand. I am the asshole, not Reed. I'm a jealous freak of an ass-hole who sends bogus emails to his wife, the woman he vowed to love, honor, and cherish. The woman who bore him this beautiful sleeping son. I am a sick man. But at least now I am free. At least now I know my nightmares aren't real. I'm just a little wacked out with jealousy. That's all. And I can at least work on that. I can fix that. Whereas Shelby screwing the whole world would have been pretty hopeless. That couldn't have been undone. My jealousy is another story. I can wrangle that in. I can be more positive. I can listen to Tony Robbins tapes and fix it.

Anyway, the three of us turn the corner onto Tokalon Avenue, a valley of a street with big green trees and wall-to-wall mansions. We walk into the middle of a lightning bug swarm. It's like the Milky Way. It's great. We stop and just kind of let it happen all around us. All this twinkling and buzzing makes us laugh. I think it's a sign of a happier future. I try to catch one, but Shelby slaps my hand.

"Don't do that."

"Why?"

"Because you'll kill them." She sighs.

"So?"

"So. Just let them be."

"Whatever." I peck her on the cheek. And she wipes it off.

"You're sweaty." She crinkles up her nose. And I think I can hear her DNA giggling like a bunch of little schoolgirls.

Tonight Shelby and I reconnect. I'll spare you the details. But put it this way, we have make-up sex. Widespread crazy make-up sex. The kind that gets angry and then tender and then angry all over again. And this time when I fall asleep, her DNA doesn't make a fucking sound.

But I do have a dream. I'm walking down I-35 here in Dallas. It's abandoned. Not a soul on the road but me. The grass is greener than Easter morning and the highway is made out of smoked salmon. And I'm barefoot. I'm walking on pink fish. It's slippery and soft. It takes me to Texas Stadium, where I stand in the middle of the football field and look up through the giant hole in the ceiling. I look up at the blue sky and I wait for God. It's a good dream.

I wake up happy and I kiss Shelby awake. We do it again and I fix us breakfast before Noah gets up. I fry up some eggs and bacon. I throw some canned biscuits in the oven. And I pour orange juice into old jelly jars. Shelby calls this my "trailer trash special." She prefers a healthy gourmet breakfast like granola, organic fruit, or yogurt. Shelby's a great cook; she's always experimenting with weird shit. But me, my tastes are fairly white-bread. And Shelby will indulge me every once in a while—especially if I've been good. And I figure after last night's little marathon, I've been very good.

"Are you frying bacon?" Shelby walks into the kitchen with Noah around her neck.

"Yeah, and eggs, too." I turn around and hold up my greasy spatula.

"Can you hold him?"

"What? I'm making breakfast." I look at her like she's crazy.

"Hold him! I think I'm gonna puke!" She tosses Noah into my arms and I drop my spatula. Shelby runs out of the kitchen and I hear vomit hit the hardwood in our living room. Noah starts crying. He's not a morning baby.

"Are you okay?" I turn off the stove.

"No. I'm not okay. That smell is making me sick!"

Noah is screaming. I bounce him around and put him in his baby chair. The bathroom door slams, followed by Shelby's retching. The toilet flushes and she shouts at me.

"Get that bacon out of here!"

I take the bacon and the eggs to the backyard and feed them to our dog, Max. When I get back, Noah is red faced and screeching so I fix him a bottle; he gets happy fast. Shelby, on the other hand, stays pissed at me for the next three days.

Shelby is pregnant. She hasn't said anything, but you don't have to be psychic to figure that out. I just hope it's mine. What am I saying? Of course it's mine. Jealousy is a very bad thing. It eats you from the inside like a worm and I need to get a grip before it ruins my life. I need things between Shelby and me to be good. Especially now, because my business is in the shitter. It's like I've woken up from one bad dream only to find myself in another. My company is hemorrhaging. Reed has completely fucked us. Come to think of it, that must have been what the Reed and Shelby dreams were all about. Reed *was* fucking me over. Just not with Shelby.

We've lost all but two of our clients and our bills are at least 120 days past due. We're going to have to let people go before we start bouncing paychecks. And Reed is freaking out. Not about letting our employees go. He could give a shit. Turns out he got a call from the IRS. Reed fucked up our taxes this year. So we're being audited on top of all this. And I have a feeling that a lot of our cash flow went straight up his nose and that's going to be awfully hard to explain to Uncle Sam.

This is all my fault. I've been fiddling around on the Internet while Rome burns. And I knew this. I wanted this. Now everything I've busted my ass for is going down the drain. And I wish I could say that I had lots of savings and that this won't affect Shelby and Noah. But it will. As CEO of Anderson-Bindler.com, I make about $250 an hour. However, Shelby spends about $260 an hour. So we're pretty much screwed. And then there're Shelby's credit cards; she's racked up platinum amounts of debt. Meanwhile, I reinvested all my capital into growing this business. This company was our nest egg. And I've let it all go to shit. Having a hyperactive imagination is a luxury I can no longer afford.

It's time I lived in the real world and got my shit together. It's time I get Reed to ask his dad for a loan.

*   *   *

It happened again today. The premonitions are back. I saw
Sarah's death. She's Reed's assistant. She has lung cancer. Or
she will have lung cancer. Which is weird because she doesn't
smoke and she's only twenty-three. But God's big cartoon
hammer will come down and bonk her on the head within the
year. The tiny spot in her lung will metastasize and it will
spread like black ants inside her. I know I was going to try and
get a grip on this, but my thoughts are too liquid right now to
control. Things spill out of me. While at other times, people's
thoughts and destinies spill into me. And this is worrying me.
This is a sign of major mental illness. This is schizophrenia. Or
if I'm lucky, I'm just bipolar.

Whatever it is, I am not right in the head, and you have no
idea how hard I am fighting to keep it good. How hard I am
trying not to snap. I am brittle and dry and I can feel a forest
fire coming my way. That's why I keep a bottle of vodka in my
desk. It's Monopolowa. A really good Polish potato vodka. It
dampens my mind and fireproofs my soul. It is my trusty
friend and thirsty savior.

I pull up the Web and I go to MentalHealth.com. I do their
little online diagnosis. According to their stupid tests I have
Schizotypal Personality Disorder, Cyclothymic Disorder, Borderline Personality Disorder, Paranoid Personality Disorder,
and Alcohol Dependence. I'm either a hypochondriac or I'm
Charlie-fucking-Manson. To keep from slitting my wrists, I
take another shot of vodka and a hit of Psychic Cow.

I should have stuck to my original philosophy: Don't go
looking for answers because you'll only find problems. That is
the only truth I know. But did I follow it? Fuck, no. I had to go

and rip the lid off Pandora's box and now my shit is flying everywhere. So I take another shot and play the sacred cow in a game of psychic prowess. I'm seventeen for twenty guesses. Damn, I'm good; I take another shot to celebrate my mighty, but defective, brain. At least there's something I can do right. Even if it is outguessing a stupid computer cow. I nurse the bottle and the vodka makes glug-glug noises like a sinking ship. I polish it off and gasp for air. My eyes tear up and the room spins. It's the first time in about a year that I feel warm and safe. However, my one moment of calm is shattered by my phone ringing.

I pick it up and answer, "Travis Anderson's Home for Wayward Girls."

"Mr. Anderson?" a woman's voice floats into my ear.

"Speaking."

"Travis Anderson?"

"Yeah. Who the fuck is this?"

"This is Debra McFadden. I'm with the IRS."

"What do you mean, he said no?" I shout.

"He said no." Reed shakes his head. "The old man said no."

"Yeah, but what kind of 'no' was it? Was it 'no' that's too much, or 'no' not right now?"

"It was 'no' as in 'no-fucking-way.' " Reed glares at me.

"Did you tell him how much trouble we're in?"

"Yes, Travis, I told him."

"And what did he say?" I sit down in this leather sling of a chair across from Reed's desk.

"He told me federal prisons have nice golf courses."

"You've got to be kidding me!"

"After the stroke the old man's become a real bastard."

"Well, get power of attorney or something. He's obviously out of his head."

"I've already tried that. Didn't work."

"Then we are fucked!" I throw my hands up. "We are completely fucked!"

"Look, we'll figure something out." Reed taps his Mont Blanc against his palm.

"*We* will figure something out? *We*, Reed? You're the one who didn't pay our taxes. You're the one who's pissed off all our clients. And you're the one whose expense reports are full of titty bar tabs."

"Hey, you've gone there as much as I have." Reed flips his hair out of his face and twirls his pen in between his fingers.

"No, I have not. Not ninety thousand dollars worth."

"It was client entertainment," he says.

"Look, Reedy-boy, all I know is I went hands off for a couple of months and in that time you managed to completely bleed this company dry."

"Hands off? Dude, you were completely checked out. And now you're pissed at me? I've been doing your job *and* mine!"

I fight my way out of the sling chair and stumble to my feet.

"That is such bullshit. You and I both know you've fucking snorted this company up your goddamn nose!"

"Get. Out." Reed points to the door.

"I'm not through discussing this with you!" I cross my arms.

"Discuss it with my lawyers." Reed clenches his teeth and holds his Mont Blanc like a knife.

I turn around and leave because the only thing left to do is punch the bastard in the nose.

Golf is not real life. In golf, there are set rules. And most important, there is always beer. This is why I like golf better than life; you can get snot-slinging drunk and you can still play, usually better than when you're sober. And there's not going to be some five hundred-pound gorilla sent by the government to chase you down because you took a couple of strokes off your score card. That's what real life is for. Real life does not have rules. Sure, people say that it does. But it's really a free-for-all. Anything can happen. The potential for disaster blows my mind. And unlike golf, people get pissy when you show up drunk.

Today I have opted for the golf course instead of the office. Because I need to drink. A lot. And I need some rules that I can rely on. I don't need to see people's malignant futures or hear their stupid boring thoughts. And I don't need to be harassed by the IRS. I feel like I am about two weeks away from making one of those aluminum foil space hats—the kind that bums wear to deflect cosmic rays and shit. That is how crazy I feel.

Anyway. I load up my clubs and cooler into my cart and I head out to the driving range. My tee time isn't until ten. I have almost two hours and at least a twelve-pack to kill. The last few times I was out on the course, I was slicing like a retard. But a good beer buzz helps me adjust my grip. Somehow, beer magically strengthens your grip and reduces your slice. However, too much beer can fuck up your aim. It's like an algebra problem: How many empty beer cans per hour equals a straight trajectory? It's a problem I've been trying to figure out since college. But before I can get down to the drunken mathematics of my golf game, my cell phone rings. I answer it.

"Hello."

"Hello, Mr. Anderson. This is Debra McFadden with the IRS."

"Oh, hi." Talk about a buzz-kill.

"Yes," she smacks. "I was wondering when we could schedule an appointment."

"Oh yeah, can I get back with you on that? I'll have to talk with my accountant."

"Actually, we could just talk one on one. Maybe work something out. That is, if you're willing to work with me."

"Work something out?"

"Oh, sure. You betcha." She smacks some more. "How about I drop by your house sometime this week. It'll take the sting out of it. I promise."

"You really think that will help?" I take another long sip.

"Cooperation always helps, Mr. Anderson."

"I guess this Wednesday would be okay. I'll have to ask my wife, though."

"Great. Wednesday it is. Let's say seven-ish?"

"Seven sounds good." I hold the cold silver can against my sweaty head.

"I'll see you then, Mr. Anderson."

I can hear the lipstick-stained smile in her voice.

"Okay. Thanks. Bye."

"Bye."

I put my cell phone back in my golf bag. I close my eyes and chug the rest of my beer. That's when this vision pops up in front of me. It's a pink and chlorine-blue morning. It's swimming lessons at the country club. I can even smell the sunscreen and diaper wipes. The water babies are wearing their orange floaties. Some are crying and spitting. Some are laughing and splashing. I zero in on this little boy with big blue eyes and a Michelin Man body. He's rubbing the water off his cheeks with his pudgy little hands. He's laughing.

And then *shlush!* The little tyke is yanked under. There's this thrashing about and a craggy tail slaps the water. Everyone around the pool freezes as the lifeguard jumps in after the kid. It takes a couple of seconds for everyone to figure it out. But it's when a cloud of blood rolls through the water that all the mothers scream and jump in after their own kids. Meanwhile, this alligator the size of a horse drags the little boy to the deep end. One orange floatie pops up to the surface while the monster rolls over and over on the child.

This is what I see when I shut my eyes. I see horrible things. I see shit that would drive most folks insane. I open my eyes; the sun gives me a headache. I pop another cold one and guzzle away all this bullshit.

After a couple of bitter cold sips, I calm down and stop thinking crazy. And this is what I figure: I reckon that little boy was me. Here I am floating in my beer all happy and shit, while Debra McFadden just sneaks up and pulls me under. I think that's my subconscious trying to tell me that I shouldn't have invited her to my house. At least I hope that's what my subconscious was trying to tell me. Put it this way, just to be safe, Noah won't be going to any more swimming lessons.

It's easy to cry. Especially when you're this drunk and this alone. Shelby's at her Bunco game tonight and Noah's asleep. It's just me and this bottle. But I won't cry. Because I don't do that. I don't care how bad things get. I don't care if I'm in prison for tax evasion and I'm getting gang-raped, I won't cry. That's because I have this theory about tears. I think your tear ducts are evolution's way of alerting others to the fact that you need to be taken out. I know that sounds rough, but if you really think about it, what other reason is there? We only do it when we're weak or wounded. As soon as your enemies see you cry, they move in for the kill. As soon as your mate tastes the salt on your cheek, she knows you're no longer a viable partner. Tears have never helped me. However, the resolve that holds them back has. After all, God helps those who help themselves.

I think some philosopher said, "Men are their actions." I'm no deep thinker, but I think this is one of the great truths of life. See, in my book, if you cry, you're a loser. If you act crazy, then you're a nut. The thoughts behind your actions are pretty inconsequential. Hell, you can think about all sorts of things. Math. Taxes. Football. Sex. Food. Or even something crazy like alligators in swimming pools. But these thoughts are not you. You are not math. You are not taxes. You are not an alligator in a swimming pool. But if you let your thoughts manifest into action, then you are that action. It's simple. If you murder, you're a murderer. If you fuck around on your spouse, you're a piece of shit. Theoretically, you can be nuttier than Chinese chicken salad, but so long as your actions are normal, then so are you. What's going on inside your head is your own business. And nobody needs to know about it.

I like this philosophy. It gives me a great deal of comfort. It's almost as good as this tequila.

3

Fluxion, Friction, Fucking, Fusion

Supper Club is this thing we do with other couples. It's this decade's answer to swinging. Except instead of swapping spouses, you swap recipes for Curried Coconut Lamb and shit like that. Tonight is our night to host the club and I've promised Shelby that I won't get drunk and start weirding people out.

Last time, Jim and Lisel Thomas hosted the club. They served Kobe steak with this jalapeño-papaya chutney. It sucked. So instead of eating, I drank gallons of hot sake and got a little sloppy. I started seeing things. Elves. Leprechauns. Lucky Charms.

According to Shelby, I had no problem with telling folks all about this. Most of that night was a drunken blur. At least it was until I got home and puked up all that Japanese rubbing alcohol.

The only person that I do remember is Blythe Mitchell, Shelby's friend from Junior League. She looked like the Blessed Virgin of Guadalupe that night. All bright light and roses. She was beautiful and I think I whispered this to her. I also think this pissed off her husband, Carter—even though he's far too moneyed and polite to say anything.

That's probably why the Mitchells aren't coming tonight. They must still be pissed. Because Shelby's grilling Chilean sea bass and nobody misses Supper Club when there's free sea bass. It's too bad. I really wasn't hitting on Blythe. I was just drunk and I thought I saw her soul. So I told her. Which is yet another example of why you should let your morals, not your random thoughts, dictate your actions.

To avoid future fuck-ups as well as get a grip on myself, I've stopped drinking. I mean, I'll still drink socially. After all, to just up and quit would smack of AA. And then the rumors would fly. I mean these Supper Club people really love to kick folks when they're down. In fact, two supper clubs ago, we found out Lisel and Jim couldn't have kids.

Poor Jimbo's impotent.

I figure my plate's full enough without a bunch of Brie-eating assholes talking shit about me over their martinis. That's why tonight it's a two-drink limit for me. That way I'll hold off the gossip and still play the good host.

People should be getting here any second now. Noah's up-stairs with his baby-sitter. And Shelby's running around in her slip making everything glow and shine. She's got fresh flowers and candles everywhere. The house is full of good smells—sesame oil, ginger root, teriyaki, garlic.

And just when I'm about to pop a cold one, the doorbell rings.

"Get the door, Travis!" Shelby darts out of the kitchen and up the stairs to finish getting dressed.

My job tonight is to man the grill, get the door, and mix the drinks. Shelby's job is to cook, make things nice, and remind me when I'm not doing my job. I run my hands through my hair, check my breath, and open the door with the most sincere smile I can muster.

It's Jim and Lisel. They're always on time. Shelby says it's because they don't have kids, but I disagree. I've known Jim since college, and he's always had this weird military compulsion about time. He goes off hitting walls and shit if he's late. In fact, I thought I saw a red mark on Lisel's arm once when they were almost late for Supper Club. But then again, I do have an overactive imagination.

"Trav!" Jim gives me our fraternity's secret handshake and Lisel smiles from behind his broad shoulder.

"I think I smell garlic and . . ." Lisel sniffs. "And ginger! Omigod, it smells like my Japanese marinade! Is that what that is?"

"I have no idea. It sure does smell good, though." I wave them in.

"Well, I bet Shelby decided to use my recipe. That little stinker." She nudges me as she walks past.

"And look at the flowers!" She surveys the house. "Absolutely gorgeous! Did Shelby pick these up at Eatzi's?"

Okay, Lisel's already being a bitch. See, when you host Supper Club, there's this unspoken rule that it's cheating to go to Eatzi's, because they'll do everything for you. But Shelby only bought the appetizers and flowers from there. She's been marinating sea bass all day long, so Lisel really needs to shut up.

"To be honest with you, I'm not sure where she got them. How about a drink?"

"Yeah, Shelby got these at Eatzi's." Lisel fluffs up the bouquet and then smells it. "I saw these there this morning. They're just *gorgeous.*"

"How about you, Jim?" I open a beer and take a swallow. "What's your poison?"

"The usual. Gin and tonic. Extra lime." Jim winks at Lisel.

"How about you, Lisel?" I take another swig to wash down the heartburn these two are giving me.

"I'll have a glass of OJ." She rearranges Shelby's flowers.

"Are you sure? We've got a really nice white burgundy over here." I hold up the bottle.

"You know, I'd love to, but I can't." She bites her bottom lip and then whispers, "I'm pregnant."

I blink at Jim as little blue Viagra pills dance around his head.

"Jim! You dog!" I punch him in the arm. "Congratulations, man."

"Thanks." He glances down at his shoes and tries to act modest.

"When's it due?" I hand Lisel her juice.

"Early to mid-February." She tilts her head and rubs what will soon be her belly.

I hold up my beer. "Here's to a healthy baby. Cheers!"

We clink our glasses and they chirp.

"To a healthy baby!"

And that's when I have to fight back the tears. Because I

see Jim and Lisel's future. I see their stillborn child and all the horrible sadness that she's swaddled in.

"Oh, look. How sweet." Lisel pats me on the back. "I think Travis is a little choked up for us."

Shelby is keeping her eye on me. She just picked up my beer and took it into the kitchen. She's a little pissed. I can tell. I haven't kept to my two-drink limit. But I have stuck with beer and I've only had four. And a half. Which is no big deal at all. Besides, she doesn't see what I see. My mind's got a mind of its own and a few beers always help it behave. So long as I don't overdo it.

Poor Jim and Lisel, they've been bragging about their pregnancy all night. And everybody is toasting them and making jokes about Jim changing diapers and not getting any for the next year. It's sick. Life is sick. It's all a cruel joke. Sure, Lisel is as fake as her tits and Jim's a control freak, but they don't deserve this. Nobody does. But what do you do? I'm not sure what I saw was even real. So I can't say anything. And if I did, what good would it do? What could I really do to fix this? Nothing. All there's left to do is eat and drink and talk about people and order shit out of catalogs. If you think about it, that's what we're all doing here. We're all in pain. But unlike all my friends here, I seem to be the only one aware of it.

I look around this living room with its big red walls and golden pillows. And all I see is death. Zombies with trendy haircuts. A bunch of Banana Republicans on Prozac and cocaine. We're all hiding in this alphabet soup of status. Our IPOs. Our BMWs. Our Starbucks CDs. Our kids' high IQs. But it's not working. Because we're all going to die. Because we're all the sons and daughters of Eve. And she ate that fuck-

ing apple. She swallowed the seeds whole and from them grew
the toil of men and the pain of women.

Jesus, I sound crazy. Sons and daughters of Eve?

Please.

Where do I get this shit? No wonder I drink so much. I
can't stand to hear myself think sometimes.

Anyway. Back to the party. Everybody's eating dried figs
smeared with blue cheese and drinking expensive white wine.
This is not of God. He did not intend for certain things to be
eaten together; it says so in the Bible. I'm sure figs spread with
funky cheese is in there somewhere. Have you ever eaten a
dried fig? They taste like raisins with a problem, and they look
like tumors. Plus, did you know that the same fungus that gives
you jock itch is the same stuff swirling around in blue cheese?
No, thank you. I'll stick with Cheetos and beer.

However, grilled sea bass is another story. It's amazing. Or
it will be amazing as soon as we get done cooking it. Shelby's
got her Williams-Sonoma apron on and she's standing over my
shoulder, telling me exactly how to cook these suckers. We are
"just caramelizing the marinade," she tells me. That's because
Shelby doesn't work the grill. I do. Shelby doesn't like to
sweat—at least not at parties. But I don't mind standing between her and the flames. After all, she's the olive in my martini. The tasty morsel in a world that's bitter and cold. I turn
away from the grill to get an eyeful of her. Her chest is full
against her white apron, and with the smoke clouds swirling
around her face, she looks like an angel.

I wink at her.

She smiles.

"Look, Travis." She points. "That one. Don't let it burn."

"You're beautiful. You know that?"

"Stop staring at me and do your job." She crosses her arms.

"I can't help it." I turn around and flip the fish in question. It sizzles.

"Thank God." She begins to breathe again. "I'll kill you if you let those burn."

Shelby is a serious hostess. She's taken classes on it. Actually, all this Martha Stewarting is what makes Shelby shine. I know that sounds sexist, but this is her calling. She's a genius at nesting. Nothing makes Shelby happier than throwing a dinner party that looks like it was cut out of a magazine. And that's exactly the way tonight has been unfolding—with all the silver and figs and white burgundies.

We go to bed with all the dirty dishes in the sink. Shelby's rule since we got married has always been "the cook doesn't clean." Which means our housekeeper, Valya, does the dishes when she gets here in the morning. Valya is great. She's this old Russian woman who came to the States during the Cold War. Her English is spotty and she's got arms the size of Christmas hams, but she's a nice old lady. Noah calls her "Baba"—that's Russian for grandma. That's because Valya only speaks to him in Russian. The cool thing is Noah can answer her back. It's a pretty sweet deal. Especially considering how hard it is to get into a good private school these days. Knowing Russian will definitely bump Noah to the top of the waiting lists.

Anyway, Valya will let herself in and we'll wake up to a clean house and a happy kid. Shelby and I always sleep in after a Supper Club. It wipes us out. So I'm really surprised this morning when Shelby wakes me up with her tongue in my ear and her hand in my boxers. She kisses and bites my chest and then she goes down on me. Shelby makes me so hard it hurts.

She climbs back up and breathes in my ear, "Fuck me."

And that's exactly what I do. She pulls up her nightgown and I pound her like she's never been pounded before. She's wet, almost too wet. Which is weird because Shelby doesn't usually like doing it in the morning. In fact, the only time she gives me morning sex is when she feels guilty. But I don't see her K-Y on the nightstand. So maybe she really is this horny. If she's not, she's putting on one hell of a show. She's moaning and groaning something fierce. And then it dawns on me that our bedroom door is wide open. What if Noah walks in? Shelby's been all sorts of kinky lately, and what if Noah walks in on something like that?

"Wait." I stop. "The door's open."

"Don't worry about it." She grabs my ass and pulls me in deeper. "Valya took him to swimming lessons."

"Where?" I see the alligator dragging Noah under a mushroom cloud of blood.

"Come on." Shelby rolls her hips. "They'll be gone for at least an hour."

I pull out and jump to the floor.

"What are you doing?" She sits up.

"I don't have time to explain!" I put on my boxers.

"Where are you going?"

I don't answer and run down the stairs.

"Travis!"

I just keep running. I grab my keys off the kitchen counter, run out to the garage in my shorts, and get into my Range Rover. The garage door creeps open and I peel out of the driveway. I keep seeing that alligator. That huge monster tearing my son apart. And then it occurs to me that I forgot my rifle. How am I going to kill the mutherfucker if I don't have a gun? What if I'm already too late? Goddamn it! I don't have time to turn around. Fuck it! I'll kill the bastard with my bare hands if I have to. I won't let this happen. So I floor it and run every red light that keeps me from my little boy.

When I do get to the club, I don't park. I leave the Range Rover running and haul ass to the pool.

I spot Noah. He's all the way on the other side of the pool with the other water babies and his swim teacher, Becky. I tear after him. My heart's beating like a caged hummingbird and my eyes are locked on Noah. He's got his orange floaties on and he's splashing and laughing just like the vision. He's rubbing the water off his cheeks. I get to the pool's edge and I dive in. I fight and slap the water that keeps me from Noah. I grab him up in midstroke and hold him up out of the pool. I get him out of there as fast as I can. Valya comes running up to us and I hand her Noah. "Here, keep him out of the water."

Valya holds Noah and he cries into her fat neck.

"Mr. Anderson, what are you doing?" Becky holds a little girl who's learning to kick.

"Get the kids out!" I grab a little boy and set him on the edge of the pool next to Noah. "Now!"

"Omigod! What's the problem?" She starts helping me.

"Just do it!" I grab the kids two by two and pass them off to the women who are now running up to the pool.

"Travis? What's wrong?" Shelby's friend Blythe asks.

"Here, take her." I hand her a kicking and screaming little girl. "Get everyone away from the pool!"

"But why?"

"Hurry!" I beg.

Blythe must see the fear in my eyes because she directs the kids and their moms to a cabana. After I hand off the last kid, I jump out, shaking with adrenaline and spitting out fear. I take Noah from Valya and we both cry like babies. I know what I said about tears, but I can't help it. I let them fall while Valya just stands there and holds a beach towel around both me and Noah. That's when Becky comes up to me, all nervous and shaky.

"Wh-what was it?" she studders. "What was the problem?"

"An alligator." I exhale, and smooth Noah's hair.

"Huh?" Her mouth drops. "Is this some kind of joke?"

"No, there's an alli—" I look over the pool and nothing is in it but a big green alligator raft and some kickboards.

"Oh" is all that falls out of my mouth.

"This isn't funny, Mr. Anderson. Safety is not a joke!" Becky puts her hand on her hip and then turns around to the scared moms and shouts, "Okay, everyone! Back in the pool! The kids are OH-KAY! False alarm!"

She looks me up and down.

"I think you need to take your son and leave." She actually snarls at me.

That's when I feel the stare of a hundred mama lions. They're holding their cubs and growling at me. These mothers are ready to pounce. Even Valya is shaking her head. She won't even look at me. She just prays under her breath in Russian and crosses herself.

This is not a good morning.

4

The Blue Guy Blues

Shelby has called all my friends and family for an intervention. She says I'm an alcoholic. She says I'm crazy. She's got everybody scheduled to come over sometime next week, after I meet with the IRS. Shelby has even talked to lawyers about our tax liability if I'm found insane. But they told her that Unkie Sam will come and take everything whether you're crazy or not. This did not sit well with Shelby. Shelby has never been poor and she's told me she's not about to start now. I think this is what's motivated her whole push for my sobriety. Because I've been a heavy drinker since college and Shelby knew that when she married me. But then again, I was a twenty-six-year-old millionaire and when you're young and rich, people tend to overlook a lot of character flaws. When you're crazy and broke, they're not nearly as forgiving.

But get this: Shelby hasn't told me she's pregnant. I don't

reckon she thinks I could handle it right now. And she's probably right. I cracked yesterday. I completely embarrassed myself in front of all of her friends at the pool. I wouldn't be surprised if Shelby didn't also talk to the lawyers about getting a divorce. I guess I really wouldn't blame her. I'm a loser of a husband. I've fucked up our lives. And the worst part for Shelby is that I'm not even being discreet about it.

I feel so hopeless that I've even thought about offing myself so Shelby, Noah, and the new baby could have the life insurance money. But I've checked my policy and it doesn't cover suicide. So I'm stuck. Here. Waiting. Waiting for this audit and intervention. Waiting for the humiliation of my friends and family telling me that they would be better off with me in a nuthouse. Waiting to have everything I've worked for taken away by this big government. Put it this way, if I didn't have a drinking problem before now, I will after this is all over.

And here's the kicker: I'm being followed. Well, I'm sort of being followed. There's this blue guy in an orange sheet and when I'm walking around town, I can feel him about two steps behind me. But when I turn around, I only catch a glimpse of him and then he's gone. I've used every ounce of willpower that I have to ignore him. To tell myself it's just my imagination. But it's seriously creeping me out. Because I know no one else can see him. I know he's a figment. Hallucinations are a major symptom of dementia. Plus, this blue dude is just so quiet and still. It's like all the noise and chatter in the world drops away when he's around. It's eerie. It chills me to the bone. He showed up a week ago when I was chowing down on some waffle fries at Chick-fil-A. There he was, sitting in the booth across from me, smiling like he knew something. Like he knew I was the only person who could see him and he thought this was fucking hilarious.

I run to the nearest liquor store every time I see that blue mutherfucker. But lately even drinking doesn't keep him away. You know what I really think? I think God is playing evil tricks on me. Just like he did to Job in the Bible. But I've got news for God: I ain't like Job. I'm just not that faithful. I'm not that solid or good. So these tests are a complete waste of His time and mine. Because I'm not cut out for sainthood, and of all people, God should know that.

Agent Debra McFadden is sitting in my living room drinking her caramel macchiatto and smoothing her hand over our silk pillows. She's nice, very nice. In fact, Debra McFadden looks like she should be driving carpool in Plano. Or making something with a glue gun. But she does not look like she should be working for the IRS. Not with her headband and her pleated jeans. Plus, she smiles too much. And she drinks caramel macchiattoes. She even apologized for not picking one up for me. But she said she didn't know what blend tax evaders preferred. She was then nice enough to explain that she was joking. But I still didn't laugh. She was also nice enough to apologize for making such an asinine remark. Agent Debra McFadden is just so fucking nice that I can't stand her.

"Okey-dokey, Mr. Anderson." She pulls out this huge file folder from her bag. "Let's get down to the nitty-gritty."

Debra McFadden speaks in rhymes. Debra McFadden was spawned by Satan.

"You, Mr. Anderson, have been a very lazy taxpayer." She

fans out my past five tax returns on our coffee table. "And from the look of this place here, I doubt you make just sixty thousand."

"What? I never filed something like that." I pick up the photocopied form. And sure enough the total income box reads 60K and my signature is at the bottom of it. "This can't be right."

"Oh, Mr. Anderson, if I had a dime for every time I heard that one." She puts her hand on her heart and laughs with her mouth closed.

"No, but really. This is my signature. But this isn't my tax form," I say.

"Well, it's right here in black-'n'-white, my friend."

"This isn't my tax form. I've never made less than three hundred thousand a year since I started my company."

"Then you admit you've been cheating the government?" She puts her hand on my knee to comfort me.

"No!" I push her hand off me. "I'm saying that tax form is a fake!"

"Now don't go and get yourself into a sticky wicket by accusing me of a trumped-up audit. Because, buster, I've got all your originals back at the office."

"Then I suggest you get the fuck out of my house and don't come back until you have them."

She gasps, "I'm just doing my job, Mr. Anderson."

"Well, if your job is to fuck me up the ass!" I stand up. "Then you're definitely doing your job!"

"I don't have to tolerate this." She gathers up her papers. "I *will* report and document this."

"Yeah, report and document this." I grab my crotch.

"Trust me, I will." She then walks herself to the door and out of my house.

I am smiling big. This would be great. This would be better than great. It would be fucking awesome. That is if it really happened. But this little melodrama is only happening in my head. Because I'm too spineless to ever do something like that. My incisors just aren't sharp enough to tear into the IRS. Besides, the tax forms are correct. So instead, what really happens is Debra McFadden and I sit in my living room, going over all my tax forms for hours. I nod my head a lot and she sips her latte and breathes her ass breath in my face. And I just sort of zone out and keep imagining different scenarios where I tell her off.

Then she asks me a question that jars me awake.

"So you like to play the Psychic Cow, I see?"

What?" I shake the cobwebs out of my head.

"PsychicCow.com. You play that game a lot." She unfolds this spreadsheet of all the sites I visit. "And you're good. Probably the best we've ever seen."

"How do you know all this?"

She puts her latte down and tucks her hair behind her ears.

"Mr. Anderson. We know a lot of things about you."

"Huh?" I rub my eyes to make sure I'm not dreaming all this.

"PsychicCow.com was a Web site developed by an independent government contractor, to find people like you." She pulls out a brochure that says Shimmer, Inc. "Here, I want you to read this."

"I don't understand." I start to shake.

*   *   *

Okay. And I thought I was crazy. Well, I ain't got nothing on the U.S. government. Hell, they've got their very own Psychic Friends' Network. Or, according to this brochure, they used to. The CIA actually had this psychic spy program called Project Stargate. It was a top secret "remote viewing" center in Fort Meade, Maryland. Debra McFadden tells me that certain right-wing types in the army and the CIA were wigged out by all this hocus-pocus. Some saw it as just plain bullshit, while others feared that it was trafficking with the devil. Consequently, these concerned folks leaked the project to the press.

Debra says Stargate was terminated shortly thereafter, in 1995. I guess taxpayers were about as fond of Army-issued crystal balls as they were of two-thousand-dollar toilet seats. So today Stargate is officially dead. But according to this brochure, many of its top brass have gone into the private sector by forming Shimmer, Inc. They offer their remote viewing services to corporations and to law enforcement agencies. It says here that they specialize in finding missing people, particularly children.

And PsychicCow.com, well, that's how Shimmer finds their new talent. That's how, according to Debra, I'm going to get a little tax break. Uncle Sam still uses these guys; Shimmer's a "government contractor." Debra says that if I pass some tests and they sign me on as a remote viewer, then Reed and I will be forgiven all our trespasses against the IRS—all five million dollars' worth.

I kick ass at Psychic Cow and some higher-ups with the government are really excited about this. And here's the best part: Shimmer will even pay me to train and then later on, I'll be on retainer with them for something like 100K a year. Which isn't a whole lot, but it'll help.

Later down the road, I'll even be eligible for stock options. Don't ask me how this all works. I didn't know the Internal Revenue Service was in the business of cutting deals. Actually, this has the CIA written all over it. But you know what? I'm not about to look a gift horse in the mouth. If being "psychic" means I'm cleared of my back taxes, then I'm the Amazing-fucking-Kreskin. I mean, if all I have to do is beat that cow in some kind of test, then I'm home free. I do that every day on the Internet.

My face is cramping because I'm smiling so hard. Maybe I'm not a wack job after all. Maybe I've got a gift. Maybe I just need to learn how to control it and then my life will be all better. Then perhaps I won't have to go into rehab. This is a very good thing. And right now, Debra McFadden is my favorite person in the whole wide world. I almost French kiss her when she leaves. But instead, I give her a big wet smack on the lips.

"Thank you," I say. "You don't know how much this means to me."

I think this kind of weirds her out. But, boy, does she have bad breath. Talk about shit mouth. I mean, they're called Altoids, Debra. Eat one. Jeez.

"Oh, and by the way, Mr. Anderson," Debra keeps me from closing the door behind her. "What we just discussed . . ."

"Top Secret. I know."

"No. It's beyond Top Secret. Don't mention this to your partner. Or your wife."

"I can't even tell Shelby?"

"Wives like to gossip, Mr. Anderson." She smiles with her mouth closed. "If this gets out, we abort and you pay us what you owe us."

"Oh. Okay." I feel dizzy. I don't have five million dollars. I also don't have a wife who can keep her mouth shut.

"Mum's the word," I say.

"I recommend that it stays that way." She tilts her head and stares at me. "Good night, Mr. Anderson."

"Good night."

Debra McFadden walks across my lawn and gets into her Chevy Malibu. She drives away into the tree-lined night. I can still smell her. Her breath is on my lips. It tastes like blue cheese and dried figs.

Shelby is not amused. My good mood only seems to piss her off. She's really upset with me. She cries a lot. And she doesn't get out of bed until noon. I want to grab her and tell her that everything will be all right. That we just won the lottery. But I can't. Because as much as I love Shelby, I know she has no vault. Hell, she told her tennis group that I had hemorrhoids. And that she didn't come for the entire first year of our marriage. And that we had to buy those "Good Sex" tapes to teach me how to get her off. Shelby blabs in confidence to her girl-friends, who in turn confidently blab to everyone in Dallas. If I tell Shelby that the IRS is cutting us a deal, I might as well announce it on a loudspeaker at the Lakewood Country Club, and then go canvass North Park Mall with flyers. Shelby thinks she's the queen of discreet, but she couldn't keep a secret if our lives depended on it. And this time, our lives really do depend on it. So for her own good, she'll just have to think we're doomed.

Don't get me wrong, the temptation to tell her is unbearable, especially when she starts to cry. That's when I want to hold her and tell her that we're okay. But she won't even let me touch her. I sleep in the guest room now—after the whole alligator incident. And there's no comforting her with silent strength. Because she doesn't think I have any. Plus, all this turmoil can't be good for the baby she's carrying. It's making Shelby really neurotic. She's pulled off all of her fake nails and bitten away at her cuticles. The fear is blistering up in her. I can see it in her pretty blue eyes. She's never had to worry about money. And for people like Shelby, being poor is terrifying, because it's the unknown. And the biggest, baddest bogeymen live in the great unknown.

I can tell all this makes Shelby want to run, and I don't blame her. Running from what scares you is natural. It's what keeps you alive. It's just sad that I've become someone she wants to run from. But I don't think she's going anywhere. At least not yet. She's pregnant and she doesn't do poor. And a divorce right now would more than wipe me out. So here we are. Together, but alone in this big house. With secrets filling up all these rooms between us.

At least Noah doesn't think I'm psycho. He's a cute little guy. He talks all the time now. He calls me Papa. (That's Russian for Dad.) He knows the English and the Russian word for everything. He's a smart one. And a bad one. Just yesterday, he snuck away from Valya and I caught him drawing all over the walls with a green crayon. When I asked him why he did it, he looked at me with the saddest eyes and said, "Da debil made me do it, Papa."

I was going to put him in time-out, but I couldn't stop laughing long enough to do it. After the whole alligator thing, every moment with my son is sacred. What if I had lost Noah?

It freaks me out just thinking about what could have happened. It's like God gave me a reprieve. What if that whole episode was some sort of miracle? What if the alligator really did sneak into the pool and God turned it into a raft? I know that sounds nutso. But God did it for Moses. He turned a staff into a snake in front of Pharaoh. And who's to say miracles only happen in the Bible? Granted, I'm not Jewish and my people aren't in bondage, but maybe I'm meant for something big.

Just maybe, this deal with Shimmer and the IRS is my calling and I'm going to do something great. Like use my gift to find all these missing kids or something. Perhaps God really is on my side. Think about it. What are the chances that the government would find someone like me and then be willing to bail me out? We're talking about a five-million-dollar tax debt here. I had a better chance of being struck by lightning while fucking Heidi Klum. So who's to say God didn't step in and save my son? After what Debra McFadden just told me, I'd say all bets are off as far as what's possible.

When I get to the office this morning, I have a voice mail from Debra McFadden telling me to meet her for lunch. She wants to go to Chumbawumba's. Which is odd, because only die-hard vegans and weirdos eat there. It's this Indian restaurant that's owned by the Holy Vishnus. It's like in their church or something. I call Debra's office to see if we can't go someplace else, but I get her voice mail. And I've been instructed not to leave messages or to call her from my cell phone anymore. Things are now officially cloak and dagger. So it looks like I'm on my way to the Holy Vishnu temple. It's over in this bad part of town, near Oak Cliff. And when I finally get there, I'm kind of worried about parking my Range Rover on the street, but that's the only place to park.

I go into the side entrance and that's when I see him. The blue mutherfucker. He's everywhere. There are paintings of him all over the place. Him playing the flute. Him without a shirt on, showing off his love handles. Him tweaking the nipple of some harem girl. This is seriously creeping me out. The blue guy is the thing that these nutbags worship. It says here on all these plaques that he's their god. He's Vishnu. And now he's somehow gotten me here. I feel sick. This can't be my calling. I'm not about to be some mental case in airports, chanting and shit.

"Excuse me," I ask this old Indian lady. "Where's the bathroom?"

She doesn't speak. She just smiles and points down the hall.

I'm about to puke. This place smells evil. It's a mixture of cheap incense and dog food. It's seriously making me sick. I run to the bathroom and make it just in time. My mouth swells with spit and then I spew and gag. That blue dude is fucking with me. I can feel it.

I flush the toilet and go to the sink and splash cold water on my face and rinse out my mouth. Water always tastes sugary after I yak. I hate it. The taste of acid is all up in my nose and throat. I just want to go home. But then I remember why I'm here. Debra McFadden. The Money. Shelby and Noah.

I pull it together. I remind myself of my original philosophy.

"Men are not their thoughts. Men are their actions," I repeat to myself.

I take some deep breaths and then I take action. I go back into the restaurant. But I don't see Debra. Just this malnourished hippie girl wrapped up in a bedsheet. She's tending to this buffet of overcooked mush. It smells like BO, and I'm using all my willpower not to hurl again. Then I hear—

"Yoo-hoo! Travis! Out here!"

It's Debra. She's sitting outside on the patio with this *skinny freckled dude*. She's not acting very CIA-like with all her yoo-hooing and carrying on. And the skinny dude is one of them. A Vishnu. It looks like someone got some chalk and drew all over his face. He's even got the ponytail on top of his bald head.

I wave at Debra and walk outside. It's actually really nice out here. In the middle there's a thin tree with white lights strung all over it and this tinkling fountain that makes me want to pee.

"Travis, I'd like for you to meet Ikshu. Ikshu, this is Travis." Debra smiles at me like a bank teller.

There's an awkward pause, and then Ikshu gets up to shake my hand. His hand is bony and clammy. He shakes like a girl.

"Nice to meet you, Ikshu."

"Nice to meet you, Travis Anderson." He smiles with a grill full of tetracycline-gray teeth.

"Travis, go grab yourself a plate." Debra holds up her pile of slop.

"No, thanks. My stomach's a little upset."

"That's really too bad. This place is like the best Indian restaurant in Dallas," she says. "Rock stars eat here all the time."

"Yeah, I know." I look around the empty patio. "I just don't feel like eating right now."

"I betcha you're stressed out." Debra points her fork at me. "But we're going to fix that. Aren't we, Ikshu?"

He nods and smiles.

"Ikshu is going to be your guru." She puts her hand over her heart. "Oops! That rhymes."

"My guru?" I can feel acid edging up my throat.

"More like your yogi." She talks with her mouth full. "He's a master yogi. And yoga is the first step in your training."

"Debra, I don't need another religion. I'm already a Methodist." I think I can hear the blue guy laughing.

"No, silly. It's not like that." She pushes her food around on her plate. "Ikshu is just going to show you how to relax."

"Look, I'm all about relaxing. Just not here." I look at Ikshu. "No offense."

He just stares at me and chews.

"Mr. Anderson, I can't force you into joining the program." She drops her fork and looks me in the eye. "This is what it is."

"This. You're telling me that this . . . that the Holy Vishnus are part of all this?"

"No, Mr. Anderson." She smooths her tongue over her teeth. "I'm telling you that Ikshu is going to be your trainer. And you can either do what he tells you or you can pay up."

"I thought you just said you weren't going to force me into anything."

"I'm simply restating your situation." She puts her hand on mine. Her fingernails look like pink Chiclets. "You're free to leave at any time."

I pull my hand away and take another look at Ikshu. He's just sitting there all starry-eyed.

"Since we're on the subject." I squint to see if anyone's

home in Debra's head. "Just exactly how are you going to fix my tax problem?"

"In due time, Mr. Anderson, in due time."

"No, right now," I say. "I want to know right now."

"Not here, Mr. Anderson." She clenches her teeth and fake-smiles. "Okay?"

I look at her. She stares back at me like she's trying to give me a mental message.

"Okay." I look at Ikshu. "But I'm not shaving my head and I'm not wearing a bedsheet."

Ikshu just blinks at me.

"Oh, Mr. Anderson, you are a funny one," she chuckles.

5

Stripped

I office in the Crescent Court. It's this Big Gulp version of European elegance. Imagine the Beverly Hillbillies mansion—big limestone and fancy ironwork. Now multiply that by the 80s. The Dallas Oil Tycoon eighties. Add some valets, some hotsy-totsy shops, and you've got yourself the Crescent.

There are two sides of the Crescent Court. The office side, where people who think they're rich come to work every day. And then across the courtyard, there's the Hotel Crescent Court, where people who really are rich come to get rubbed on, eat lunch, and shop.

I'm, of course, on the side where people work.

My office has a balcony that faces the hotel and overlooks the courtyard. And today, I am sitting out here, sipping my Bloody Mary, hoping to see a naked woman. I shit you not, it happens all the time. Some souped-up trophy wife doesn't realize that there's an office building just across the way; she steps out on her balcony, throws open her robe, and greets the morning sun with open arms.

It's poetic.

Sometimes these ladies come to their balconies sans robe. A lot of times, they are completely shaved like Barbie dolls. Or strippers.

Come to think of it, maybe they do realize what they're doing. Because these women have the best bodies money can buy. Perhaps these women get some cheap thrill out of showing off their turbo-engineered bodies to the world, or, at the very least, an office building full of men. But then again, maybe they're just too dim or self-centered to realize that just because they don't see us, doesn't mean we can't see them. Who knows? Whatever the reason, it's a phenomenon that happens at least once a month. And it adds a certain element of excitement to an otherwise boring morning. I admit, I really like the fact that wealthy naked women give free peep shows at the Hotel Crescent Court; it reminds me that life can be full of all sorts of little surprises.

"I see you haven't wasted any time getting started this morning." Reed's two-pack-a-day voice startles me, causing me to spill my drink.

"Aw, shit!" I wipe the tomato juice and vodka off my shirt. "Look what you made me do!"

"Tsk-tsk-tsk, Trav-o, my boy." He shakes his head. "You're loaded."

"Why don't you go fuck yourself?" I take the celery out of my drink and eat it.

"Shelby just called." He lights a cigarette. "She wants to throw a little surprise party for you."

"Please don't tell me that you're coming."

"Now what kind of friend would I be if I missed your intervention?" He takes a long drag.

"It's really not something you'd like, Reed. There won't be any hookers or coke."

"That's okay. I can bring my own." He cocks his eyebrow at my drink. "After all, we all have our habits."

"I don't have a habit, asshole."

"You know, Trav-o, denial, they say, is the first sign of a problem."

"No, the first sign of a problem is a lame-ass partner who fucks up your taxes." I dig the lime out of my drink and suck on it. "That's the first sign of a problem."

"You are such a little bitch. You know that?" He runs his fingers through his Hair Club membership. "Need I remind you, this place was built on my money? Or have you forgotten?"

"Don't even start with that shit. I've paid you back a hundred times over."

"The fact remains." He points with his cigarette. "You owe me."

"What-the-fuck-ever, dude."

"Face it, Travis. You used me." Reed looks away and clears his throat. "And now that the money's gone, I guess so is your friendship."

"Oh, Jesus." I roll my eyes. "Man, that's so not true. I started hating you long before the money ran out. I promise."

"Fuck. You." Reed stares at me. We're about to come to blows.

Our hatred for each other is out in the morning light.

Naked as those rich women who stand out on their balconies. And it's just as ridiculous, too. In fact, we both start to crack up. First with a couple of stifled snorts, and then with hard laughter. The kind that spews and rattles out of you like steam from a pressure cooker. We both stand out here and howl. At each other. At this fight. At this mess we've gotten ourselves into.

Reed's laughing because I'm laughing and I'm laughing because he doesn't know we're in the clear with the IRS. It's this circle of hysteria that feeds on itself.

"You-you are such . . ." I gasp for air. "Such a worthless pebble of shit."

"F-f-f-fuck you." Reed wipes the tears from his eyes. "You bastard fucker user mutherfucker."

Everything is hilarious. We're gagging and delirious. Reed slaps me on the back and then our mania just kind of putters out. A couple of sighs. A few groans. And then an awkward silence. Our unsaid apologies hang in the air like farts. I nurse my Bloody Mary and look out at the hotel. Reed stands beside me. Both of us caught in this thick sentimentality. Finally, Reed saves us the embarrassment of any touchy-feely apologies.

"So have you seen any snatch out here today?" He cups his hands over his brow and scans the hotel balconies.

"No, not yet."

"Too bad." He sighs. "I guess since Shelby's pregnant, you're probably a little hard up."

"What?" The hair on my arms stands up.

"You know, Shelby being knocked up and all. She's probably not giving you any." He turns and looks me in the eyes. "Or is she?"

"How did you know that?"

"Everyone knows that pregnant chicks don't like to throw a leg."

"No, how did you know that Shelby was pregnant?" I stare at him.

"Oh, um, yeah." He rubs the back of his neck and puts out his cigarette. "She just told me. In there. On the phone."

I can feel his lie hit me square in the jaw. But maybe it's not a lie. Maybe it's just my paranoia. It's my paranoia. It has to be. I would get a vision or something if it was a lie. Or at least, I hope I would.

"I can't believe she told you that." I crunch the ice from my drink.

"Don't worry about it. I won't tell anyone." He pats me on the shoulder. "Come on. Let's see if we can grab an early lunch at the Gold Club and forget about all this bullshit."

I go with Reed, not to grope the strippers, but to get some kind of psychic impression off him. However, the only thing I'm getting is a vague headache from all this worrying. Why would Shelby tell Reed? But then again, she did invite him to my intervention. So maybe she told everybody. Maybe she thinks Reed will pitch in some cash to help her. But that doesn't make sense because she knows Reed hates kids and that I've already asked him to hit up his dad.

This is giving me colon cancer; I can feel my lower intestines eating me from the inside. This baby can't be Reed's. It can't be. Because Shelby passed my email test. And even by the off chance she did—God forbid—fuck him, I've been taking extra vitamin C and yohimbe to fortify my sperm. My little guys would have annihilated any foreign troops in Shelby's canal. It's got to be my kid she's carrying. I just need to get a grip. But why hasn't she told me? And why would she tell a son-of-a-bitch like Reed Bindler that she's pregnant and not her own husband?

"Look at you." Reed lowers the top on his Boxster. "You need to relax. I'll buy you the first lap dance."

"You've got blow on your face," I say.

"Oh, thanks." He wipes the coke off his cheek and blows his nose a couple of times before starting the car. We peel out of the underground garage like Batman and Robin, and tear down Maple Avenue in the blistering Dallas sun. The heat blows over us and we listen to talk radio all the way to the Gold Club. Reed valets the car and we dash into the tit-cave. Reed gets us a table right on the stage and we order lunch. Filet mignon and martinis.

Reed's new "girlfriend" is here. Her name is Tamber. She's up on stage, bumping and humping to the Dixie Chicks. Reed licks his finger and then rubs his nipple; Tamber throws her head back with laughter and then shakes her crotch in his face.

I can't get the martinis down fast enough.

"Yee-hah!" Reed stands up and makes ass-spanking, ride 'em cowboy gestures. I just sit here tonguing my olive like a sore tooth. Tamber tries to get my attention with her Texas flag beach towel. She snaps it at me and starts playing naughty matador-girl. A smile sneaks across my face. Then Tamber lays the towel down, kicks off her G-string, and grinds the floor. Reed goes crazy, hooting and hollering with a mouthful of steak. He starts putting ten-dollar bills in his teeth and Tamber collects them by sandwiching his face between her tits.

"Lunch is served!" He does this snake thing with his tongue.

That's when I get this vision of Shelby doing the same thing to Reed. And that's when I call a taxi and leave.

When I get home, Valya is in the kitchen, making her Russian pancakes for lunch.

"Where's Shelby?" I brace myself on the butcher block.

"At z'grocer," she says.

The room is swirling around me. The copper pots and pans dangle and wobble from the ceiling. And my eyes are watering from Valya's scorching butter.

I sit down at the kitchen table and watch her cook. Her fat arms jiggle and her old neck sways back and forth. Normally, I don't notice this stuff about her. But for some drunken reason, I am seeing all this in slow-mo. And it's pissing me off. I want this Russian woman and her smoke out of my house. I want Shelby home, where she belongs, taking care of me and my boy.

"Where's Noah?" I say.

"Vaud-ching *Barney.*" She smiles at me and holds up two of her pancakes. "You like bliny?"

"No, I don't like bliny!"

Valya says something in Russian. Probably, "Asshole capitalist, I kill you!" But the room's spinning too fast for me to do anything about it. I just lay my head down on the kitchen table and shut my eyes. I can feel the drool pooling up around my face, but I don't care. It feels kind of good and warm.

It does at least until Shelby comes home. She drops her plastic grocery sacks by my head.

"What?" I sit up.

Shelby doesn't speak to me. She just opens and shuts cabinet doors and rattles cans.

"How long has he been there?" she asks Valya.

Valya shrugs. "He shout me. He no like bliny."

"Don't act like I'm not here!" I wipe the slobber off my face with my sleeve.

"Don't tell me how to act." Shelby slams the pantry door.

"Goddamn it! I'm your husband!"

"You're drunk." She opens the fridge and puts away the oranges.

"I might be drunk. But—but—you're—you're pregnant!"

"Valya," Shelby touches her arm. "Could you take Noah upstairs, please."

"Da, sure." Valya wraps her butter-soaked pancakes in paper towels. She sneers at me as she leaves. "I take bliny with me."

"So how did you find out?" Shelby puts a bunch of grapes in a colander and washes them in the sink.

"Reed told me! My goddamn partner, that's how I found out!"

"Well, I'm sorry." She pops a grape in her mouth. "But I didn't think you could handle it."

"Why?" I start to cry and I can hear Shelby's DNA taunting me for it.

"Why, what?" She shakes her head at me. "You're an alcoholic. You're not real stable these days."

"No! Why did you tell Reed?" I choke on my tears and spit. "Is it his?"

"I'm not even going to dignify that with an answer." Shelby calmly looks away and picks a few bad grapes out of the bunch and throws them down the sink.

"So the baby's his?"

"Travis, you're drunk and now you're being ridiculous."

"Then why did you tell him?"

"Because I threw up on the phone when I was talking to him today," she says. "And he asked me if I had morning sickness. And I told him, yes, I did. I'm pregnant."

I just sit here, holding on to my chair, trying to make the world stop spinning.

"Then the baby's not his?" I say.

"Look, Travis, you're drunk." She folds her arms. "I won't be talked to like this."

"Like what?" I shrug. "I just need to know."

"Are you trying to hurt me?" She covers her mouth and tears squeeze out of her blue eyes.

"No, of course not."

"Yes, you are, Travis. First the drinking and now this. Why are you doing this to me?" She cries into her fists.

I get up and walk over to her. She backs away from me. But I try to hug her anyway.

"Get off of me!" She hits me in the chest. I just stand there and let her use me as a punching bag. She gets it all out and then collapses into my arms.

"Why are you doing this to me?" She hiccups and gasps. "Why?"

"Shhhhh. Everything's going to be all right. I promise."

"No, it's not, Travis," she sobs into my shoulder. "No, it's not."

6

Divine
Intervention

The weird thing about my relationship with Shelby is that the worse things get between us, the better the sex gets. After our little fight at lunch, later on that night, we fucked like weasels. You always hear that your marriage in the bedroom is a direct reflection of your marriage outside of the bedroom. Well, that's bullshit. I mean, if that's the equation, then somewhere along the line, Shelby and I have inverted it and multiplied it by eleven. Because last night, we spanked it nasty. I'm not kidding; you could rewrite the *Kama Sutra* with the shit we did. We've never had sex like that. Never. Not even make-up sex. It's like the more Shelby hates me, the more she gets off on me. It's sick, I know. But at this point, I'll take whatever I can get.

Actually, there is a downside to all this wild ass. I hate to sound all sappy and shit, but it's making things a little confusing. After last night, you'd think she'd let me sneak a little kiss here and there. But, no. This morning Shelby was cooking breakfast so I snuck behind her to give her some loving. And she hauled off and punched me. Hard. It was as if last night never happened. I guess the bottom line is Shelby will fuck me, she just won't forgive me. As a matter of fact, today is my intervention. And despite all my promises that things will be better, she's set her jaw against me and is going through with it.

Shelby spends the better part of the morning making a cake and arranging flowers for the "Intervention Team." Valya runs the vacuum cleaner all over the downstairs and scrubs the guest bathrooms. As usual, Shelby is playing the good hostess. And I've been given strict instructions to act surprised when everyone shows up. Like I said, Shelby can't keep a secret.

"People might think we're going for melodramatics if they find out you knew this was coming." Shelby finishes the icing on her dark-chocolate raspberry torte. "So just go in the den and watch football or something. And try not to mess up in there."

Get this. I've also been allowed a six-pack of beer so that our dear friends can see that this isn't a false alarm. Shelby really wants this whole intervention to come off without a hitch. She wants me with my beer breath in front of all our friends. It's the lesser of two evils for her. Now instead of everyone thinking I'm insane, they'll just think I'm a drunk. Plus, there's no telling what kind of whoring around she'll be able to do while I'm gone. That is, if her DNA really does make her do that sort of thing.

"Don't be getting too drunk in there, Travis!" Shelby shouts from the kitchen. "Because people need to tell you their issues. And the least you can do is be sober enough to hear them!"

I just shake my head. It's enough to make me want to stop drinking just to spite everyone and their fucking issues. All this bullshit for something that's supposed to be confrontational and spontaneous. Jesus, this isn't an intervention, it's Supper Club. So as my final act of rebellion before I'm locked up, I sit in my den with Noah and read him a story. When those mutherfuckers get here, I'll be sober as a judge. Then I'll act like they're the ones who are crazy. Then I'll tell them my issues with their problems. I might be going down, but I'm not going down without a fight.

After reading a story, Noah and I dozed off in my chair. So you can imagine my surprise when I wake up and see Debra McFadden standing over me with her bank teller smile.

"What are you doing here?" I shift Noah to the other side of my lap.

"Just play along," she whispers. "I'll get you out of this."

"What?"

"Hi, Travis, my name is Debbie McMullen." Debra McFadden barks. "I'm an intervention counselor."

"Oh."

"Okay, everyone!" she shouts. "Come on in!"

Shelby and all our friends file into my den and line up against the wall. Valya swoops in and picks up Noah and takes him into the other room. I just sit in my chair, half asleep with an untouched six-pack of beer by my side.

"Travis, I know this may be a surprise, but we're here to help you." Debra offers me her hand to help me get up. I don't take it, but I do stand up. I look at her like she's crazy. What the hell is Debra McFadden doing here, acting like she's my intervention counselor? I scan all the scared faces in this room. Shelby's holding a Kleenex and Lisel's got her arm around her. Jim is standing next to them, but he won't look at me. I can hear his thoughts; he feels bad about this. And then there's Reed. He's all snuggled up with Tamber. I can hear his thoughts, too. He's jonesing for some coke. And then there's everyone from Supper Club. Even Carter and Blythe showed up. Blythe is bubbling over with compassion. But Carter has a shit-eating grin on his face. He's imagining what it would be like to punch me out.

"I don't get it." I act surprised just like Shelby wanted.

"It's your drinking." Debra looks at the lineup and then at me. "We're not all standing up here because you're healthy, Travis."

"Oh, Jesus, Debra!" I throw up my hands. "Do we *really* have to be doing this?"

"First of all, my name is Debbie." She smiles with gritted teeth. "And I'm doing this to help you."

"To help me?"

"Yes, we're all here to help you get into rehab. You have a problem, Travis." She nods a lot in sympathy.

"Really." I shoot crusty looks at each and every one of my so-called friends. "So I'm supposed to just up and leave my wife and kid and job? Just go into rehab?"

"Yeah, that's the plan." She winks at me.

"Why can't I just stay home and join AA or something?"

"I'm afraid that's not an option." Debra adjusts her headband. "I think you know that."

"Travis! Please. Just do it!" Shelby breaks down crying.

"I can't believe you people are making me do this." I look at all of them. I can see their darkest, dankest secrets lingering over their heads and I could tell them all. Right here. In front of everyone. But I resist. I bite the inside of my cheek, and keep their nasty little histories in my mouth. I need to forget about how humiliating this is and just go with Debra. After all, she's obviously got a plan.

"So are you going to let us help you?" She puts her hand on my shoulder and massages it. "Or do you want to hear all the reasons that brought everyone here today."

Carter Mitchell raises his hand. "Can I go first?"

"No, you can't, asswipe."

Debra widens her eyes at me. And I widen mine back at her.

"Look, let's just stop right here," I say. "I'll go. Okay?"

Everyone stands there with blank faces. Obviously, they thought I should have put up a bigger fight. And I think it shocked them that I gave up so easily. But this was getting old and I'm not about to stand here while these sons-of-bitches tear me apart.

Shelby breaks up the silence with a crying jag. Blythe and Lisel huddle around her—each jockeying for the "best-friend-in-a-crisis" award.

"Very wise decision, Travis. This is the first step to a better life." Debra pats me on the back. "Come on, let's go. Valya's already packed your bags."

"We're leaving, like right now?"

"Yep, that's how this works." She escorts me out of my den. Shelby and our friends file into the kitchen. No see you laters. No take cares. No nothing. I don't even get to kiss Noah and Shelby goodbye. Debra's Chevy Malibu is waiting outside. We get in and drive away. Meanwhile, Shelby and the rest of the "intervention team" are in my kitchen, eating chocolate cake and washing it down with the milk of their so-called human kindness.

I am obviously a very important person to Shimmer. Because according to Debra McFadden, they've been monitoring my every move since the day they found me. This seriously pisses me off. See, as soon as Shelby contacted our health insurance about my coverage for rehab, Shimmer put Debra McFadden on the job. In fact, Debra is the one who helped Shelby arrange this whole intervention. Shimmer has literally stepped in and taken my life away. And I guess I'm supposed to be okay with this.

"Cupcakes, stop pouting. You're not a regular citizen anymore," Debra says to me as we drive to the Vishnu temple. "You're a spook for hire now. And we do things like this."

"Like this? Like kidnapping people and ruining their reputations?"

"Travis, you had to have an alibi to work with us. Lucky for you, rehab's a really good one."

"Yeah, real fucking lucky. Now everyone thinks I'm a drunk." I look out the car window. "You should have discussed this with me beforehand."

"Actually, you should be very thankful. Shimmer had to act really fast for me to intercept you," She says. "Besides, Shelby's the one who made the call about locking you up, not us. Okay?"

"No, this is not okay." I rub the stubble on my chin.

"I know. I'm really sorry." Debra gives me that plastic smile of hers. "It's just two months of work for five million dollars. I think you can handle it."

"Look, Debra, or Debbie, or whoever you are, you need to tell me how this is going to work, right now, or you can turn this car around and take me home."

"Oh, dear, someone got up on the wrong side of the bed this morning," she says.

"Yeah, someone fucking did!"

"Calm down. It's real simple. Shimmer has set up a bank account in your name. When you pass your tests, we deposit five million into that account. Then we'll issue a wire transfer from it to the IRS."

"And that will call off the audit? It's that simple?"

"Well, there is a ton of paperwork involved. So you'll have plenty of hard evidence that you paid your taxes. The CIA has also filed some special something or other that will end any future investigations. It's a pretty sweet deal."

"Almost a little too sweet."

"Travis, I'll level with you." She looks at me. "You're a very special case. If you are who we think you are, you'll be a very important agent in the welfare and security of our nation."

7

The Powers
That Be

"One truth leads to another." Ikshu sits cross-legged on the floor of the Vishnu temple. I sit next to him. The wood floor is cold and hard; it's making my butt fall asleep.

"Sounds kinda like beer," I say. "You know, drinking one usually leads to drinking another."

Ikshu closes his eyes and exhales in disgust.

"Hey, I was just kidding. Come on."

"I am sorry I cannot laugh with you, Travis Anderson." He opens his eyes and smiles. "I do not find foolish ignorance funny."

This is what I have to put up with. Ikshu and his holier-than-thou bullshit. The Holy Vishnus don't believe in "polluting the body." No booze and no meat. And I guess that also means no jokes about them, either. I haven't had a drink in two days and it makes me sweat just thinking about it. I am about an hour away from hijacking one of these hippie mutherfuckers with a plastic fork and making him take me to get some cheap malt liquor and a Big Mac.

I've been locked up here since my intervention. I haven't been allowed to leave because if I'm spotted by somebody I know, the powers that be will pull the plug on my mission. Which means I haven't had a sip of alcohol in two days.

Two very long days.

And there's no liquor or beer or wine anywhere in this place. I've looked. There's not even any mouthwash that I could swallow. This place is driving me bananas. The food is horrible. The incense burns my sinuses. And they play this whiny music all goddamn day long.

You know what this place reminds me of?

Nashville.

Like one of those tourist traps dedicated to old *Hee-Haw* stars. Roadside shrines full of sequins and big-haired wax figures and flowers left by crazy fans. That's what this temple is like. There's even a wax statue here that people leave flowers for. It's an old Hindu man sitting in a plush purple throne worthy of Elvis. It looks like he's about to open his eyes and stand up. They dress the thing in an orange sheet and white tube socks. You know, the cheap kind you get at Target with the green stitching at the toe. It's bizarre.

"You are not meditating. I can feel it." Ikshu touches me on the shoulder. "Your mind is the monster. It tortures you with desires, my friend."

"I was too meditating." I open my eyes.

"But you are not meditating on God." Ikshu shakes his bald head.

"Yes, I was." I smirk. "I was asking for Him to deliver me . . ."

"That is good, Travis Anderson. Because He can deliver you!"

"Really? Do you think He could deliver me a meat lover's pizza and a case of Shiner Bock?" I crack myself up.

"Travis Anderson, you are not on the path of the yogi."

"And you know what, Ikshu, I probably never will be. At least not without a couple of beers under my belt."

"I would not be so sure about that." Ikshu opens his palms to me. "Lord Vishnu is the all-attractive one. His perfumes have brought you to us."

"Vishnu? The blue dude with the love handles?"

"Yes, yes, yes." Ikshu laughs deep and low like the blue dude does when he's following me. "I am talking about God."

"You're saying He brought me here?"

"Of course. He has plans for you."

"And what are those exactly?"

"I am not sure yet." Ikshu looks deep into my eyes like he's trying to steal my soul. "But I do know this. A man can only know his true destiny by knowing Vishnu. And the only way to know—to truly know Vishnu—is to chant his holy name."

"Well, looks like the blue dude will have to take a rain check because I ain't chanting shit."

"My friend, Lord Vishnu is everywhere. You will find him no matter what path you choose . . . But some paths, they are easier than others."

"Okay, Ikshu!" I am burning up for a beer. "I've about had

it with your Holy Vishnu humma-humma-humma bullshit! Okay? I told you, I'm not into this shit! Okay? I'm not into chanting! I'm a fucking Methodist! We don't do that! So cut the crap, and just teach me what I need to pass my fucking tests!"

The bastard shuts his eyes and starts chanting.

"Holy Vishnu Vishnu Vishnu Holy Holy." His eyes roll back in his head. "Holy Rama Holy Rama Rama Rama Holy Holy."

What a piece of fucking work. I literally have to sit on my hands to keep from killing the bastard. I take a couple of deep breaths, shut my eyes, and come up with a chant of my own.

"Five million dollars. Five million dollars," I say out loud as I sit here and pray that God will turn the water into wine at dinner tonight.

I'm going on day three without a drink. I feel all shaky like I have the flu and every time I shut my eyes I have bad dreams—night terrors that cut me to the core. Last night I dreamed about vampires. A man and woman vampire were sucking on each other and getting blood all over the backseat of my Range Rover. They were also cuddling Jim and Lisel's baby like it was their own. It was one of the sickest things I've ever seen.

The girl vampire was some kind of ugly, with long white hair and zits; she kept crawling over the seats, trying to kiss me while I was driving. Once I realized who these freaks were, I pulled over and ran for my life. They chased me all the way to Texas Stadium, where I thought I could wait for God under the giant skylight. But He never showed. He just left me a message on the scoreboard. It was flashing in big bright lights: LAUGH-TER IS GOD'S MUSIC.

The vampires eventually caught up with me. As a last resort, I laughed at them, which really pissed them off at first, but then they couldn't resist; they started to belly laugh with me. I had them rolling on the Astroturf. And that's when I put a stake through their miserable black hearts.

"We just wanted to be your friend." The girl vampire gurgled up dark blood and that's when I woke up in a cold sweat, lusting for just the smallest bottle of vodka.

Debra McFadden says this is normal.

"Bless your heart, you're just going through withdrawals." She pats me on the back.

I have never wanted to hit a woman before, but right now, I could drop her. I feel like a broken tooth, all pulp and exposed nerves. I throb with pain and I don't need some Plano housewife patting me on the back and telling me about my withdrawals.

"Look, I don't think you understand." I stare hard into her eyes. "I just need one beer. I can't meditate without it."

"Oh, it's a Catch-22, isn't it?" She unwraps some bubble gum and puts it in her mouth. "Want a piece?"

"No, I don't."

"Come on." She nudges me. "Chewing gum will help get your mind off drinking."

"Trust me, it won't."

"Well, I'm sorry, but according to Ikshu, you can't effectively meditate with alcohol in your system." She smacks. "Lowers your vibration."

I find myself wishing she'd choke on that gum. I imagine her face turning blue and me refusing to give her the Heimlich until she gives me a six-pack.

"Look, the first week is always the hardest." She nods. "If you think it would help, I could bring in an AA meeting to the temple and you could start doing your twelve steps here. I heard that really helps."

"Actually, Debra, that sounds about as helpful as a fucking piece of gum right now."

"Well, you don't have to get crabby, buster." She adjusts her headband. "I'm just trying to help."

After lunch today, I go with Ikshu into the temple. The Vishnus, young and old, have also come here and we all stand before this big black velvet curtain. Everyone seems to be brimming over with anticipation. I think something big is about to happen. Then suddenly the ding da-da ding of finger cymbals starts. Then the chanting, "Holy Vishnu, Holy Vishnu." Cymbals. Drums. Chanting. More cymbals and drums. More chanting and carrying on.

That's when the curtain swings open. Grown men weep. Some throw themselves flat on the floor. The women smile and laugh and sing. Ikshu's eyes start fluttering like he's having a fit. Meanwhile, I just stand here and try not to let any of these mental patients touch me.

Everyone here is going ape-shit over what's behind the curtain—these "It's A Small World" looking dolls. They don't even spin or sing or do anything. They just stand there in this Mardi Gras float. One is black as tar—kind of a do-it-yourself lawn jockey. And the other looks like it was carved out of soap. They've both got a bunch of plastic beads and flower necklaces draped all over them. This is what all these people are losing it over. Fucking dolls. It's the twenty-first century and

I'm standing here watching people throw hissy fits over some stupid dolls.

After it's all said and done, I ask Ikshu what's with all that.

"They are not dolls!" His face turns bright red. "They are the Arca Vigraha of Lord Vishnu and his consort, Lakshmi!"

"Hey, you don't have to get so defensive about it. If you want to play with dolls, that's your business," I say. "You're a grown man. I just happen to think it's a little strange. That's all."

Ikshu walks off in a huff. I guess I pissed him off. And in my book, when you're pissed off about something said, then there has to be at least an ounce of truth in it or you wouldn't care. I think Ikshu knows that it's twisted for him and his little friends to be getting off on a bunch of dolls. It's retarded and weird. I don't care what he says about Arca Viagra whatevers.

But you know what? It's the first time this week that I haven't wanted a drink. So maybe those dolls do have a purpose: they give me something to torment Ikshu over. Which in turn, makes me forget about my drinking problem, i.e., the fact that I can't get anything to drink here. I can't wait until the dolls come out again tomorrow. Messing with Ikshu is the only fun I've had since I've been here. There's no TV and the only books to read in this joint are comic books about the Hindu gods. And I've read all I care to about the wacky adventures of Shiva and Ganesha.

I go to my room and I practice my breathing. I do like Ikshu taught me and imagine that there are "chakras of light" lining up from the base of my spine to my head. Starting with red and going all the way up the spectrum to indigo at the top of my head. I charge them with "white light," and I hate to admit this, but I think it's working. I don't know how to describe it. Except that I'm starting to feel like, like . . . a cinnamon roll. Yeah, a cinnamon roll—all sticky and warm and sweet inside. I feel electric. Free. High. It's like taking a Valium or something better. Nothing bothers me.

And I can see for miles in all directions. It's wild. I can actually see the blue skies outside. I can soar past them and see the American flag on the moon. Past Jupiter's big red birthmark and Saturn's icy rings. Maybe Ikshu's not as big of a crackpot as I thought. But I don't care how blissed out you get, you still shouldn't play with dolls. There's just some things a grown man shouldn't do.

Tonight, I lie here in bed and stare at the ceiling. I can't sleep. It's too hot to sleep. And my thoughts keep turning to Shelby and Noah all alone in that big house. I miss them more than I miss my beer. Which, now that I've had some time to clear my head, is really why I'm here—at least it's why Shelby thinks I'm here. She told me to pick her or my bottle and she thinks that I picked her. But I didn't pick anything; I faked it. I'm not in rehab. I'm here, doing God knows what. And if I'm going to be honest, the first thing I'm going to do when I get free isn't going to be running home to my family—it's going to be running to the nearest liquor store and gulping down whatever I can get to first. That's what I'm going to do. That's what I have to do. And that's a problem. A huge fucking problem that I've been trying to solve like algebra—taking from one side of my life to balance the other and then dividing it all by my addiction. Shit. I said it. *Addiction.* I think I'm an alcoholic. Did I just admit that? Fuck, I am an alcoholic and I need help. God, I need help.

It's this silence. This fucking meditation. It's making things bubble up in me like hydrogen peroxide on a wound. Which, if that's a proper analogy, maybe it'll help me heal this addiction. Maybe, meditating is my way out of drinking. I can't believe I'm even saying this. Meditation? Addiction? This isn't me talking. What's next? An hour-long discussion about aromatherapy? I've got to get out of this place. That Ikshu flake is rubbing off on me. I need to get home to Shelby and Noah. I need to get these tests over with and get on with my life. I need to get to sleep.

But now, the couple next door is knocking their headboard against my wall and making all sorts of racket. I guess they're having sex. Which I thought was against the rules for these weirdos.

"OH! GOD!" the woman shouts and the headboard knocks, knocks, knocks at my wall.

Okay, they're definitely doing it next door. Which, now not only makes me wide-awake, but wide-awake horny. Which is a problem. Why is it that all you have to do is hear people doing it and it gets you wanting to do it as well? I've got all these vivid images of some new-age Playboy bunny getting her brains fucked out from all this wall banging. But the truth is, it's probably just some gross hippie woman with weird boobs. However, no matter how hard I try not to think about it, the Playboy bunny keeps popping up in my head. And it's getting me all wound up.

So I close my eyes and picture doing Shelby. God, I miss her. Her fingernails scratching right under my shoulder blades. Her lips, dry from breathing hard, just barely against my neck. And then a completely uninvited and completely unwanted

mental picture jumps into my head: Shelby fucking Reed. My
heart starts racing. I need to leave. I need to stop this!

I have to calm the fuck down. I'm just freaking out. After
all, Reed brought Tamber to my intervention and he wouldn't
do that if he and Shelby were screwing around. Or would he?
Maybe that was a cover. And then it dawns on me: Why don't
I just see for myself what Shelby's doing? I mean, what's this
remote viewing crap good for if you can't spy on your loved
ones?

I take long, deep breaths. I imagine lighting up my chakras,
but nothing happens. Not a goddamn thing. So I keep trying. I
breathe deeper. In and out. Out and in. I visualize balls of light
at the base of my spine to the top of my head. I light them up
and still nothing happens. I'm still here sitting in this bed, hear-
ing those two assholes knock their headboard against my wall.
Maybe it doesn't work when you're horny. I close my eyes and
try to wait. I exhale for a long time and that's when I fall down
the rabbit hole and into outer space.

I see the earth. It's a small blue swirl. So I fall fast and
bright like a meteor, straight for Dallas. And then I'm there, in
my house—downstairs in the kitchen. All the lights are off. I
walk up the stairs to my room. It's dark. I can barely see a
thing. I open the door to my room and walk over to the bed. I
see Shelby's head on her pillow. And then I see someone else's
head on my pillow.

It's Noah.

He's sucking his thumb, and holding Peanut Butter, his
stuffed bunny.

I reach down and kiss his head and that's when it happens:
Noah pees the bed.

"Oh, baby, no," Shelby groans.

Noah starts crying, "Papa! Papa!"

She picks him up out of the wet sheets and turns on the light.

"I'm sorry, baby. Shhhh. I should have put some pull-ups on you." She hugs him close to her breast. "It's okay. Mommy will change you."

He just squalls, "Paaaaapaaaa!"

I feel terrible. He's crying because I'm not there.

"Papa's at work, honey. He'll be back soon." Shelby unsnaps his PJs, tosses them on the floor, and puts a diaper on him.

I stand over them and watch Shelby strip the bed while Noah cries. I watch them and feel like crying myself.

This morning I wake up a little tired, but not feeling nearly as desperate for a drink. I sit outside on the patio of Chumbawumba's and have breakfast with Debra McFadden—if that's what you can call this shit. There's all these morning mosquitoes out here and they're hungry. I slap away the bloodsuckers and tell Debra all about last night.

"See, I told you. Ikshu knows his stuff." Debra gloats. "Minds are like parachutes, Travis. They don't work if they're not open."

"Well, mine is fucking open and ready for landing." I sip my hot tea over my breakfast of Vishnu mush. "So when can I take these tests and get out of this place?"

"First we have to get you on a plane to California, to Shimmer's research center."

"California?"

"Yeah, the problem is getting you out of Dallas." She puts a big heap of mush in her mouth and smacks. "You know what? I think we might drive you down to Austin and fly you out of there. Less risk of you seeing someone you know."

"Let's do it."

"Not so fast, Speed Racer." She winks at me and puts more mush in her mouth. "We've got to get you geared up with a disguise."

"Hey, whatever. I'm just ready to get this over with."

"Why? So you can go get a little drinky-winky?"

"No." I glare at her. "So I can see my family."

8
Third Eyes And Second Glances

This is so not funny. I'm standing here in the Austin airport with my head shaved, wearing an orange muumuu, and yellow greasepaint all over my face. This is my disguise. Or as Debra calls it, this is my "gambit." (That's CIA-speak for a disguise that changes your ethnicity.) Debra thought that since I would be traveling with Ikshu, this would be the easiest way to conceal my identity. I told her there was no fucking way that I was chanting at the airport. And that's when she painted the yellow lines on my forehead.

"This way," she chirped, "no one will mistake you for a Buddhist or some other religion."

So here I am, looking like a freak, waiting for my Southwest Airlines flight to San Jose. The airport is full of cowboys, businessmen, would-be rockers, students, moms with babies, and little Mexican grannies. Not one of them smiles at me. In fact, they all keep their distance and kind of sneer. People really don't like Holy Vishnus. And after spending a week with them, I can see why. They're annoying and they don't use deodorant. I guess Debra's making me dress like this was a pretty smart idea. Because I'm definitely in no danger of someone talking to me and blowing my cover.

Even Ikshu won't talk to me. But that's because he's still mad about the whole doll thing. He's trying to be all Holy Vishnu happy, but I can tell he's really pissed. I can feel it coming off him like stink off a turd. I know Ikshu acts all gentle and kind, but there's a brutal silence about the man sometimes. Maybe something dark lurks behind all that inner peace crap. I'm not sure what it would be. But I think I see it slip out of his eyes every once in a while when he flashes those partly-cloudy teeth of his.

Or more likely, I'm just being an asshole because I need a drink. Ikshu's probably a nice enough guy. I mean, for all my talking shit about him, I will give him this: he at least tries to be a nice person. And that's a lot more than I can say for most normal people. I should cut him some slack. So what if he worships dolls? Looking for flaws in people is a bad habit of mine. And I need to quit. After all, Ikshu has only tried to help me out and all I can seem to do is rip on the guy.

Once our plane takes off, Ikshu falls fast asleep next to the window and I sit on the aisle. Big surprise; nobody wanted to sit between us. I read a *Newsweek* while the stewardess walks around throwing peanuts at everyone.

"What can I get you to drink, sir?" she asks.

I pop a handful of peanuts in my mouth.

"You have Absolut?" I look over at Ikshu to make sure he's still asleep.

"No, sorry, only Smirnoff."

"I'll take it."

She hands me a little jewel of a bottle. I can see my distorted reflection in it.

"Would you like some ice or maybe some tonic with that?"

I don't answer her. I turn that bottle full tilt and gulp it down like cool, cool water.

It burns. My eyes water and I have to shake it off. But, boy, it feels good.

"Excuse me, sir. That'll be six dollars."

"Can I have another one, please?" I pull a wad of cash out of my wallet. "Actually, make that a double, and let me buy a couple of Jack Daniel's for my friend over here while he's sleeping."

The stewardess rolls her eyes. She's definitely heard that one before. She makes all sorts of clinking when she hands me my vodka and I shush her.

"My brother needs his sleep," I whisper.

"Sorry." She gently hands me the Jack Daniel's.

I give her a ten-dollar tip and open another baby vodka. This one I sip on and contemplate whether to save the other bottles for later, or down them now. After all, Ikshu could wake up at any moment.

I turn to look at him, and then the blue dude suddenly appears in the seat between Ikshu and me.

"Holy fuck!" Every hair on my body stands on end and I almost drop my vodka. I stare at him and hold very still like

I'm sitting next to a rattlesnake. He stares back at me with eyes as black as outer space. His eyelashes are long and curly like a cow's. His doughy body is the color of the sky and he's not wearing a shirt. Just gold genie pants. I wonder if he heard me talking shit about his dolls. What am I saying? Of course he didn't. It's a fucking hallucination.

"No, my child. I am no hallucination."

It talks.

I can't breathe so well.

I scramble to gather up my bottles and run to the bathroom. I lock my ass in and try to take some deep breaths. I try to meditate and calm down.

"Fuck that." I open the whiskey and down it. It warms my throat and head.

I look in the mirror. My face is painted with three vertical stripes. My head is shaved and I'm wearing a bedspread and wooden love beads. Shelby is right. I am fucking crazy.

Someone knocks on the door.

"Go away!" I shout. "I'm in here!"

A ghostly blue hand passes through the door. I freeze. It reaches inside of me and my head buzzes with the joy of glitter gold. I feel like a cinnamon roll again. The hand withdraws and waves good-bye. And then all the alcohol and peanuts that were in my stomach come rushing up out of me like a geyser. I vomit all over myself and the bathroom.

By the time I get cleaned up and back to my seat, Ikshu is awake.

"The blue guy just attacked me." I buckle my seat belt.

"He did not attack you. He saved you."

"What do you mean he saved me?"

"He saved you from your alcohol." Ikshu looks repulsed.

"How'd you know that?"

"Besides the fact that you reek of it." He covers his nose. "I am at one with Lord Vishnu, my friend."

"Oh." I pick up my magazine and we continue to ignore each other the rest of the way to San Jose. I flip pages and try to make my heart stop racing. I either just experienced a major psychotic episode, or that blue mutherfucker is for real.

As soon as we get off the plane, Ikshu rents a car and drives us to Shimmer's office in Menlo Park, just outside San Jose. It's right around the corner from the Stanford Research Institute. Ikshu says that back in the day, the Institute used to work very closely with the CIA's remote viewers and that's why Shimmer is located here today.

Anyway, Shimmer, Inc. is your typical glass and concrete corporate campus. The lobby feels outdoorsy with all its natural light, babbling waterfalls, and tightly manicured plants. Aside from the security guards with Uzis, it looks like any other high-tech office. One of the security guards checks Ikshu's ID and the other one pats me down and runs me through a metal detector.

"I'll see you later, my friend." Ikshu steps into a waiting elevator and disappears. Meanwhile, my security guard holds me by the arm and walks me down a very long hall where he deposits me in what looks to be a doctor's office.

I am greeted by Dr. Jude Solomon, a psychiatrist with prematurely gray hair and a slight lisp, along with his pudgy assistant, Grace. They introduce themselves, and Dr. Solomon gets right down to business.

"Remove your clothes, pleath. We need to get you wired."

"Gee, doc, I usually don't go this far on the first date." I pull my Holy Vishnu getup over my head. The good doctor and his assistant don't laugh.

Instead, the assistant pulls out some surgical shears and turns them on.

"We're going to have to shave your chest." She tilts her head to the side and goes to work; she doesn't even wait for me to say okay. I look up at the ceiling as the shears jerk and buzz the hair off my body.

"Shit! That hurts!" I flinch.

"Sorry." She just keeps buzzing away. "Try to hold still."

"So how long will this test take?" I stand there, sheared and in my boxers.

"If everything goes well, two days." Dr. Solomon checks his Palm Pilot. "Grace, once you have him wired, put him in 2A."

"Sure, doc." She brushes all the loose hair off me.

The doctor walks out without saying good-bye.

"Man, he's a friendly guy," I say.

"Oh, he's just tired." She hands me some electrodes. "Hold these. Now, the glue's going to be a little cold at first."

She sticks electrodes all over my stomach, chest, neck, and head. And she wasn't lying about the glue. It's ice cold. Anyway, after I'm all dotted up with electrodes, I wrap my sheet around my waist, and she walks me down yet another long hall. She takes me to a small windowless room full of equipment and a Barcalounger.

"Have a seat and I'll hook you up." She smiles.

I sit down and see a video camera staring back at me.

"Here's a pad and paper. Just close your eyes and then draw or write whatever comes to mind."

"What for?"

"We're going to monitor your brainwaves and vital signs while the person in the other room sends you messages. It's a piece of cake." She plugs me into a bunch of machines and flips some switches.

"Okay, let's rock and roll." She dims the lights and leaves.

I shut my eyes and I don't see anything. Nada. Zip. Zilch. No visions. I guess I shouldn't have had that vodka on the plane. Maybe that's what's fucking this up. Maybe this is the blue guy's way of punishing me. Who knows? Vodka or blue guy or whatever, I've always hated Pictionary and I especially hate this lab rat version of it. It's stuffy in here and I'm starting to sweat. If I don't pass these tests, I don't get to be a remote viewer, which means I'll still owe the government five million dollars. Which means my life is over. Thinking about this puts my heart so far up in my throat I could chew on it. What if I can't do this?

I'm trying everything I know to get this to work. All the tricks I learned from Ikshu about chakras and breathing and shit, but nothing seems to help. When I shut my eyes I don't see anything. Actually I do see something—those two vampires from my dreams. The hideous white-haired girl and her Eddie Munster boyfriend just keep dancing around in my head and they won't go away.

After a couple of hours, Dr. Solomon comes in and turns up the lights.

"Let's see what you got." He pushes his glasses up his nose and picks up my blank paper. "Not much, I see."

"I think I have jet lag." I squint.

"Then how about we continue this tomorrow?" He rips the electrodes off me one by one.

"Ouch!"

"Sorry. They're like Band-Aids, you've just got to pull them off fast." He rips three more off my shaved head.

"Ouch!"

"See, all done." He holds the electrodes up.

"Maybe tomorrow I can play the cow?"

"Not likely," he says. "We're trying to find out what you can do under certain controls. So tomorrow, we'll run you through a series of diagnostics. But the cow game won't be one of them."

"So what happens if I don't pass?"

"Try not to worry about that, Mr. Anderson. Besides, our tests show worrying tends to block anomalous cognition."

"Anoma-what?"

"Anomalous cognition. It's the scientific term for what you allegedly can do."

"Hey, there's no allegedly about it." I put my Vishnu getup back on. "I mean, have you seen my PsychicCow.com scores?"

"I'm afraid that's hardly scientific," he says.

"What do you mean hardly scientific? That game is how you people found me."

"Exactly, and these tests are how we decide whether or not to throw you back." He carefully wraps the electrodes into something that resembles a noose.

Grace escorts me up in the elevator and drops me off at my dormitory room.

"I'll come get you tomorrow morning at seven." She unlocks my door and walks back to the elevator. "Get plenty of sleep. You'll need it."

I'm actually quite surprised with my room. It's nice. Not what you'd expect from the government. It's a top-floor suite, with a king-size bed and mountains of white feather blankets and pillows. There's even a Jacuzzi and a fully stocked kitchen. However, there's no mini bar—which I guess is for the best. And when you punch a button next to the couch, a big-screen TV and stereo is revealed from behind fancy wood panels.

Shimmer definitely wants to keep their guinea pigs happy. I go to the fridge and open a Coke. There's even a phone on the counter. So I call Shelby and Noah. It rings and rings. The damn machine picks up. I hang up and try Shelby on her cell phone.

"Hello." Her voice sounds clipped and robotic.

"Shelby?"

"Travis?" She sounds annoyed. "Travis, what are you doing? I didn't think you could call."

"I got a free one for, uh, good behavior." I clear my throat. "So what are you doing?"

"Trying on shoes." She sounds distracted.

"Oh. That's good . . . Where?" I ask.

"Stanley Korshak." She sounds pissed.

"Well, that's good." I keep waiting for her to say something like I miss you or I love you. Instead, I just get static.

"Travis," she says with a sigh, "I can't really talk right now."

"I miss—"

"Why don't you call me later?" she says.

"Wait . . . Where's Noah?"

"He's with Valya."

"Well, how is he?" I'm almost begging her not to hang up.

"He's fine. Look, I'll talk to you later. Just get better, okay?"

"Okay . . . I-I-I love you."

"You're breaking up. I gotta go. Bye." She hangs up.

I put the phone down and back away from it like a smoking gun. I shouldn't have called. She's not ready to talk. She probably won't be ready to talk until I'm stone cold sober and I've gotten our life back together. I guess I don't blame her.

God, I wish this room had a mini bar. A little bottle of Cuervo would make this all better. What am I saying? I want a drink because Shelby wants me to quit drinking. Now, that's circular logic if I ever heard it. I just need to get a fucking grip. I can do this. I can stay sober. I just need to take it one step at a time. One step at a time? Oh, Jesus, I really do need help. I'm starting to talk in bumper stickers.

I should just go to sleep, but after that depressing conversation only a mighty big nightcap would bring it on. Maybe I'll meditate. Maybe I can make myself feel like a cinnamon roll again. I sit on this big white bed in the lotus position, as Ikshu would call it, and I meditate. It takes a while, but I get there. My chakras are all lit up. But this time I don't feel like cinnamon, and I don't leave my body. I just stay inside myself and practice breathing and being here. It helps.

Not as much as a double martini would have helped. But it helps.

"All I can say, Travis, is even a busted clock is right twice a day." Debra McFadden reshuffles some papers on her desk.

"What is that supposed to mean?" I say.

"Well, from the look of your test results, that means maybe we made a mistake. Maybe you're not the person we thought you were."

"What about Psychic Cow? Let me play the cow and I can prove it."

"Travis, we already know you can play the cow." She drums her pink fingernails on the desk.

"Why are you fucking with me?"

"No one's"—she makes twitching rabbit ears with her fingers—"'fucking' with you." What we needed from you were consistent results in a controlled environment."

"I can be consistent."

"Yeah, you can, but the problem is you seem to be consistently wrong."

She's about to let me go. I can feel it coming. And I can feel my life going with it.

This is a major intersection of fate. The kind of turning point you hear from bums when they give you their hard luck stories of why they're in your face with their onion and piss breath, begging for change.

"Look, Debra, please. I need this." I find myself silently praying for a miracle.

"I know you need this, but the U.S. government doesn't just give five million dollars away for the heck of it." She clasps her hands and tilts her head.

"Jocelyn!" I involuntarily shout—almost like a sneeze.

"What?" Debra leans forward. "Jocelyn, what?"

"Jocelyn says that . . . that she loves you?" I look around the room.

Why am I saying this shit? "And that she misses you and Shasta?"

"Jocelyn?" Tears well up in Debra's eyes.

"Yeah, Jocelyn." I nod. "Who the hell is Jocelyn?"

Debra starts to cry. She pulls a Kleenex out of the box on her desk and blows her nose.

"Jocelyn was my sister." She sobs. "She died two years ago in a car crash. Shasta was her cat."

I just sit here, feeling like I should apologize to Debra for making her cry. But there's another part of me that wants to get up in her face and do the cabbage patch.

Who's not psychic now, Debra?

Debra sees to it that I get another chance. Which means seven more days of testing. On Monday, I have to roll dice and predict how they will fall. Tuesday, Dr. Solomon wires me up and we play with Zener cards, little flash cards with plus signs, circles, squares, stars, and wavy lines; I have to tell Solomon what cards he's thinking of. Wednesday, I graduate to the remote viewing tests. Grace wires me up and puts me in the room with the Barcalounger. She gives me map coordinates and I have to describe in detail what the location looks like. Thursday, she gives me a picture of a person and I have to tell what city that person is in and try to guess his or her name. Friday is wristwatches and wedding rings; I have to give physical descriptions of the people they belong to. Saturday is back to the map coordinates and finding a particular target, like an ink pen or a laptop. Sunday is a little medley of map coordinates, flash cards, and dice. By Monday, I've got visions of little beers sweating in buckets of ice on a beach. I'm beat and just want a drink.

But instead I have a meeting with Debra and Dr. Solomon to discuss my test results. I have no idea how I did. Solomon was his usual aloof self this past week. He and Grace never gave me any indication of how I was doing. When I would ask, Solomon would say the same thing.

"Remember, let's limit the casual talk, Travis. We don't want to contaminate the data."

Whatever. I don't want to talk to that boring asshole anyway. But I haven't had a real conversation in over a week. I'm starting to feel like a lab rat that just wants to be petted. I keep getting poked and prodded and shaved and wired while nobody smiles or talks to me. It's really starting to depress me.

"You're a fifty/fifty." She won't look me in the eye. Instead she picks at her fake nails.

"That doesn't sound good," I say.

"Actually," Dr. Solomon interrupts, "it's statistically improbable. Which indicates anomalous cognition. But it's still not what we were shooting for."

"Most of Shimmer's viewers are eighty/twenty." Debra purses her lips.

"What does that mean?"

"It's actually quite phenomenal." He pushes his glasses up on his nose. "It means under test conditions, they're correct at least eighty percent of the time."

"And you were only correct half the time." Debra sighs. "But that's way more than the average Joe gets."

"So what are you telling me here?"

"Well, I think you have talent," Dr. Solomon says. "I'm just not sure how valuable you would be to Shimmer at this point."

"What?" I feel like I've just been hit in the face. "But I'm hundred percent when I play the cow."

"That's just the problem, Travis. Some days you're hundred percent, others you're zero percent." Debra shakes her head and I see five million dollars flying out of her bouncy hair.

"I just need to practice. I can do this. I know."

"Travis, I would be incurring a great deal of risk to sign you on at this point." Solomon chews on his pencil.

"No, you wouldn't. I can do this. Ask Debra, I pulled her dead sister's name out of thin air."

"Yeah, doc, he did do that. And he knew her kitty cat's name, too."

He sticks out his bottom lip and squints.

I want to knock that smug look off his face.

"So you can communicate with the deceased?" he asks.

"Yeah, I guess."

Okay, I'm lying here. I've never even used a Ouija board, but for five million dollars, I can learn.

"Well, that is a skill set that we've been hoping to acquire." He scratches his head. "Problem is how to test it."

"Hey, I'm your man. I see dead people."

"You see dead people?" Debra lights up. "What about aliens?"

"Are you nuts?"

"No, seriously, have you ever seen aliens?" Solomon's eyes widen.

"Only on *The X-Files*."

"Too bad. That's often a marker for extreme talent, Mr. Anderson," Solomon says. "That and near-death experiences."

"Well, I've seen a blue guy. Does that count?" I ask.

"You've seen a blue man? An angel or apparition of sorts?" He pushes his glasses up on his nose.

"No, more like a Hindu god."

They both just look at each other. And that's when the albino vampire girl and her boyfriend waltz into the room and I scream for the Holy Mother of God to save me.

9

Mysterious Ways

Her name, or rather their name, is SageRat. The albino girl and her, uh, brother are remote viewers for Shimmer. Of course, they're not real vampires. They've just read one too many Anne Rice novels. They're Goths. But the girl really is an albino, and the poor thing really is ugly. Her milky blue eyes are crossed and her long hair is the color and texture of cornsilk. Her skin is whiter than Ivory soap and thin, too: you can see the blue veins on the side of her head and she's got bad acne. She looks down at the ground a lot.

As for her brother, he's scary, too. But unlike the girl, most of his freakiness is self-induced. He's got a jet black mullet with a rat tail. And he's pierced everything. His tongue, his lips, his eyebrows, his cheeks, every inch of his big ears, and probably other places that I really don't want to know about. He's also got flame tattoos shooting up his neck and he wears Marilyn

Manson contacts that make his eyes look like black, shiny orbs.

They're quite the gruesome twosome with their fangs and all. But the weirdest thing about them isn't how they look. It's how they act. Dr. Solomon calls it a conjoined consciousness. They're joined at the mind. Which is why they insist on being called the same name. Which is why they speak and blink and breathe and do everything in unison. At first, it was really creepy. But after you talk to them for a while, it becomes profoundly annoying.

I'll admit I could have handled myself a little better when I met SageRat. Screaming bloody murder when you meet people is never a good way to win friends and influence people. But then again, SageRat didn't have to hiss at me, either. Those two should realize that if you go around dressed like a freak show, you can't just pop in unannounced without eliciting a few screams. They acted all offended that I was startled. Like I was being prejudiced, or something. But let's get real. Here these two are showing up in my dreams, French kissing each other, and then one day they just walk into my life. And I'm supposed to be okay with that? All I know is I'm already playing fast and loose with my sanity, and I really don't need this.

And get this: Ikshu and I have developed something that resembles a friendship. I'm not about to take him for a round of golf at the country club or anything, but we talk. He says that I'm very lucky to have seen the blue guy. He told me that it was nothing to worry about and that I should actually count it as a blessing. I told him that since I hadn't had anyone to talk to at Shimmer, I read the *Bhagavad Gita*–one of the Holy

Vishnus' books he gave me—and that seemed to make him proud. I didn't have the heart to tell him that I couldn't finish it, though. Talk about a bunch of mumbo-jumbo.

"*Bhagavad Gita* is a book of mighty wisdom in times of war," Ikshu says. "And whether you realize it or not, we are at war."

I'm starting to see what he's talking about. If war is hell, then working for Shimmer is war. But instead of getting in a tank or a fighter plane, I get into a Barcalounger and spend eight hours a day battling my sanity in the psychic trenches. This week my mission was to find a boy who had been kidnapped by his Mafioso dad. I found them dining with the beautiful people at Caffe Ponte Vecchio in North Miami. I even got their address, right down to the street number.

Today, I tracked down this lady, a pretty blond accountant, who had fled to Canada with over a million dollars of her boss's money. I found her living like a rock star in Vancouver, staying in the Westin Grand on Robson. They deployed a team of agents to arrest her almost immediately.

Ikshu says that I have great potential, and he should know. He's the best remote viewer this place has got. Dr. Solomon and Grace treat him like a god. I'll admit I thought Ikshu and all his Hindu bullshit was strange, but his yoga lessons have really paid off. I guess I owe him big. Debra McFadden says that my viewing has now far exceeded their expectations and that when I get home there will be five million schamolies waiting for me. If Ikshu wasn't a vegetarian weirdo, I'd take him out for a big steak dinner and cigars at Del Frisco's once we get back to Dallas.

I'm psyched. It looks like I'm on my way to getting my life

back. I just hope that I still have a life to get back to once I'm finished here. Hopefully, Shelby can forgive me and we can get on with things. Hopefully, I'll have a reason to be forgiven. Hopefully, I won't start drinking again.

I have to face it; I only quit drinking because I didn't have any other choice, not because I wanted to. What happens when I'm back out in the real world? There will be liquor stores full of choices. I need to stop thinking like this. I need to stay positive. At least, now I know that I'm not a psycho. Just psychic.

Which raises the question: Just how thin is the line that separates a psychic and a psycho? I think it's a fucking tightrope walk, and I'm not too sure how well I'm doing. Take all those bad dreams and visions I had. Were those psychic or just plain psycho? Has Shelby's DNA really talked to me? Is she fucking the whole world? Or just fucking Reed? It's this kind of shit that blurs my line. Once you start messing with how you see reality, then it becomes really hard to know what's real and what's not. And that's where I believe a psychic like me starts going mad.

Maybe Shelby really is a slut. But the truth is, I love her. And this tears me up inside. It feels like I swallowed a bucket full of broken glass and it's shredding me into ground meat. It's setting off little earthquakes in my heart, making me shake with tears. Tears that I don't believe in. Tears that prove that I'm too weak to keep her.

I try to take comfort in what Ikshu told me about being psychic. He says not to take my dreams and visions literally. He says that the language of the mystic comes to him in metaphors and symbols. But what could Shelby fucking Reed symbolize? What the hell kind of metaphor is that?

"Are you okay?" The albino girl suddenly appears in my doorway.

"What the fuck?" I get up from my couch.

"I could feel it," she mumbles. "Your sadness."

"How-how'd you get in here?"

"Your heart is broken. I felt it as I was walking by." She plays with her long white hair and looks down.

"Where's the rest of you?" I peer around her, looking for her punk-ass brother.

"Rat's practicing aikido." She floats toward me, her long cobweb dress flowing behind her.

"Rat?"

"Yes, Rat. I am the Sage, and he is the Rat." She looks at my neck like she's hungry.

"But I thought you two were joined at the brain, or something?" I try to look at her, but she's so ugly, she makes my head spin.

"Only when we're working." She locks into my eyes. I'm a rabbit caught in a cobra's gaze—woozy and frozen. My blood thumps and swishes in my ears. I'm about to black out. I try to yell, but it only comes out as a whisper.

"Get out of my head!"

"I wasn't in your head." She wets her lips. "I was in your heart."

"Stop it!"

"She still loves you, you know." Sage rolls right up to me like a thunderhead; she accumulates in my face. I can feel her hot breath on my cheek.

"Don't," I say through clenched teeth.

"I know what love is. She loves you." Sage smoothes her hand across my chest.

It takes every ounce of willpower that I have to slap her hand away.

Her crazy blue eyes ignite like a gas flame.

"Just because I don't look like someone you'd want to fuck, doesn't mean I don't know what love is! And it doesn't mean I don't deserve to be treated like a fucking human being! You asshole!"

She turns on her heel and runs out of my room in a gossamer blur.

And then I can breathe again. My head is pounding. I'm hyperventilating. What a crazy bitch. I think she was doing some kind of Jedi mind trick on me. I could feel the pressure the moment she walked in. It made me feel thick and slow and stupid. She was in my head, controlling me and digging around in my thoughts. I feel dirty, like I need a long shower. I need to go out and buy a gun, and extra deadbolts for my door. But that won't keep her out. I have a feeling she can come and go as she pleases. And that makes my skin crawl.

"Sage prays to a darker god." Ikshu flips the channels on his TV and sips on a Perrier.

"A darker god?" I sit up.

"She is a vulgar soul, Travis Anderson." He turns off the TV and looks me in the eye. "It would be best to stay away from her."

"Trust me. After yesterday, no problem." I laugh it off.

"Sage is nothing to laugh at. She is a wicked, wicked woman. And this lifetime she is reaping the evil that she's sown for hundreds of lifetimes."

"What are you talking about?"

"I am talking about karma."

"Karma? You're fucking kidding me, right?"

"No, I would not kid you." He fingers the wooden beads on his necklace. "Sage was given her frail skin to blister in the loving sun as a penance for crimes committed long ago."

"Okay, let's have a little reality check here." I shake my head. "Sage being an albino has nothing to do with karma. It was a genetic mishap."

"There are no mishaps, Travis Anderson."

"So what are you saying? That if Sage had been a good little girl, she wouldn't be an albino?"

"Yes, she would have been rewarded." He steeples his hands together. "The beautiful and the wealthy are surely the righteous reborn into reward."

"Look, I'll admit Sage is a scary bitch. But that's just fucked up."

"I beg your pardon?"

"Ever been to India? Caste systems. Karma. Untouchables. Come on."

"You and your Western foolishness, my friend." He exhales.

"Don't give me that hippie enlightenment crap."

"Perhaps your mind is not ready for the truth."

"Or perhaps you're wearing me out with all this bullshit," I say. "Besides, I've got bigger fish to fry. I've got freaky vampire girl stalking me."

"That is quite a problem," he says.

"Well, what can I do about it?"

"Threaten her with her kid fears." He flashes his storm-cloud smile.

"I'm sorry. I don't speak fortune cookie. What did you just say?"

"The next time she approaches you, reach into her black heart and pull out her kid fears."

"And just how do I do that?"

"Chant and visualize." He shuts his eyes and starts doing his humma-humma Holy Vishnu bullshit.

The pretty blonde in Vancouver got away. So my new assignment is to find her. I've spent the last two days searching, but for some reason, she's completely off my radar. And it's starting to screw with my confidence. What's really weird is that I've been dreaming about her ever since Dr. Solomon told me she escaped. She shows up every night, begging me to leave her alone. She's beat up and crying and there are hundreds of needles stuck in her arm like a pincushion. It's a haunting dream, a nightmare, really. I wonder if she knows I'm tracking her. Maybe these dreams are some part of her reaching out to me, asking me to stop. This is the kind of shit that pushes a psychic across the line. And even if she is asking me to stop, I've got a job to do. I've got five million dollars in taxes to pay. Why can't my bad dreams be simple anymore? Like going to work naked or spitting out my teeth? Why do my dreams always have to mess with my head?

When I wake up this morning, I know that I will find her. My head is clear and I have that certain buzz that I get when I'm really on—like I drank too much coffee. Anyway. Grace wires me up in 2A. I shut my eyes and leave my body. I float out of the Shimmer office park, past the cloudy skies, and into outer space. I think about my target and who she is. Then I feel this tug at my chest. And I descend. I rocket back to earth and land on a ferryboat somewhere in British Columbia.

The blonde is here. I can feel her. The only thing is, SageRat is also here. Not physically, but mentally. I can feel them. I think they followed me.

"What are you doing here?" I call out.

"Solomon didn't think you could find her," they say in unison.

"Well, I did. So you can leave now."

"Good for you, asshole! Solomon was about to fire you if you didn't!"

And then their presence disappears.

I turn my attention back to the woman. I don't see her right off. There are a lot of people on this boat. Which means a lot of psychic noise. I look around at the passing landscape. It's really quite beautiful. I'm in a part of the world where the mountains meet the sea.

I smell cigarette smoke. I follow it across the deck. There's a woman with a stocking cap and gash on her head, chain-smoking Marlboro Reds. Her hair is short and hot pink. Pink? She's reading a John Grisham novel and wearing rhinestone sunglasses. I reach out to touch her and I see her cutting her blond locks and dying them pink. This is my target. I found her.

I hear a bell ring, and a whistle blows. I'm losing her. Too many people moving in and around my target. Too many thoughts. Too much going on. I concentrate on the pink hair, and I follow that thought through the clutter and noise. It moves me off the ferry and onto a bus where I see these big Neo-Gothic buildings on the waterfront. I look for a sign or landmark to tell me where we are. A vision of Queen Victoria pops into my mind. Queen Victoria—Victoria! My target is in Victoria.

Things are starting to blur. I refocus and follow the pink hair to a small, white, waterfront building. I smell fuel mixed with the salty air. I can also hear propellers sputtering. I see small seaplanes taking off and landing. And then I see my target in the waterfront building, paying for a ticket. I can't hear what she's saying. It's just a bunch of whispers. But I do see that she's paying with Canadian money. Where is she going? I can't make out what her ticket says.

I'm pulled outside of the building for some reason. There's a sign out here. But I can't make out what it says. I zoom in, but it's still blurry. I try to make the letters out one at a time. I get an H, then A-R-B-O-U-R-A-I-R. *Harbour Air.* I think that's it.

Everything begins to sparkle and fade. I'm getting dizzy and kind of motion sick. I'm losing her. I can't find her pink hair. So I race back to my body before I forget all this.

I dive back in and jerk awake. I tear off the electrodes and yell for Grace.

"I found her! I fucking found her!"

10

Rat Bastard
Son of a Bitch

I woke up this morning and found a scratch-off lottery ticket on the pillow next to me. Someone broke into my room last night while I was sleeping and left it there. My heart is racing. Someone was in here, watching me sleep, leaving a lottery ticket at my head. It was probably Sage. Gross. What if she did something to me? What if she used her Jedi mind tricks and fucked me or sucked my blood? I run to the bathroom and check my neck and chest for bite marks. I look down my boxers and check the inside of my thighs.

Nothing. Not a mark. Thank God.

Okay, she didn't suck my blood, and let's pray that she didn't molest me. Maybe she was going through my things. I grab my suitcase and throw my stuff out on the floor; I check everything. But why would she break in to do that? She could just use her remote viewing to go through my stuff. I wad everything up and put it back in my suitcase.

I inspect my sheets and pillows. No sign of wet spots or blood. I pick up the ticket and look at it. I'm too freaked out to try to be psychic about this. So I grab a quarter and scratch it off. There are three matching numbers. It's a winner! Someone broke into my room last night and left me a ten thousand dollar winning lottery ticket. I don't get it. I just won ten thousand dollars.

I take a shower and get my clothes on and go downstairs to Debra McFadden's office. She's in there, sitting at her desk, working the *New York Times* crossword puzzle. She looks up at me.

"Do you know a six-letter word for fate or fortune, beginning with the letter K?" she asks.

"Kismet. K-I-S-M-E-T," I say.

She scribbles it down in the newspaper. "Oh, you're good. That's it!"

"Look, I've got a problem." I hand her my lottery ticket.

She inspects it. "Ten thousand dollars. That's hardly a problem, Travis." She looks up at me. "Where'd you get this?"

"I woke up with it on the pillow next to me."

"Were you missing any teeth?"

"Uh, no."

"That was a joke. You know, tooth fairies? Teeth missing . . . anyway."

"This isn't funny." I cross my arms. "Someone broke into my room last night and left that. I think it was Sage."

"Oh, Sage. That would make sense." She winks at me. "I think she's got a little crush on you."

"Ikshu says she's crazy. I think we've got a situation here."

"Boy, have you gotten yourself into a sticky wicket." She leans forward and whispers, "Ikshu used to date Sage. Sounds like he's a little jealous."

I flinch. "What?"

"He was in love with that little freak. But I think he was put off by how close she was to her brother." She smoothes her tongue over her teeth. "I don't blame him, that whole SageRat routine of theirs really is codependent, if you know what I mean."

"Ikshu and Sage dated?"

"Not really dated so much as just screwed around." She scrunches up her nose.

"And you act like this is normal?"

"Normal? What's normal? When you've been in Clandestine Services for as long as I have, normal is a very relative term. Granted, Sage isn't the prettiest pie on the counter, but some men are into that sort of thing, I guess."

"Well, I'm not, and I really don't want her breaking into my room anymore. Okay?"

"Why don't you just let this one pass?" she says.

"Look, if you don't say something to her, I will."

"Travis, let me clue you in on something real fast." She gives me her best bank teller smile. "SageRat is a lot more important to Shimmer than you are—sorry, that's just the facts—and I'm not going to risk upsetting two of our top operatives just because you found a lottery ticket on your bed. So get over it."

"How are they more important than me? I've completely outscored both of them for the past two weeks."

"SageRat is our leading remote *influencer.* Those two can

bend people to their will like a wet noodle. At this point, they're not all that consistent, but when they do pull it off, it's like, 'watch out.'"

"You mean they can make people do what they want?"

"In a way. So you can see why we don't want to piss them off?"

"Then where does that leave me?" I ask.

"It's just a little crush, Travis. Deal with it. Besides, we're real happy with your work. Don't screw this up." She digs her fake fingernail around in her ear, scoops out a gob of wax, looks at it, and then flicks it.

I have to look away to keep my gag reflex in check.

"Speaking of work." I look around at all the have-a-nice-day-kittens-playing-with-yarn posters in her office. "Did you ever find the blonde in Victoria?"

"We sure did. Found her exactly where you said she was. In Victoria, boarding a Harbour Air seaplane. And she had pink hair—just like you said."

"Really?"

"Yeah, really. I'm quite proud of you. So be happy. Besides, maybe this winning lottery ticket was 'kismet.'" She makes little rabbit ears with her fingers.

"You think the lottery ticket was kismet?"

"No, not really. I just wanted to say my new word. Kis-met. I like that."

Walking back to my room, I catch my reflection in a mirror. And I don't recognize myself. I'm a wreck. I'm this stubble-headed, hollow-eyed mutherfucker. I want to go back to normal. I've had enough of this crap. The vampires, the Holy Vishnus, the CIA, the chakras, the electrodes, and the constant itching of my shaved chest. I'm headed for a major breakdown; I can hear it coming like a heat-seeking missile. It's this forced isolation, this harsh sobriety. It's even the word "Shimmer." Everything here is bugging the shit out of me. I spend all day in this dream state, and then I spend the rest of it locked up in my room, watching bad cable TV. I'm so lonely for Shelby and Noah that it gives me neckaches. I've got a collection of holes in my wall where I've punched it, over and over, until my knuckles are mincemeat. I don't want to be here anymore.

I want to go home. I want to wake up late on a Saturday, roll out of bed, skip the shower, and take Shelby and Noah to Legal Grounds Coffee for pancakes. I want to be bored by Jim and Lisel over a plateful of pecan-encrusted swordfish. I want to play the back nine at Lakewood. I want to be stuck in line at Target with Noah pitching a fit and throwing packs of sugarless gum everywhere. I want my life back.

You know, you always see movies about the CIA or you read a Tom Clancy book, and you think, "Gee, that spy shit sounds cool." Well, it's not. It's a pain in the ass. At least this psychic spy stuff is. There aren't beautiful double agents offering to blow me for international secrets, and there aren't *Dukes of Hazzard*–style car chases. There aren't even any martinis. That's the movies. The reality is, my day-to-day operations and missions are butt-numbing, mind-rotting crap. Instead of Pussy Galore, I've got a dippy bureaucrat in a headband with stupid kitten posters on her wall; a toga-wearing cult member telling me what to do; a disturbed albino screwing with my head; and instead of jetting all over the world, I sit in a Barcalounger in San Ho-fucking-zay.

And if all this isn't enough to push me over the edge, I keep having these bad dreams about the woman I found in Canada. I keep seeing her with all these needles stuck in her like a life-size voodoo doll. I keep seeing her screaming and running and running with the needles breaking off in her skin. When I ask Dr. Solomon about what happened to the woman, he tells me that she was taken into U.S. custody, and she's in a federal prison, awaiting trial. He says she's fine and nothing bad, aside from going to jail, has happened to her. He thinks that my dreams have more to do with my mental health than they do with prophesy.

"Remote viewing tends to amplify the viewer's shadow. It can drive you crazy if you let it," he lisps. "Maybe you and I should set some therapy sessions to help you deal with this."

"Can't you just give me some Prozac or something?" I ask.

"Meds would most likely block anomalous cognition."

"But what if this anoma-whatever-I-do is, you know, driving me insane?"

"That's highly probable." He pushes his glasses up on his nose and stares me down. "That's why we need to get you into psychotherapy before that happens."

The lottery ticket is a fake. A mutherfucking joke! I didn't win ten thousand dollars. After work was over today, I went up to my room. And while I was watching SportsCenter I ate a TV dinner and read the legal copy on the back of my winning ticket. It says shit like "Prizes over $5,000 may be redeemed after validation by standing on your head and spitting wooden nickels. Prizes must be claimed at your mamma's house no later than 30 seconds after scratching your head."

What kind of asshole does that? I'm sure everybody here knows how desperate I am for money. I'm sure they all know that I'm about to lose everything—that my company's a train wreck and my marriage is in the shitter—and that I could have used that ten thousand. I'm definitely not in the mood to be fucked with. I'm going to give that creepy bitch a piece of my fucking mind. I don't care what Debra McFadden says, you don't just break into someone's room and screw with them like that. I grab the bogus ticket and I march down the hall to Sage's room. I bang on her door.

"Sage! Open the door! It's Travis!"

She opens up and there she is, all cross-eyed and wearing this black leather cat suit, with fake blood smeared around her mouth.

"Can I help you?" She licks the blood off the edge of her lips.

I shove the lottery ticket under her nose. "This!"

"I didn't do it." She sways back.

"This is not funny!" I shout.

"Don't yell at me!" She puts her hand on her chest.

"Stay the fuck out of my room!" I throw the ticket at her feet.

She just stands there and lowers her gaze. I can feel her thickness coming at me.

So I close my eyes and I visualize reaching into her heart, just like Ikshu said. I say the words "kid fears" over and over to myself like a chant.

That's when I hear her scream, and the thickness stops. It's overtaken by this tidal wave of blackness. I don't know what I've just done, but a cold ocean wave crashes down on me and pulls me under, washing me away. It spits me out on a middle-school playground where Sage is a little white-haired girl, a child who's being tortured by her classmates. They have her cornered and they're singing and throwing grass and clover at her. They're singing the Oak Ridge Boys' "Elvira." Only they've changed the words.

"Om-bopa, om-bopa. Mau-mau. Al-bino! My hair's on fire! Al-bino! A om-bopa om-bopa! Mau-mau!"

Sage is huddled up, crying harder than any child should ever cry. I see this happen to her day after day like a Xerox machine making copies of crime scene photos. I see the little girl discover that when she acts like an animal and growls at the children, they run away and scream. I see this little kid learn that the only way to survive is to make people fear her. I see deep inside a heart so tender and young that she feels everyone's pain and she turns that pain on herself by cutting at her own skin. I see the only person who has ever loved her. Her scrawny brother, Rat. And I understand who these two are, and how they came to be so profoundly fucked up.

This pain pushes on my eyes so hard that water gushes out of me. I sob. I wail. I howl. I can't help it. My heart's been cut wide open, and it's tangled up with barbed wire. I can't bear what Sage carries; it's all over me. And now I'm sure I've lost my mind because I walk over and hug her.

Even weirder is she lets me. She doesn't try to bite my neck or do anything weird. She doesn't even cry. She just rests her head on my shoulder, and I bawl my eyes out. Something is happening here. I'm not sure what. But whatever it is, it's seriously fucking with my head because I'm hugging this albino vampire freak and telling her that she's okay. And I don't go around hugging people, even when they're normal. I'm just not that kind of person.

Tonight is beyond the dark night of the soul. Tonight, I fight insanity with my bare fists. I beat hole after hole in the walls in my room. I keep having flashbacks of what happened between me and Sage. I keep seeing that horrible childhood. I've become her personal Bill Clinton. I keep feeling her pain, and the only way to get rid of it is to hit it into the wall.

I think this is it. I've officially flown over the cuckoo's nest.

What I really need is a drink to wash all this crap out of me. I need one so badly that I'm shivering. I can almost feel the sting of liquor hitting the back of my throat. I check my toothpaste and deodorant ingredients to see if I can eat them for some alcohol. But I'm out of luck. They're both alcohol free. So I just give up. I don't have anything left in me; I feel completely broken in two.

I quit hitting things. I go to the bathroom, run cold water over my bloody knuckles, and wrap them in toilet paper. Then I get into bed and hide under the covers, like I used to do when I was a kid. I rock myself to sleep. But sleep only makes things worse. I have this mixed grill of nightmares. The alligator killing Noah. The woman in Canada being stuck to death with needles. SageRat in my Range Rover. And of course, the blue dude shows up. Except he shows up in between dreams when I'm awake with the cold sweats. He stands at the foot of my bed with his arms crossed. He's darker this time, more indigo than blue, and he doesn't look happy. He starts talking shit that doesn't make sense.

"I am the thunderbolt among weapons. Among cattle, the

magical wish-granting cow; I am the procreative god of love, the king of snakes. I am the purifying wind, the warrior Rama bearing arms, the sea monster crocodile, the flowing river Ganges."

"What do you want from me?" I call out.

He doesn't answer. He only darkens into the night and disappears, leaving my room steaming hot and stinking of magnolias and orange peels.

I wake up, with my hands swollen with cuts and bruises. I roll over to get away from the pain, and see Rat crouching by my bedside, staring me in the face.

"What did you do to my sister?" he growls.

"How the fuck did you get in here?" I jump up and stand on my bed, looking for something to hit him with.

He moves slow and spider-like around the room, and then suddenly he does this ninja flip and lands standing on the bed in front of me, ready to fight.

"Look, I didn't do anything to Sage. I promise." I back up against the wall, hedging toward the nightstand lamp.

"Liar! She's fucking catatonic! She won't speak!"

"I didn't do anything. It just sort of happened." I feel around for the lamp while keeping my eyes on the little psycho. And that's when Rat's fist hits my face, again and again. And before I can grab the lamp and break it over his head, he grabs my arm and flips me off the bed and onto the floor. I land hard; it knocks the wind out of me. His feet land only inches from my head and then he grabs my left arm and twists.

It hurts like fuck.

"What did you do to her?" he spits.

"Ouch! Shit!" I scream. "I didn't mean to do anything!"

He twists my arm tighter. "What did you do to her?"

"Ikshu told me–fuck!–to pull–pull out her kid fears or something like that."

"What? Explain!" He twists even harder; it hurts so bad I can barely breathe.

"I-I-reached into her heart and try-eye-eye-tried to see her childhood fears. I guess."

"You fucking bastard!" He steps on my back and twists my arm until it snaps.

The pain is so bad I black out. He kicks me again in the side, which sort of wakes me up.

"And by the way, fuckhead, I'm the one who left the lottery ticket, not Sage," he says. "It was just a joke."

Then he leaves me here, all beaten to shit and squirming with a seriously broken arm.

11

Shits and Giggles

"I want to press charges." I sit across from Dr. Solomon in his office. I'm covered with purple bruises, and my hand and wrist are swollen. They put a neon green cast on, and I might have to get some pins put in. I've had three Percodans and I'm still in a world of hurt.

"You can't press charges, Travis." Dr. Solomon smirks.

"Oh, yes, I can," I slur. "Breaking and entering, assault, attempted murder. That little psychopath needs to be put under the jail."

"That little psychopath doesn't exist." He pulls out his Palm Pilot and starts fiddling with it.

"What do you mean he doesn't exist?" My head wobbles like a baby's. I think I'm drooling, but I don't care.

"When you join Shimmer, we issue you a death certificate. We erase your identity." He looks up at me and puts his Palm Pilot away. "You've got something on your chin."

I wipe the slobber off with my good hand. "You mean sort of like the witness relocation thing?"

"Similar, but not exactly."

"You guys haven't done that to me, have you?" I moan; my arm hurts like holy fuck.

"You're a little different story. We're going to have to issue a death certificate for your wife and your kid, so that paperwork's a little harder to get through. Plus, you have this whole IRS problem that we have to resolve before we can properly erase you."

I don't really hear Dr. Solomon as much as see images of Shelby and Noah in white satin-lined coffins. I smell the embalming fluid mixed with carnations and roses.

"I don't want to be erased!" I shout. "That was never part of the deal!"

"Travis, calm down. Let's talk about this."

"Sorry." I shake the funeral images out of my head.

"Don't be so rash. Look at the facts first. Think about it. You'll never have to pay taxes again. And you can never be charged with a crime." He multiplies into two Dr. Solomons and then kaleidoscopes into one. "It's not a bad deal, trust me."

"Look, doc, I just want to go home, and I don't want a fucking death certificate!"

"How about you just get some rest? And we'll talk about all this when you feel better." He swirls into this Van Gogh painting of himself.

And before I know it, I'm waking up in my bed with Grace putting a blanket over me. I must have passed out in Dr. Solomon's office. Anyway, I feel the warm tug of heavy sleep and it pulls me under, into a deep dreamless night that I wish I could stay wrapped up in forever.

*   *   *

Something happened while I slept.

Something bad:

People are laughing.

I'm not talking about a chuckle here or there. I'm talking about busting up, milk-through-your-nose, you-can't-stop-even-though-you're-in-church kind of laughter. People at Shimmer are falling down with it. Everyone is cracking up, left and right, for no apparent reason. This has really gotten Dr. Solomon worried. He's called in a special team to investigate the Shimmer air-conditioning system. He thinks it's nerve gas. So this morning, there are men in spacesuits scouring the place, looking for bombs or gas. But they haven't found a single molecule of anything that would cause this. Which worries Solomon even more.

He thinks a terrorist group has figured out that we're a spook operation and that this is going to get ugly. He's all doom and gloom about the roaring laughter. He thinks whatever's causing it is just the beginning of some serious neurological damage. In between his own laughing fits, he's scheduling everyone for MRIs and CT scans. Meanwhile, the Uzi-toting guards downstairs are wearing gas masks. But they're still having these ridiculous attacks, too. Personally, I don't think it's nerve gas. I think it's some kind of mass hysteria.

Because get this: I'm the only person who hasn't gotten the giggles. I was asleep through the worst of it. And to be quite honest, after what Rat did to me, there's not a whole lot around this joint that I find all that funny. But Debra McFadden thinks everything around here is a laugh riot. She's taken to wearing Depends because her tiny bladder can't handle all her snorting and guffawing; she's constantly wetting herself. It's disgusting. And Ikshu will just be walking down the hall and he'll drop to his knees, holding his stomach because he's so hysterical. It's crazy. Sage and Rat have locked themselves in their rooms. I guess uncontrollable laughter kind of blows their whole morbid gig.

Anyway, I sit here and take more Percodan and watch TV. Now, that *SpongeBob* is a funny show, and I find myself sort of laughing here and there. But nothing like what everyone else has been doing. And that's when I hear a knocking at my door. It's a serious drag getting up off this sofa with my fucked-up arm, but I do it. I steady myself and take a deep breath. I get up and answer the door.

And lo and behold, it's Ikshu and Dr. Solomon, leaning on each other, laughing.

"Travis, it's you." Solomon giggles and can't catch his breath. "It's you-who-who-who . . ."

"Oh, man, I just took a couple of Percs, I don't feel like dealing with this," I groan. "What do you two want? Come on. Spit it out."

"No, my friend." Ikshu chokes and sniggers. "It's your darshan. It-it-it-it's making everyone laugh." And then he just falls to his knees and doubles over.

"Why don't you two talk to me when you're over this laughing shit. It's getting on my nerves. My arm hurts."

I slam the door and lie back on my couch. There's nothing more annoying than people laughing when nothing's funny.

And just when I settle back down and relax again, my phone starts ringing. And it won't stop. It just keeps ringing and ringing. That stupid phone just won't shut up. It's tap dancing on my last nerve. I think about throwing my shoe at it. But then, I realize I don't have on shoes. I have to answer the mutherfucker.

"What!" I yell into the phone.

"Travis. Dr. Solomon."

"Yeah? What?"

"You've got to stop taking the Percodan." Solomon sings like he's telling me a joke. "Ikshu says that's what's causing the laughter."

I'm waiting for the punch line.

"Are you fucking kidding me? My arm still hurts!"

"It's affecting your morphic resonance," he chuckles. "The closer people get to you, the worse the paroxysms get." He loses it and I hang up on him.

I'm sick and tired of this *X-Files* bullshit. Morphic-fucking-whatever. I'll be damned if they're taking my pills.

They took my Percodan. They stormed in here, about ten of them, all laughing and shit, and they took my goddamn pills. Lucky for them I was doped up. Because otherwise, I would have been kicking some security-guard asses. God, I'm pissed off. My arm and face throb. I hurt all over. I've got this constant headache, and I can't sleep. But Ikshu and Solomon were right. Now that I'm off the pills, the plague of laughter has stopped. It *was* me, and this makes Dr. Solomon's eyes twinkle when he starts talking about it. He's thrilled. You'd think he'd just discovered that I could shit golden eggs or something. In fact, he won't shut up about it.

"Do you know who Rupert Sheldrake is?" he asks.

"No." I sneer at him. "And unless he's got a bag full of Percodan, I don't want to know him."

"He's a cellular biologist from Cambridge," Solomon lisps. "Basically, he's proven the principle of morphic resonance."

"And I should give a fuck about this because . . .?"

"Because, Travis, what just happened here is textbook morphic resonance. You became a disturbance in the field. And if we can figure out how you did this, well, then we could make you a very rich man."

"A rich man?" My ears perk up. "Keep talking."

"See, Sheldrake discovered nature's universal memory. Take a squirrel living in Dallas. That squirrel is being influenced by all the squirrels that came before it. Even ones, in say, Menlo Park."

"Yeah, no shit, squirrels act like squirrels. So what?"

"Well, there's more to it than that." He straightens his glasses. "See, this collective memory is expressed through morphic fields, the fields within and around each squirrel or person, or amoeba for that matter."

"Okay. You lost me. I'm in serious fucking pain here and you're talking about goddamn squirrels and amoebas and shit."

"It's amoebae." He smiles with a shrug.

It takes everything I've got not to knock him upside the head with my cast. Instead, I bounce away my anger with my knee.

"Look, just bear with me." He sighs. "There's a morphic field connecting each of us. It's an organizing intelligence. It evolves us. When one squirrel learns a new habit, it's transferred through the field to the rest. And there are some people, you, for example, who can manipulate these fields. That's why everyone started laughing when you took the Percodan."

"So how is this going to make me rich?"

"Travis, do you know what this means? Do you?" He shakes his head and grins. "You better believe Shimmer will make you *very* rich."

"All I know is things had better start to change around here, or you people can kiss my morphic-resonating ass good-bye. That's all I know."

"I can assure you, Shimmer will do everything we can to make you happy. Our remote influencers are very well taken care of, trust me."

"If that means erasing my identity and all that bullshit, then you can forget it." I sit back and cross my arms. "Not gonna do it."

"Look, you can call the shots, Travis. This is your game now."

"So I can go home if I want?"

"Of course. You always could." He nods with a grin.

"And that's okay?"

"Sure. We could have you out on a flight tonight."

"Then do it."

"Done." He smiles.

12

Back to Normal

Before I can go home, Debra has to create a "legend" for me.
That's CIA doublespeak for a lie that explains what I've been
doing all this time. And so far, it's not really sounding all that
convincing. Debra wants me to tell Shelby that I broke my
arm in the shower. She also wants me to tell her that I chewed
gum in rehab to replace my alcohol addiction and, boy, was I
stupid, but I fell asleep and it got all stuck in my hair. So, I had
to shave my head.

I'm sorry, but nobody is going to buy that. Especially my
wife. As for my bruises, Debra's trying to cover them up with
her gambit makeup. But I think Shelby is going to be more
freaked out by a face full of makeup than a face full of
bruises.

"Maybe I should just tell her the truth," I say.

"Travis, you've got to realize that by telling your wife about this operation, not only do you compromise your mission, but you also compromise your wife's safety."

"How so?" I sit here while she wipes this little sponge over my bruises.

"If she tells anyone, I mean *anyone,* and the truth about you and Shimmer gets out, then you open your family up to all sorts of threats. Terrorists and the like. So for your family's sake, follow the legend."

"Well, I'm just not buying it. I mean who falls asleep with gum in their hair and then has to cut it all off? Who breaks their arm in the shower?"

"An alcoholic." She smears flesh-colored goop under my eye. "Now stop moving so I can finish this."

I look in the mirror; my bruises have completely been erased.

"Amazing." I turn my head from side to side. "You can't even tell I have on makeup."

"Your tax dollars at work. Those are space-age polymers developed by NASA," she chirps. "You know, we could glue a wig to your head. That might work."

"I'll stick with the chewing gum story," I say.

"Oops. You made a funny." She pokes me. *"Stick* with the gum story. Get it?"

"Yeah, I got it." I wet my lips and imagine what just the tiniest sip of Jack Daniel's would taste like.

"That looks pretty nice if I do say so myself." She steps back and looks at her handiwork. "You know, I'm flying back with you, so I can do touch-ups once you're home. But you're going to have to be real creative about taking showers until these bruises heal. Okay?"

"But what if I get close to Shelby and she can tell it's makeup?

"Trust me, cupcake. I've talked to Shelby. You won't be getting that close to her."

"What is that supposed to mean?"

"It means Shelby and you still have 'issues,' and that means you'll be sleeping in the guest room until you can resolve them . . . Sorry."

On the plane back to Dallas, I sit next to Debra, and this time I stay away from the booze. Instead, I go to sleep to escape the pain of my hidden bruises. And I dream. I dream about the woman I tracked down in Canada, and it's not good. I see these two thugs beat the crap out of her and then tie her to a metal bedpost. She's screaming for help. One of the thugs takes off his sweat sock and crams it in her mouth. They've stripped her down to her bra and panties; her belly button is pierced.

Then all of a sudden, I see things from the girl's perspective. Now it's *me* writhing against the ropes, struggling to get away. I feel wild—terrified. I see one of the thugs remove the cover from a syringe. He squirts out a drop or two. I scream through my gag; I can taste the nasty funk of the sock in my mouth. And then they jab the needle into my arm and push the heroin into my veins. The warm rush makes me gasp. I fight it, but it only takes a couple of seconds, and it takes me under. The thugs keep shooting me up and eventually, my heart stops. There's no pain. The smack makes everything just fall away. I feel the girl's last breath leave my lips. And then I find myself standing outside of her, watching the thugs loom over the half-naked body.

The thug without a sock checks for a pulse. He finds nothing. The woman's given up the ghost. Her eyes are open and her hair is bright pink. The thug takes his sock out of her mouth and puts it back on his foot. Then I see both of the men get into a Chevy Malibu and drive away. I wake up with a start.

"Shimmer!" I blurt out.

"God bless you." Debra pinches my thigh and scowls at me.

I look at her and she raises an eyebrow. So I keep my dream to myself. After all it was just a dream, and Debra's told me a hundred times never to discuss Shimmer in public—not for any reason.

I flip through a wrinkled *Newsweek*. But the pink-haired girl won't go away. She's hovering around me, whispering in my ear. She's desperate and needy. I look over at Debra to see if she hears this, too. Obviously not. She's busy with her needlepoint and humming Karen Carpenter songs.

I put on my headphones and watch the in-flight movie, but the whispers don't go away. That's because they're not being whispered into my ear; they're being whispered into my soul.

Why do I feel so guilty about finding that woman? She was a criminal. So why do I keep coming up with all these doom and gloom scenarios involving her? I think Dr. Solomon was right; I need some serious head shrinking to deal with this shit.

But before I can get too freaked out by all this, Debra nudges me and pantomimes taking off headphones.

"Yeah?" I pull them off.

"Can I ask you a question?"

"Sure."

"It's personal." She shrinks down in her seat.

"Yeah?"

"Well, it's about my sister, Jocelyn." She adjusts her sweater. "Do you think you could contact her again?"

"I didn't think we were supposed to talk like this in public," I whisper.

"Oh, nobody knows what we're doing." She looks around the plane. "Please. It would mean a lot."

I shut my eyes, and a vision comes barreling at me. It's blurry at first, and then it develops kind of like a Polaroid.

It's a housecat dressed up in a tuxedo. That's all I see.

"It's not working," I say.

"I saw your eyelids moving. You must have seen something."

"I saw a cat dressed in a little tuxedo."

"Really?" Tears well up in her eyes and spill over onto her cheek.

"Yeah, does that mean something to you?" I ask.

"Shasta, that's her cat. We dressed him in a tuxedo for Jocelyn's wedding and had him give her away since, you know, we never really knew our father."

"Her cat was in the wedding?"

"Oh, Shasta wasn't just a cat. He was like a little person. He could be such a little Mister Grumpy Bumps when he wanted to be." She shakes her head and wipes away her tears. "She loved that cat. He was her best friend."

"I'm sorry. You must really miss your sister," I say.

She nods and weeps. "Do you see anything else?"

I shut my eyes and I see the cat being put to sleep just like the girl in my dream.

"Yeah, who put Shasta down?" I ask.

"Oh, I did that. I know that sounds kind of weird, but after Jocelyn was killed, I couldn't bear to look at him." She sucks on her teeth. "I put him to sleep so my sister could play with him in heaven. It was the most humane thing to do, really. You know, with all the traveling and everything that I do."

My blood runs cold. I can't bring myself to even say anything.

"Boy, that really is quite a gift you have, Mr. Anderson. Thank you." She pats me on the leg and picks up her *Cat Fancy* magazine. Then she flips the pages and coos at the kitten photos.

"Omigod, Travis! What happened to you?" Shelby is slack jawed.

I stand at our front door with my suitcase in my good hand and my broken arm in a sling. The A/C in the taxi went out on the way over here. And the Dallas heat got its hands all over me. All of my gambit has melted away; I'm covered in sweat and bruises. But I don't care. I just stand here. Stunned that I'm actually married to this woman. This goddess whose belly is swelling with my child. And this is my house.

"I fell down some stairs and broke my arm," I tell her as she helps me inside.

"And they shave your head for that?"

"They had to X ray my head," I say.

"Are you sure you're okay?" She studies my face.

"Looks worse than it is. I'm fine."

I scan my house; it feels like a stranger's. Did we really paint the living room red? I forgot about that. Who paints a room red? I guess I did.

Shelby doesn't hug or kiss me. She just kind of circles me, inspecting my wounds and cast.

"Travis. I can't believe they let this happen to you." She furrows her brow and shakes her head. "Was this covered by our insurance?"

"Yeah, I think so." I put my suitcase down in the living room. Shelby looks me up and down. The silence is so heavy between us, it's hurting my back. Neither of us knows what to say. She doesn't recognize me and I don't really feel like I know her anymore—at least not like I used to. I mean, this is the woman who wanted our living room red. And I have no idea why I would have agreed to paint it that color. I feel like I'm lost in the grocery store and can't remember what aisle my life is on.

"I missed you." Shelby leans on the staircase banister. The sunlight shines through her dress. She's not wearing a slip.

"I missed you, too." I feel my blood rushing back with the memories of who we used to be.

And then another heavy pause falls on us; it's the awkward gravity of being apart for so long.

"Where's Noah?" I ask.

"He's taking a nap. He's got a summer cold." She folds her arms and looks down at the hardwood. "But you can go upstairs and see him if you want."

"Can I?"

"Just don't wake him up. He's sick."

I walk over to the stairs and stop in front of her. She looks me deep in the eyes. She's sad. I'm clumsy. I move in to kiss her on the lips, but instead, she gives me her cheek.

"Not yet," she murmurs.

My heart drops; it's sore with disappointment.

I smile back at her anyway as I go up the stairs, but she just looks away.

The upstairs part of the house smells like the past, like Shelby and me. Our dirty clothes, her lotion, my leather coat, the cedar chips in the winter closet, Max's wet dog smell. It all swirls around me and I feel sort of light headed. I can hear these smells like a song. They sing to me and they tell me that I'm back home.

I tiptoe into Noah's room. Pew. His diaper pail reeks to high heaven. But Valya has tried to mask it with some kind of industrial-strength baby powder. A two-year-old's poops shouldn't be put in a diaper pail; they should be flushed. Noah ought to be potty trained by now. It's probably my fault that he's not. My fault that I had to go away and leave him and his mother. I carry this guilt with me as I walk over to his bed. I don't know what to do with it. But I completely forget all this self-pity bullshit when I see my boy sleeping. He's sucking away on his pacifier and holding Peanut Butter. I put my hand on his little head. He's sweating. I lean down and smell his neck. He smells like sweet potatoes, like dirt after the rain. He smells like Noah, my son. I stand over him and smile so hard my face hurts.

This little boy is my home and this is where I want to stay.

13
Bringing Down the Moon

Like magic, Shimmer has deposited five million dollars into my account. Just like that. So I go to my bank and have them wire the money to the IRS. And that's it. I'm done. My problems are over. No more audit. No more IRS breathing down my back. I'm square with them and I'm a free man. I can have my life back. And get this; Debra says that I can expect to receive the first of my retainer checks from Shimmer this week. Those checks will add up to right around a hundred grand this year. I'll also get another hundred thousand for all the training I did at Shimmer HQ.

I can't lie. I think Debra and everybody at Shimmer are a bunch of freaks without a circus, but so long as they keep paying me, I'll keep working for them. That's how bad I need money right now. However, I do have a problem with this remote influencing stuff. I'm not sure it's right. I mean, they want me to make people do things.

The problem is who decides who needs to be controlled, and how? This is a huge responsibility and I'm not sure I won't abuse it. Imagine I've got some jackass at Home Depot who won't let me return something that I bought there. You better believe I'll turn it on and make him do it. So what's to stop the government from giving me assignments that are just as questionable?

Say Shimmer offered me a million dollars to make someone like Fidel Castro shoot himself. I think I could rationalize that. He's a Communist. He caused the Cuban Missile Crisis. And he's a Communist. I'd probably do it for a million bucks and I'd probably feel like a patriot about it. But does that make it right? I don't know. It's not in the world's best interest for me to be making these sorts of decisions; I can't even decide if sending my kid to private schools is socially irresponsible or not, much less what world leader needs to be taken out.

I mean, here I am born and bred to look out for me and only me, and now I'm about to be saddled with the welfare of the entire free world. There's something wrong with this picture.

"What the hell happened to you?" Reed stands up from his desk.

"Rehab. That's what."

"Man, do you look like shit or what?" He shakes his head. "What happened?"

"I fell down some stairs and broke my arm."

"Bullshit *you fell down some stairs.* Someone fucked you up. Who was it, your dealer?"

"I don't have a dealer, Reed."

"Well, somebody kicked your ass. You don't get that way from falling down any goddamn stairs."

Okay, this is one of those times I was talking about. If I knew how to remote control people, right now, I'd make Reed shut the fuck up and maybe have the bastard punch himself in the face a couple of times.

"Just drop it, okay?" I say. "Look, we've more important things to worry about than my face. Namely, the IRS."

"What about the IRS?" Reed's nose starts bleeding.

"Have you talked to them? . . . Dude, your nose."

"Oh, shit." He grabs a wad of Kleenex off his desk and holds it over his nose.

"Have I talked to them? Travis, the bastards put a lien on everything I own. Of course I've talked to the mutherfuckers."

"They put a lien on you?"

"I guess Shelby didn't call you in rehab and tell you. The IRS has frozen all my assets. We're fucked. I can't even get our accountant to call us back; that's how fucked we are. Real good time for you to take a monthlong vacation, asshole. Thanks."

A dark red spot grows on his white tissue. Blood drops onto the papers on his desk.

"I worked a deal." I smile. "Tilt your head back and squeeze your nose. That should help."

Reed throws his head back and keeps talking, "A deal? Whatever, man. Don't even fucking joke about this."

"No, seriously. As far as the IRS is concerned, Reed, we're free men."

"Travis." He looks down at his bloody Kleenex and then back up at me. "You're about to get your ass kicked a second time. I'm not kidding."

I stand here with the biggest shit-eating grin on my face and hand Reed the paperwork from my five-million-dollar transfer. He holds his nose with one hand and the photocopies in the other.

"How'd you do this?" His left nostril is gushing blackish blood. He grabs some more tissues.

"I did it the old fashioned way," I say. "I earned it."

"Holy shit!" He squeezes his nose and tilts his head back again. "You paid them five mill?"

Reed sits back down in his chair with his head back, holding wads of Kleenex over his face.

"You owe me, Reedy-boy. You owe me big." I walk out of his office with my paperwork and a little piece of my reclaimed pride.

However, in true Reed Bindler fashion, he doesn't even say thank you. He just keeps stuffing tissues up his rusty pipes.

I hope his nose bleeds like this if he's ever with Shelby.

Ikshu is back at the Dallas Holy Vishnu temple. We have a standing lunch appointment every weekday so that he can teach me how to remote control people. I pick up a Burger King before I go; this really pisses him off.

"Eating living creatures lowers your vibration, Travis Anderson." Ikshu bows his head. "It is offensive to Vishnu and extremely disrespectful to bring it into my temple."

"Oh, go fuck yourself, Ikshu." I munch down on my burger. "I've seen your blue guy hanging out in the Chick-fil-A."

He stares at me like he's trying to remote control me.

"Want a fry?" I offer.

He shakes his head. I think he mumbles a little prayer against me.

Anyway. At these lunch sessions, Ikshu doesn't really teach me anything that I don't already know. Basically, I just meditate and try to make myself feel like a cinnamon roll. Then we go into the restaurant and I select a target and try to make that person do something. Like get up and fix a plate of couscous off the buffet. I'm not very good at this. In fact, I can't seem to do it at all.

Ikshu, on the other hand, is so good that it's scary. He's like a psychic puppeteer. He picks out this hippie chick at the table next to us. He shuts his eyes and chants. Then he makes the hippie chick pop up out of her chair, run around the room three times, and sit back down. I try to take over where he left off and I can't even make her use her spoon instead of her fork.

"How did you learn to do this?" I ask.

"It was my karma." He shuts his eyes and hums some whiny Indian song.

"No, really. When did you know you could do this?"

He opens his eyes and smiles. "Since I was a child. Here in the boarding school."

"You went to school here? What did you take, Remote Controlling 101?"

"No, these gifts were given to me in a time of desperation . . . to save me."

"Save you from what?"

"From the rats." Tears well up in his happy eyes.

"Rats?"

"I had stolen milk sweets from the offering in the temple. As my punishment, my teachers put me in a closet full of starved rats to teach me the evils of desire."

"Shit! How old were you?"

"Maybe four or five," he says.

"So you got your teachers to let you go?"

"No, I got the rats to stop hurting me." He pulls up his robe and shows me this shiny ring of scars all around his ankles.

"I don't know what to say, Ikshu. I'm sorry, man."

"Do not be sorry, Travis Anderson. It was my karma. That dark moment revealed to me who I really am."

"Who you really are?"

"Yes, I am Kalki, the Tenth Incarnation."

"You're Whatty, the what? I don't understand. If this place did that to me, I would be so fucking out of here. What are you still doing here with these assholes?"

"I am here to destroy them, Travis." His eyes look dead and his smile is mean and gray. "I am Kalki the destroyer."

He looks at my head and my eyes, but he's not looking at me. It's that penetrating stare you hear about serial killers having. I can't explain it. It's just weird. He's seriously creeping me out. I feel like I just turned over a stone and discovered a snake or something writhing with evil.

Maybe I can't remote control anyone yet, but I sure do seem to have a talent for making people tell me their wack job stories. Why are all these Shimmer people so profoundly fucked up and why do they think I want to hear about it?

Speaking of wack jobs, I haven't seen the blue dude in weeks. It seems that the Vancouver girl has stepped in to take his place. I keep seeing her pink hair all over Dallas. I see her jogging down Turtle Creek. I see her drinking margaritas outside at Primo's. I see her sunbathing at the country club. She's haunting me. Perhaps Solomon was right. Perhaps I'm a spook who's scared of his own shadow.

But why do I have a pink-haired thief and a blue god lurking in my subconscious? I guess that's what Dr. Solomon could tell me. I call Debra to see if we can set up an appointment before I lose it like Ikshu. She calls Solomon and the good doctor jumps on a plane to Dallas immediately. We have our first therapy session tonight in a dorm room at the Vishnu temple. This troubles me. Solomon must think I'm really on the edge to get here this fast. Maybe I really am on the edge. I mean, I am seeing things. Wouldn't that just be my luck? I get the IRS off my back and then I go stark raving mad before I can get the rest of my life together.

"Go ahead and get comfortable, Travis." He offers me the small twin bed and he takes a seat in an old office chair. "What seems to be the problem?"

"Everything, doc. My wife . . . I keep finding myself driving by liquor stores . . . I don't think right . . . I'm seeing things." I lie down on the bed. It smells like curry and sex. I think this is the room I heard all those fuck noises coming from.

"What kind of things do you see?" He scribbles in his Palm Pilot. "The blue man?"

"No, he's lying low these days. I keep seeing that girl I found in Vancouver."

"I told you, Travis, she's okay."

"I know that. But I keep seeing all this weird shit. I dream about her getting killed and now I'm starting to see her when I'm awake." I can't seem to get comfortable on this bed. I keep thinking about the pubic hairs and dried body fluids that are probably all over the covers. I keep seeing Ikshu and Debra McFadden bumping nasties. Were those the two people I heard in here?

"Okay. Calm down and take a deep breath." He squints at me and takes a deep breath himself. "Let me explain some things to you. I've been studying your EEGs and your personality tests. And by standard psychology, I would diagnose you as having a schizotypal personality disorder."

"I'm schizo?"

"Schizotypal, but if we don't watch you, we could lose you."

"This is not making me feel better." I can't take it anymore. I think this bed is giving me lice. I jump to my feet.

"Why did you just get up?" He raises an overgrown eyebrow.

"That bed. It's dirty. I, uh, prefer to stand."

"Oh-kay." He writes something about me in his Palm Pilot.

"What did you just write?"

"Don't worry about it. I'm just taking notes. Now where were we?"

"You were saying I was borderline schizo." I scratch my neck and arms; those nasty-ass sheets gave me crabs or something.

"Oh yeah, we were talking about your diagnosis." He chews on his plastic pencil. "I would prescribe some antipsychotics. But they would block your anomalous cognitive abilities. And after your little episode with Percodan, I don't think meds are an option anyway."

"So what can you do for me?"

"What you're experiencing is what all great sages and prophets have experienced. You have opened the Door. And it will only be your internal fortitude that will get you through to the other side."

"Jesus, doc, if I had wanted some kind of retarded riddle, I would have gone to Ikshu for help. I want you to fix me. Just give me some pills."

"Trust me, if things get too hard, I'll get you the help you need. Just hang in there. The hallucinations and the paranoia are just part of the process. You're discovering that reality is fluid. You're expanding your perceptions. It's unsettling to say the least."

"No shit, it's unsettling. You don't see what I see."

"Travis, you have no idea how much potential you have."

"Oh, really? Because a few days ago you were ready to send my lame ass packing."

"We had to be sure."

"I think you were fucking with me."

"I think you're paranoid."

"Should I be?"

"No, Travis. Your EEGs and recent scores actually show more promise than Ikshu or SageRat."

"Ikshu and SageRat are psycho."

"I would concur. From a traditional view, they are quite psychotic. But everybody, especially a remote influencer, has his own reality. And if you're going to keep your sanity, you're going to have to deal with that."

"Okay. That's another thing I'm not sure about; this remote influencing bullshit."

"What's there not to be sure about?"

"Lots of things. Do you really think it's okay just to take people over? Come on. The government is paying to research this?"

"What if that person was about to kill your wife and child?"

"I don't know. I guess it would be okay then."

"You *do* know. Reality is subjective and so are morals. Unfortunately, there is a time to kill—a time to protect, Travis. And there are times when remote influencing is more than okay. There is a time when it's for the highest moral good."

"Yeah, so maybe you're right. But who decides when it's okay?"

"Who decides if a war is for the greater good? It's determined by military intelligence and the President."

"Kind of like Vietnam?" I ask.

"Look, Travis, you don't live in a perfect world. And Shimmer is not a perfect organization. But we are a very important service to U.S. military intelligence. And we do a lot for the safety and security of this nation, and the world for that matter."

"What really happened to the pink-haired girl?" I try to make him look me in the eye, but he's shifty.

There's a long pause. He lets out a heavy sigh. He knows what I've been seeing. And he knows what really happened to the girl. He knows they didn't just lock her away.

"She was a spy." He glances down and then meets my eyes.

"So you offed her?"

"Goddamn it, Travis!" He leans forward and whispers. "She had information that could have launched a nuclear war."

"Then why didn't you just tell me that?'

"Did you hear what I just said?" he lisps. "Everything involving that woman was classified. We were dealing with a highly inflammatory situation."

"Well, what do you think I'm seeing? Her ghost?"

"I don't know what you're seeing, Travis." He shakes his head and rolls his eyes.

And that's when I get the chills. I think the Vancouver girl is in the room with us. I don't see her. I just feel her. It's like the tense feeling you get in the back of your head when someone's staring at you. I don't say anything to Solomon about it. Maybe it's some paranoid side effect of remote viewing, but something or someone is telling me he can't be trusted.

The moon hangs fat over White Rock Lake and it's pink, like in that Nick Drake song. I'm parked at the water's edge in my Range Rover. Shelby's still ignoring me. I figure if I'm going to feel this alone, I'll do it without her around. So I sit here and stare at the moon's reflection in the water and think about the pink-haired girl. Pink. Pink. Pink. Pink. I wish I had never seen that fucking color. I wish I had never found that girl. Because then I wouldn't be feeling like this.

Like I killed her.

I guess this is just part of the job. When you're a spook, you get people killed. After all, this is exactly what I was wondering about; what if it's in the world's best interests for someone to die? What if it's my job to make it happen?

I guess I should be proud of what I did for my country. But I'm not. I feel like shit. I try to tell myself that I saved hundreds of lives by finding that girl. But my guilt is heavy. It lumps up in my throat when I think about how she died; how those thugs tied her up and stuck her full of needles; how violating that was to the soul.

I can't wash that dirty image out of my head. For some reason, I don't think the pink-haired girl really was a spy. She didn't feel like a spy to me. She felt innocent and scared when I found her. But what do I know? I'm barely sane.

I suppose this is just what you feel when you kill someone—even if they were bad. I try to stop thinking about her. I just look up at the pink moon. And make a wish that I can somehow find some peace and that I won't have to kill anyone else.

After I finish feeling sorry for myself, I start up the Rover and drive over to Hasting's Liquor. I park in the handicapped space. I look at all the liquor shining under the fluorescent lights. The bottles are so pretty in there, all lined up and begging like puppies for me to take one home. My broken arm throbs for one. But no matter how hard those bottles beg or how bad my arm aches, I stay in the truck. It's safer that way—sort of like going to a titty bar; I'm just going to look. That's it. Just going to look for a while, maybe get a little adrenaline going from thinking about it, and then I'll go home to my wife.

Who am I kidding? Eventually, if you look long enough, you're going to taste it. I open my door and start to get out. I don't want to just taste it, I want to swim in it. And then something strong and silent jerks me back into my Range Rover and makes me peel out of the parking lot. I feel the pink-haired girl sitting next to me, giving me a shitty look.

14
Rasputin's Eyes

I wake up this morning alone, in the guest room, with a hard-on so tight that my eyes are crossed. I get up to go to the bathroom. I try to take a leak, but can't. I try to will myself to go down, but mind over hard-on isn't a super power that I come equipped with. Jesus, my bladder is about to bust.

Shelby's boycott on sex is really starting to take its toll. We haven't done it since before my intervention. I have this fleeting thought that maybe I should just remote control her into doing me—just nudge her a little bit. And almost as soon as I think this, I wish I hadn't. I can't believe I would even entertain such a slimy thought. What the hell's the matter with me? Why don't I just slip her a Mickey? Thinking about how sick I can be sometimes makes me go a big rubbery one.

Well, at least now I can piss.

Anyway. I haven't told Shelby about how the IRS is off our

backs yet. Maybe she would start sleeping with me again if I told her. Only thing is, Debra didn't give me a legend for that. And unlike Reed, who knows better than to ask where a magic five million dollars came from, Shelby doesn't. She's going to ask me over and over how I got that money and she's going to want to know why I can't get more. I'm going to have to talk to Debra and get a legend. I'll do that today because this celibacy bullshit is for the fucking birds. It makes you think bad thoughts.

I throw on a T-shirt and go downstairs in my boxers. Valya's in the kitchen, making breakfast for Noah and Shelby. She's got a big Russian breakfast going. Which I hate, but I would never tell her that because Shelby and I think it's important to expose the boy to different cultures. Anyway, Shelby and Noah are eating big bowls of kasha. (That's Russian for Cream of Wheat.) Actually, it's more like Noah's wearing his. And Shelby's busy reading the "Living" section and ignoring me.

Valya slings a big steaming bowl under my face.

"Thank you." I smile at her.

"You velcome." She turns around and starts getting the second course going. It's some kind of pink fish. Lox or something.

"Pap-pa! Pap-pa! Pap-pa!" Noah bangs his spoon, splattering the mush everywhere.

"Come on, biggin', eat your stuff." I point to his bowl.

He touches the bruise on my face. "Ouchie!"

"That's right, Papa's got an ouchie." I wipe his cereal off my cheek.

"So is Papa going to work today, or is Papa going to lie around the house all day in his underwear?" Shelby hides behind her paper.

"Well, good morning to you, sunshine." I put some butter in my kasha.

She rattles her paper and turns the page.

"Jesus, who pissed in your Cheerios?" I grin.

"I'm seeing a lawyer this afternoon," she announces from behind her paper wall.

"You're what?"

"I think I want a divorce." She puts the paper down.

"You *think* you want a divorce?" I stare at her. "Well, have you thought what this would do to us financially? To N-O-A-H?"

Tears well up in her eyes. "This isn't what I signed up for, Travis. We're poor! You're probably going to jail. And I feel fat. My ankles are swollen. And I hate you!" She breaks down. Valya rushes over to the table with a plate of smoked salmon and puts her arm around Shelby.

"You want a divorce because you feel fat? Isn't that how you're supposed to feel? You're pregnant." I pour a heaping spoonful of sugar into my kasha. "I mean, come on."

"We're broke, Travis."

"And you think paying a bunch of lawyers to rip our family apart is how to fix that?"

"At least it's *doing* something." She pats Valya's hand to let her know she doesn't need her anymore. Valya goes back to her dishes.

"What do you mean, *at least it's doing something?*" I grind my teeth. "Goddamn, I've been doing something. Trust me."

"What? Like rehab?" she scoffs. "Is that what you call 'doing something'?"

"No, for your information, I've been doing a lot. I've been busy getting the IRS off our fucking backs."

"You what?" She looks at me like I'm crazy.

"Thanks to me, we don't owe them a dime."

She smiles despite herself. I'm expecting her to jump up for joy, but instead this is what I get:

"And when were you planning on telling me this?" She does this head bob-and-sway maneuver she learned from her daytime talk shows.

"It just became final yesterday. I didn't want to get your hopes up."

"Fuck you, Travis! I can't believe you kept that from me. You are such an asshole!" She gets up in a huff. "Valya, do me a favor and make sure Noah gets a bath before you take him to nursery school, please. I have an appointment downtown."

"Da, sure." Valya nods.

I shut my eyes and light up my chakras. The smell of cinnamon and warm butter swirls around me. I make that smell reach out to Shelby like smoky hands in a cartoon. I pull her back to me. I fill her full of sweet kisses and slow fucks in the afternoon. I make her feel like we used to feel. I stir her like sugar that's settled in the bottom of a cup of bitter coffee. I sweeten her. She turns back around and walks over to me.

"Oh, I'm sorry. That's great news. My hormones are all over the place this morning." She touches my hand and kisses me on the forehead. "I don't want a divorce."

"Neither do I." I wink at her. "Sorry I snapped."

I stand up and we hug. She's warm and soft. We hold each other tight, in the middle of all these cinnamon roll feelings. Then Noah screams bloody murder. He wants someone to hug him, too. I pick him up. He's gotten into Valya's smoked salmon and he's squishing it between his fingers.

"Uck." Noah looks at his hands and then wipes them on me.

He giggles. And we all laugh together for the first time in what seems like forever.

Okay, I know, I said I would never remote control Shelby. And I didn't.

I just kind of reminded her of how she used to feel. It was no more manipulative than say, wearing her favorite cologne or buying her flowers or doing anything that I know would make her happy. I just happen to be able to do it with my mind. It's not like I forced my will on her and even if I did, it was to save our marriage. It's not like I was doing it to get off or anything. So why do I feel so guilty? I don't know what I'm moaning about. It's no different than Shelby coming on to me when she wants a new car or a vacation.

After breakfast, I go with Shelby to the gyno for her sonogram. She's just starting her second trimester and today, we found out the sex of our baby. We're having a little girl. A little girl! Noah's going to have a sister. I'm going to have a daughter. I overflow with pride and happiness. And so does Shelby. But this time she does it on her own. No help from me. Well, I did knock her up. So I guess I did have something to do with her good mood. At least I hope I did. What am I saying? Of course this is my little girl Shelby's carrying. I can feel it. At least, I think I can.

When Shelby and I get in the Rover after the appointment, we make out like high school kids. She tells me that she loves me, and all is right in my world. Even though this world is now

full of passive-aggressive Holy Vishnus and histrionic vampires. Shelby and Noah and this new baby are the fulcrum that
helps me balance all this bullshit. My family is my strength and
as long as I have them, I can handle anything.

Even Debra McFadden's bad breath and kitten posters.

Speaking of Shimmer, I have an appointment at the temple, so I drop Shelby off at our house and head over to meet
Ikshu. I go to his room and knock. But he doesn't answer. I jiggle the doorknob and it's open.

"Ikshu? You home?" I call out, but he doesn't answer.

I feel the pink-haired girl standing over my shoulder. She
pushes me into Ikshu's room, even though I know better than
to be snooping around like this. She wants me to see something.

And this is what I see: a shrine to Charlie-fucking-Manson.
There's a poster and candles and stacks of books about Helter
Skelter and Sharon Tate. What the fuck? He's also got a
framed picture of Rasputin. This old black-and-white photo of
the grizzled Russian with eyes so deep and monstrous that you
can't look away from them.

Eyes like Ikshu's.

Then it occurs to me why all this shit is in here. These people are like me. They're like Ikshu. And they're like SageRat.
They're remote influencers. And then I have this terrible real-
ization: this is not a gift. It's a curse—a blight carried by mad-
men. I feel nauseated when I think about what both Manson
and Rasputin were capable of. I don't want to be like them. I
want out of this. I want to go to church and Sunday school. I
want to fear God and not ask any more questions.

"I see you let yourself in." Ikshu walks in the door.

"Oh!" I almost jump out of my skin. "Sorry, the door was open and . . ."

"And you saw the poster and had to see what else you could find."

"No, I just . . ." I don't know what to say. I'm cold busted.

"It is okay, my friend." He smiles softly. "I can feel your repulsion. I can see your fear. It is okay."

"What do you mean it's okay?" I point to the poster. "You've got a shrine to Charlie Manson in here!"

"Travis, calm down. I am a student. I study him. That is all."

"You study him?"

"He was a great influencer. So were a number of people in history. I study them so that I can perfect my work for Shimmer." He walks closer to me.

"But why the poster? The candles?"

"The only way to find the truth about someone or something is to meditate on it."

"You meditate on Manson?"

"Yes, and from this, his truth, his secrets are revealed to me."

"Ikshu, I don't mean to be closed-minded, but this is where you lose me. Manson was a cold-blooded killer. I don't know why you would want to meditate on that."

"And you aren't?" he asks.

"Aren't what?"

"A killer." He moves into my personal space. "You with your sex drive and your meat lust? You slaughter factory workers and animals every day with your compulsive spending. You are a murderer, too, my friend." He puts his hand on my shoulder.

"Eating meat is not the same"—I jerk my shoulder away—"as killing Sharon Tate, Ikshu."

"Both destroy life. All life is sacred." He gazes into my eyes and tilts his head.

"Look, you can speak in riddles all day long, Ikshu, but your man-crush on Charlie Manson is just plain fucked up. Sorry." I try to step away from him.

He leans forward and whispers, "To own is to fear, Travis. Let go of this world."

And before I even realize what he's doing, he kisses me on the goddamn lips.

I wrestle him off me, but he just laughs.

"Fuck!" I spit and hold my fists up, ready to kick his hippie ass. "What the hell are you doing?"

"Anointing you."

"Do that again and you're a dead man."

"Indeed, Travis Anderson, you are my Judas."

I keep wiping my mouth and tongue on my sleeve. My lips feel fat and full of novocaine, and I keep seeing horrible images of people burning alive. I'm caught in this flypaper of confusion. Ikshu is messing me up inside. I try to squeeze his visions out of my eyes. I do my best to focus on getting to my Range Rover. Somehow I manage to get away from his Vulcan mind-grip. I tear down the hall, through the restaurant, and outside.

My hands are shaking. I can't get them to stop long enough to put my key in the car door without scratching the paint. Then I remember that my key chain unlocks the doors. I hit the button. My Range Rover beeps and I jump in. I fumble for the ignition, start the engine, and loud static fills my speakers. I think I hear Ikshu's voice coming through my radio.

"You can't run away from God, Travis." It hisses. "You are the Judas." It fizzes.

Then another surge of static rolls through my speakers, and Faith Hill sings about "this kiss, this kiss."

I turn it off.

Ikshu's screwing with me. He's trying to remote control me. I take a couple of deep breaths and roll down my window. I spit repeatedly and try to get him out of my head. I drive down Gaston, and I remind myself that I'm the one in control of my body. I'm the one in control of my mind. Not Ikshu.

15

The Evil Kid

"I'm over it," I say. "Fucking over it."

"Travis. Let's talk about this in person." Debra's voice streams into my ear from my cell phone.

"I'm over all this Shimmer bullshit. I'm over Ikshu and I'm over being a spook!"

"I really can't discuss this with you over a cell phone, Travis," she sings. "You know that."

"Really nothing to discuss, Debra. I quit."

"Travis. Please. Let's talk about this. I love you."

She's playing the good spy and dropping weird shit into our conversation. Fuck her. I hope some counterintelligence hears every word of this.

"Please, Travis, let's have lunch at the temple," she begs. "How about tomorrow?"

"How about never?" I push the "End" button and throw my cell phone on the passenger seat.

I don't care if Shimmer did pay me five million dollars, the government doesn't print enough money for me to hang with a nutbag like Ikshu. And I've got news for him; I don't play games. He's fucked with the wrong man. I'll kill his Kalki the destroyer–ass if he even thinks about messing with me or my family. I have no problem, no problem at all, telling those other Shimmer assholes hasta la vista, either. I don't owe them a god-damn thing. I've put up with enough. Now that I've got my money, I've got zero-fucking-tolerance for freak show bullshit. I'm not their trained monkey. They can kiss my ass good-bye.

And if Shimmer wants to sic the IRS on me, let them. I'll sing like a fucking canary. My ass will be on *60 Minutes* so fast it will make their heads spin. If I have to, I'll leave the country like some kind of John Grisham character. I'll go to the Cay-mans or something. If I have to, I'll live on the beach and do Shelby under palm trees and raise my kids on coconuts. I have no problem with that at all. Sounds a lot better than dealing with Ikshu and his serial killer worshipping–ass.

From here on out, no one is the boss of me. I'm a free agent.

Okay, I lied. I do have a boss. Her name is Shelby Anderson. And this is what she tells me: Tonight is Supper Club and we're going. It's at Jim and Lisel's house. Shelby says that if we don't go, everyone will think I'm still mad about the interven-tion. (Which I am.) We *have* to go, she whines. She has laid out my new clothes that she bought at Harold's today and I have to put them on, like right now, while she watches me. She gives me strict instructions to play nice and act normal.

"Our reputations are on the line here, Travis," she says as she curls her eyelashes. "Please, just do this for me."

"Okay, okay. Just get off my back," I say. "I'll go."

I do exactly as she wants. Half because it will make her feel better, and half because it might get me laid tonight.

Jim and Lisel live in this monster of a Tudor-style mansion, just one street over on Tokalon. And tonight we're dining al fresco by their pool. Lisel had Jim string thousands (of white lights) over the patio. She also probably had him up in their magnolia trees, hanging all the Chinese paper lanterns that are glowing like little friendly ghosts tonight. There are citronella candles burning by the truckload, but the mosquitoes, because of our neighborhood's obsession for summer yard parties, have evolved an immunity to them. There's a Gipsy Kings CD blaring over the outdoor speakers. All our friends are here, wearing their cotton summer best, sweating to death and slapping away the no-see-ums.

Away from everyone is a small Hispanic woman, tending to the makeshift barbecue pit that Jim dug out of his yard. It's for the cabritos. Those are milk-fed baby goats that have been roasted underground all day. The maid is unearthing them and getting them ready to serve. From here, they look more like skinned Cocker Spaniels. But they do smell good.

Shelby grabs me by the belt loop and whispers, "They're cheating."

"How so?"

"Their maid. She's the one cooking the cabritos."

"Let's just hope those really are cabritos, and not Fidos."

"Eww. Gross, Travis."

Lisel walks up to us, holding two bright orange daiquiris.

"Welcome back, Travis!" She gives both of us a frozen drink. "Nonalcoholic Mango Madness Margaritas!"

Shelby and Lisel air kiss. I keep my distance. She knows better than to even try that with me.

"Mmm." Shelby sucks on her straw. "This is delicious. Thank you."

"Well, they should be. Fresh mangos are such a pain in the ass to fix." Lisel fake-laughs and touches Shelby's arm, "You know, they're just so messy with those seeds and all."

Shelby smiles at me as if to telepathically tell me that mangos don't have seeds; they have pits. Lisel's lying. Their maid chopped every one of the mangos in question.

Anyway. I just hold this ridiculous drink. Not really sure what to do with it. It looks like a margarita, it smells like a margarita, it's frozen like a margarita, but it's no margarita. This is not a very nice thing to do to a recovering alkie. This stupid mango thing only makes me want a real one. I want to toss it into the pool. But I do the polite thing: I hold it and let it sweat in my hand.

"So, where's Jimbo?" I look around at all the wives gossiping by the poolside.

"Oh, he's down there." She points past the festooned magnolias. "Playing horseshoes with the boys."

I peck Shelby on the cheek, and go take my place with the men. I walk under the glowing paper lanterns and take a sip of my fake margarita. It tastes like Pine-Sol. Mango anything always tastes like pine trees to me. I'm tempted to dump it out. But then again, I figure it might be easier to resist replacing it with something alcoholic if I just keep it.

Jimbo and the boys are all huddled together, whoopin' it up and tossing shoes. This is a game that Jim insists on making you play whenever he has you over. I don't know why. It's ob-

viously a game invented by bored cowpokes. So to make your
guests play it, seems to me, to be an admission that you and
your party are boring. But then again, Jim is a native Texan
and playing horseshoes might be a tradition or something. Sort
of like his putting a Lone Star flag doohickey on the back of his
BMW or carrying a concealed handgun.

"Trav-o!" Jim calls me over. "Look at you. Welcome back,
bud."

I walk over to him and we shake hands and slap each other
on the back.

"Damn. Look at you and that cast. Where did Shelby send
you? Auschwitz?" he laughs.

"That's not funny, man," I say.

"I see Lisel hooked you up with the good stuff." He points
to my drink.

"Yeah."

"Look, we have a whole case of Shiner Bock iced down
over there, if you, you know, want to upgrade." He smirks at
me and takes a swig.

"Uh, thanks, man, but I'm kinda not supposed to have that."

"Oh, man. Shit. I forgot, people like you can't drink at all,
can you? Sorry, man." He takes another swig and ribs me.
He's drunk.

I just look at him with his beer in one hand and his horseshoes in the other. I think how that used to be me. How I used
to be this obnoxious overgrown frat boy with too much money
and not enough humility.

"Jesus, man, don't be so uptight. Come on." He hands me a
horseshoe. "You can still have fun."

Now I know why I used to drink so much. It was Jim. He

made me do it. He and the rest of these assholes got on my nerves so bad, I had to get drunk in order to deal with them. It's pretty much all their fault.

The rest of the night is one big brag-fest in reverse. See, our friends are a modest bunch. Instead of boasting, we bitch. We grieve over our golf handicaps and we whine about our vacations to Bora-Bora and Ibiza. We moan about our Saabs being in the shop. We one-up each other with these high-dollar tales of woe. It's like if you camouflage enough of your boasting with complaining, you won't come off looking like a dick.

Anyway, Shelby seems to be having a good time tonight. And this makes me happy, I guess. Her friends are clamoring around her. She's like a movie star to them. This beautiful creature scandalized by tabloid gossip, but revered just the same. Her friends all live vicariously through Shelby's plight. These women horrify and titillate each other by imagining themselves in similar circumstances. They are full of wonder at how Shelby has pulled it off. How she had the strength to send me into rehab and take care of Noah all by herself. How she kept our home and marriage together despite my financial incompetence. And how she had time to find "such cute maternity clothes."

I don't want to steal Shelby's spotlight with my cast and bruises. So I walk over to the roasting goats and inspect them. For some reason, I just don't have a good feeling about eating something that basically looks like roadkill.

"Sheep go to heaven. Goats go to hell." That song by the band Cake blows across me. "Sheep go to heaven. Goats go to hell."

I see the image of Lisel and Jim's dead baby. It's this goat

that's going to do it. It's riddled with *E. coli*. The flames aren't
hot enough to kill the bacteria. And when Lisel eats the meat,
it will cross the placenta and kill her baby.

"The secret to the goat sauce is two cups of black coffee," Lisel
announces as the maid brings the roasted carcasses to the table
on a silver tray. "It gives it a nice, earthy flavor. I also use it
with brisket or mutton."

The maid fills up our plates with black bean salad, blue
corn tamales, and salsa while Jim tears the goats apart to serve.
The tender carcasses just fall to pieces—all shreds of rare meat
and tiny bones.

"Nothing like a little cabrito," he says.

"You got that part right." Lisel slurps on her virgin Mango
Madness and rubs her pregnant belly. "The key here is finding
the right goat. It has to be a suckling kid and it *has* to be
slaughtered at thirty days of age. Or you can forget about it. I
can't tell you how hard these little rascals were to find. I had to
go to this little Mexican grocery store in this really bad part of
town and all these Hispanic children started yelling at me. Talk
about scary."

I lean over to Shelby and whisper, "Don't eat it. It's got *E.
coli.*"

"Travis, don't be ridiculous." She pushes me away.

"Don't eat it. I'm serious."

She just rolls her eyes. I don't know what to do. So I try to
remote control everyone at the table and make them not eat
the goat. But I can't seem to hook them. And now Jim is serv-
ing up our plates with the poisonous meat. Everybody's
mouths are watering for these bacteria-infested kids.

"Look at how tender," Blythe says.

Her dippy husband nods.

"Smells great." Some dude at the end of the table leans over his plate and takes in the steaming meat.

Since we are a polite group, everyone waits until the last person is served before we dig in. The last person to be served will be Lisel. She's going to eat this goat and it's going to kill her baby. And what if Shelby eats it and it does the same thing to our baby? Fuck, this is bad.

Jim puts half a baby goat on Lisel's plate. And she picks up her fork, as if to say it's time to start, and that's when I lose it.

I scream an eternal "NO!"

I grab the tablecloth and tear it off. Goat sauce, black beans, blue tamales go everywhere. In Shelby's hair. All over Lisel's white linen dress. Splattering in Jim's face. Spilling into Blythe and Carter's laps. The dishes crash onto the patio and the meat and bones rain down on us like some kind of plague.

After the last piece of silverware clinks on the ground, there is a silence so awkward and heavy that it almost pushes me under the table to hide.

Shelby can feel it, too. Her shoulders and head drop under its weight.

"I am so sorry." She covers her mouth, but instead of crouching under the table, she runs out of the backyard.

Meanwhile, Lisel slings the black beans and salsa off herself. She glares at me. I keep looking under the table and decide that maybe Shelby had the right idea, maybe I should just get up and run away, too.

"Why did you do that?" Lisel shakes her head. "Why?"

Jim stands up, ready to kick my ass.

"I think you need to leave, Travis, before I have to make you." He sneers and clenches his fists.

Everybody at the table is stunned. Not sure what to say. Not sure if I'm crazy or what. Most of them just sit here with food all over them, being really still and quiet. But Blythe and Carter Mitchell are actually laughing at me. Assholes.

These people have no idea what I just did here. They have no idea that I just saved Lisel and Jim's baby. And there's no way I can ever explain this to them. There's no way to convince them that I'm not crazy. So I leave.

I run out of the backyard to find Shelby, to explain to her why I did what I did. Why I embarrassed her when I promised I wouldn't. But I'm out of luck. She's taken the Range Rover and left without me. I have to walk home, down Tokalon to our house on Lakewood, covered in blood-red goat sauce and Mango Madness.

I am the crazy dumb saint of Lakewood. And like most saints, I have just been martyred in order to save souls. But nobody knows it and nobody cares.

16

Kicked in the Crystal Balls

Shelby is devastated. And I don't blame her. For all appearances, what I did to Jim and Lisel was insane. It was crazy. And because of it, we will probably be kicked out of Supper Club. I can't say that I'm all that broken up about that, but Shelby is. These past few months have stripped Shelby of all her dignity. I have taken away all the comfort and joy that she has ever known. The money. The status. And now the friends. Her life here in Lakewood was her god, with all its parties and fancy foods and new clothes. What I did tonight was nothing short of blasphemy. She can't even begin to fathom why I would do something like that. She wants nothing to do with me. She wants a divorce.

I have no other choice but to tell her the truth.

"I've been working for the CIA." I just blurt it out.

"You what?" She freezes.

"That's where I was during rehab." I shrug. "It was this special program."

"You're serious, aren't you?" She slowly shakes her head while her bottom lip quivers. "And wh-what exactly were you doing for the CIA?"

"I was a spy."

"Oh. My. God." A tear runs down her face.

"Just calm down and let me explain."

"I am calm." She breaks down.

"Why are you crying?" I touch her hand and she jerks it away.

"I can't raise these babies alone. I can't," she sobs.

"Shelby, honey, you're not alone. I'm here. Right here."

"No, Travis, you're not." She shakes her head and the dam breaks.

She's full-on hysterical. That's when I realize why she's crying. She's not afraid of losing me to the CIA. She's afraid she's already lost me to insanity.

"No, really, Shelby. The CIA is real. It's how we got our taxes paid. I swear. I'm like this psychic spy and they had me track down this girl. See, there's this place called Shimmer and . . ."

The harder I try to explain, the harder Shelby cries.

Needless to say, going to Supper Club didn't get me laid tonight and telling Shelby about Shimmer hasn't saved our marriage. In fact, it looks like another night alone and hard up in the guest room. Considering how upset Shelby is I'm lucky she didn't kick me out of the house. She thinks I'm certifiable. Maybe I am. Who tells their wife that they're a psychic spy for the CIA and expects her to believe them? How stupid can I get? That's such a wackjob thing to say it's almost a cliché. But then again, how do you convince your wife—a woman who knows all too well that your prime motivators in life are food, beer, and sex—that you, in fact, possess this superhuman brain that the government wants to use as a weapon? You know, whoever said that shit about the truth setting you free obviously never had to tell his wife that he was a psychic spy.

At about three A.M., Noah wakes up screaming. Since I'm right next door in the guest room, I go get him. He must have had a nightmare. Poor little guy is almost purple, he's crying so hard. I pick him up and carry him into bed with me. He grabs onto my neck and holds on for dear life. He's shaking like a Chihuahua.

"Come on, biggin'. Shhhhh. What's the matter?" I rub his little back while he holds me in this two-year-old version of a full nelson.

"Monsta, Papa, a monsta!" He bawls and points to his room.

"Noah, it's okay." I rock him. "No monsters. Just a bad dream. Bad, bad dream."

I can taste Noah's fear like a battery on my tongue. It's a vicious buzz. This dizzy free fall of adrenaline and night-lights.

"Monsta bwack eyes." He nuzzles his head into my neck, getting his slobber and snot all over me. "Monsta."

I shut my eyes and I see Noah's monster. I see Rat's big black eyes. He was in my son's room. I can smell him. He's in my house. What the fuck is he doing here? I don't care how much kung-fu the little freaker knows, I'll kill him if I find him.

But what do I do? I can't leave Noah; he's too scared. But what if Rat's after Shelby? I'm paralyzed. I have no way to protect my family. My shotgun and hunting rifle are locked away downstairs. The knives are in the kitchen drawers, and my golf clubs are in the back of my Range Rover. What do I do? I close my eyes and I try to scan the house. I don't pick up anything. Either he's no longer here, or I'm just not able to turn it on right now. I scan Shelby's room and all I see is her sleeping; I see her hugging a pillow instead of me. I mentally go from room to room. And everything checks out clean. Maybe I was just picking up Noah's fear. Maybe that's what triggered the vision of Rat. Maybe I'm just being paranoid, as usual.

Once I get Noah back down to sleep, I physically check every room in the house. I was right. The house is clean and we're safe. But I'm so ramped up I can't go back to sleep. I lie here in the guest room and watch Noah breathe as the sun comes up. That's when I notice a fake lottery ticket on the pillow next to me.

The mutherfucker was here.

Today I bought a gun. A really good gun. A Glock 10mm. I'm not real crazy about keeping a handgun around the house with Noah. But I'm also not real crazy about self-proclaimed vampires breaking into my house and leaving phony lottery tickets. Besides, I won't keep it loaded and it's staying in the glove compartment of my Range Rover, or under my bed at night. It will always be in reach. If these Shimmer fucks want to play around, they can play around with the business end of my Glock.

I keep freaking myself out with bad mental pictures of Shelby and Noah in coffins. It's those same images that kept popping in my head when Dr. Solomon was talking about erasing our identities. I would never forgive myself if I let anything happen to them. I mean, what's the use of being psychic if you can't foresee certain disaster for yourself? But all this psychic knowing has done is get me into trouble.

I just need to calm down. I mean, two months ago I was certain that this was all some sort of miracle from God. Now I'm not so sure the Big Guy's not getting me back for something. Maybe I shouldn't have sent that email to Shelby. Maybe I shouldn't have keyed Reed's car. Maybe I should have tithed more to my church. What if God is like the Godfather and so long as you pay up, he won't break your kneecaps? What if the Old Testament was right, and you shouldn't suffer a soothsayer to live—which—that would be me. Fuck, what if this is God's way of getting rid of me?

What am I saying? Why would the same God, who created me with this so-called gift, want me destroyed because I used it? That just seems kind of petty and mean for an omnipotent being. Especially when He had Moses turning wooden staffs into snakes. Plus, I've never asked for anything that big anyway. No burning bushes or plagues of locusts. I just want a good and normal life. Which I guess that is something of a miracle these days. But for some reason I feel like I should have that, like for whatever reason, it's my birthright. And I think I could even create that kind of life—one far away from Shimmer and Supper Club. One where both Shelby and I could be happy. Why would God begrudge me that just because I'm a little psychic? Why would He begrudge anyone that?

When I shut my eyes and get still, I can feel the smallest seedling of a plan growing in me. Maybe it's God's plan. Maybe it's my own DNA's urgings. Whatever it is, hopefully, it will be in full bloom by the time SageRat or Ikshu show up. Because I can hear them coming, like a train whistle blowing out past the horizon. I can hear them building steam and it doesn't sound good.

Debra McFadden has left voice mail after voice mail on my cell phone. She's gone *Fatal Attraction*. She's acting like she's my jilted girlfriend, wanting me back, begging me to please see her "for at least a cup of coffee." She uses all these stupid metaphors for my relationship with Shimmer like "after all I've done for you." And "we could have had a future together!" And my personal favorite: "I won't be ignored." I take that as a threat. In fact, I take that as a sign. A sign from God that I need to buy some new bullets. The evil kind, with Teflon tips.

And guess who I see at the gun store while I'm buying my bullets?

The blue bastard.

At first, I thought he was here to stop me. But he just looks at me with his big cow eyes and smiles. I buy my bullets, and I get right up in his face and I flip him off.

"Fuck you," I growl.

He leans forward with a big goofy smile and then goes up into a puff of smoke like *I Dream of Jeannie*.

"Son? Are you okay?" the old man calls out from behind the counter.

"I'm great. Fucking great!" I shout as I bolt out of the store.

I know I look crazy and I don't care. I've had it with the prank calls from Debra and I'm sick of being stared down by some secondhand god. That's why I take my ammo and head straight for Diamond Dave's Shooting Range. I find myself here a lot these days. I imagine Ikshu's or Debra's face on my targets. I bite my bottom lip, and I unload round after round. I shoot them the fuck out of my life. I breathe in the gunpowder and smoke, and I feel strong like I haven't in a long time.

I'm getting really good with this Glock. The people here at the range have started to call me Travisaurus Rex, because I'm such a monster with this gun. Folks watch me empty round after round into bull's-eye after bull's-eye. The owner wants me to shoot in some local tournaments. He says I've got real talent.

Just let those Shimmer fucks come and get me. Let Debra McFadden try and cook my family's rabbit; I'll blow her tits off. And if Ikshu wants to play crazy, I can play crazy with a gun.

I think they know this. Because I can feel Ikshu and SageRat backing off. I think they've seen me shooting at the range and I think they know they better back off. Because the calls from Debra have stopped, and I don't hear the train whistle anymore. In fact, this week my life sort of feels normal again. Shelby hasn't brought up the CIA thing and I don't think she will. I think she wants to act like that didn't happen. That makes two of us.

I'm still sleeping in the guest room, but Shelby hasn't hit a crying jag in a good while now. I take this as a sign that maybe things are on the mend. Her friends from Supper Club have totally stood by her, and she's off as usual to her luncheons and Junior League meetings. She leaves me alone a lot with Valya and Noah. But I'm not complaining. I think that maybe our life will be okay. Maybe not great. But at least manageable. And at this point, just the possibility of leading a humdrum life makes me smile.

Just to be on the safe side, though, I visualize shooting my gun. I send a little psychic postcard to Ikshu, SageRat, and Debra just to remind them that I have it and I know how to use it. So long as I don't have them snooping around, looking to freak me out, I think Shelby and I can lead a normal life. Which might not be happy, but then again, whose life really is, anyway?

I found a brand-new bottle of vodka yesterday. It was out in the garage, under a bunch of junk. I guess Shelby forgot to check out here. I hate to admit this, but just being near this bottle gives me butterflies. I've snuck it up to my room. I just want to look at it. I'm not going to drink it. It's just me and my two best friends—my bottle and my gun. I think about the torture of the virgin margaritas at Supper Club. And how long it's been since I've been able to relax and just have a drink. I go back and forth on it. Yes. No. Do it. Don't do it. Maybe just a sip. Maybe the whole thing.

It's a big plastic jug of Taaka. It's cheap, but I don't care. It tells me that it missed me. It sings sweet lullabies to me. It tells me this could be the last time we could ever be together. It wants me to hold it. It wants to kiss.

And I do. I kiss that bottle full on the lips, and drink it deep, like I wish Shelby would drink from me. I polish the vodka off in just a matter of minutes. Damn, it feels good. I fall back on my bed and let the world spin. Then, in the middle of all this sloshy goodness, it occurs to me what I've done. I'm getting drunk—really drunk. And Shelby will be home any minute. I can't let her find me like this. So I stumble down the stairs and out of the house. Boy, I'm already fugged up. I stagger down Lakewood Boulevard to White Rock Lake. I'll just ride this out down here and Shelby will never have to know about this.

I forgot how disconnected you feel when you get this drunk. Actually, it's kind of nice to be unplugged for a change. My teeth are numb. I would feel guilty for what I just did, but my buzz is too happy to let me feel anything but good right now. Vodka is magic. The sky is blue, the sun is golden, and God is in His heaven (where He should be) and all is right in my world.

I stumble down to the water. The lake is black and shiny and rippled like an empty garbage bag. It looks good from here. The sun is a little too golden, a little too hot. I'm sweating. But I just keep walking toward the lake. In fact, I walk right in. I wade in up to my waist, and skim my palms across the water. I remind myself of a Baptist preacher getting ready to dunk people. I feel like an apostle ready to save a world full of wretched souls.

In fact, a baptism seems like a really good idea right now. I hum a few bars of "Amazing Grace." And I pinch my nose and fall back into the water. I hold my breath and open my eyes. The sunlight shines through the diarrhea water and the slush of the lake floods my ears. It's kind of pretty in a perverse sort of way. It makes me want to pray. I'm not really sure what to say;

all that comes to mind is "Forgive me" and then I come up choking and gasping for air.

The water is lukewarm and it smells like dirty feet. I just want to get out of here and go home. Why am I in this lake? I start walking home and then I discover that I've lost a shoe. It was a Cole Haan. Shelby's going to be pissed if she finds out. But she's not going to find out, because I'm going to drink a bunch of coffee before she gets home. That's what I'm going to do.

Besides, I deserved this little bender. Shelby's been a real bitch lately. Making me go without any loving for almost two months. *She* made me do this. I was looking for love in that bottle. That's what I was doing. This was Shelby's fault. If she'd just throw a leg, I wouldn't be doing this. I'm only human. You can't take away every single vice a man has and expect him not to do something like this. Everyone's got their breaking point. Mine is having blue balls for over two months.

Anyway, I walk up to our house and the front door is wide open. Both cars are in the driveway. My heart stops. And then starts.

And then stops again.

Fuck. Shelby's home.

I sneak around back. And that's when I remember, I left the empty bottle in the guest room along with my gun on the floor.

FUCK!

What if Shelby finds that? What the hell am I doing leaving a gun on the floor with Noah in the house?

I AM SO FUCKING STUPID!

I run up the stairs to the guest room and my bottle is on the floor, but my Glock is gone. I freak. I run to Noah's room and I see blood splattered everywhere and there are bullet holes in the wall.

"Noah!" I cry, but he's not in here. There's blood all over the place, but no body.

I can't breathe. What the hell have I done? I run to Shelby's room and there's blood on those walls, too, and more bullet holes. I can't feel my head. I can't feel anything. I am numb with shock and booze.

This is not happening.

I tear through the room looking for Shelby and Noah, but they're not here, either.

"Shelby! Noah! Please!" I scream.

But there is no answer. Just dead silence. I walk up to the bullet hole and finger the hot metal. And even though I'm out of my head drunk, I talk to the bullet, and this is what it tells me: Shelby and Noah are alive! Debra and Ikshu have taken them. They've told Shelby that I'm some kind of schizo–serial killer and for her own safety, she and Noah have to come with them. Debra drives away with my family in her Chevy Malibu. Then Ikshu takes my gun and fires it into the walls.

I touch the wet blood and it's also willing to talk. It tells me it came from a needle that was stuck in someone's arm. I start to cry. I slide down the wall and look at the blood on my hands. I can't stop shaking. How did I let this happen? Ikshu was watching me.

The fucker put that bottle in the garage.

He knew I would drink it, and when I did he came in and stole my family.

I squeeze my eyes hard and try to zoom in on Shelby and

Noah. I try to make it work, but the vodka and my fears keep getting in the way. I can't locate them.

I open my eyes and that's when I hear someone coming down the hall. It's Reed.

"Shel—holy shit!" His fake tan evaporates.

"Reed, please, it's not—"

He turns around and hauls ass out of my house.

I'm too drunk to chase after him and too crazy to think of what to say. I just sit and rock back and forth. In between my own sobs, I hear the pink-haired girl's whispers. I try to ignore them, but they keep ringing in my head like an alarm clock. Eventually she's screaming at me so hard that my ears hurt.

"Go! Go! Go!"

17
Gun Rhymes
with Run

I get up and go like the pink-haired girl told me. I wash the blood off my hands. And I put on my running shorts and shoes just like she tells me. I fill up a backpack with a sports bottle of water, a change of clothes, my cell phone, Noah's stuffed rabbit, and a small photo album. I splash my face with cold water and try to shake off this drunk.

"Now!" The pink-haired ghost screams. So I put on my sunglasses and backpack and run out the backyard gate and down the alley to the woods around the lake. I run as hard and as fast as I can because I can hear the sirens coming.

This pounding the concrete is hurting my broken arm. Bad. But I just push myself past all the pain. I blast past all the burning in my lungs and legs. I concentrate on Shelby and Noah, and I feel like I could run all the way to Mexico if I had to.

Yep, the pink-haired girl was smart, real smart. Since I'm dressed like a runner none of my neighbors are giving me a second thought. They just see me as any other health-Nazi who hits the Lakewood streets, with their fancy sports injuries and backpacks full of sand.

Down by the park, I run past a bicycle cop. I almost shit myself. But he doesn't even see me. At least that is until he gets my description. What if he already has it?

I kick it into turbo and I run away from the lake. I take off into the wooded area of the park. It's where all the bums hide out and the kids come to drink, smoke, and screw around.

Once I make it to the woods, I stop running. I bend over with my hands on my knees. All I can do is spit and gasp and wheeze. I try to catch my breath as I stagger around the nature trails. A pack of punk-ass kids on dirt bikes blazes past me. I look down at the ground and hide my cast from them. They yell something at me in Spanish. Maybe they know who I am and they're taunting me. What am I saying? I'm just freaking out. I need to sober up and calm down. I take a couple of deep breaths, but I couldn't make myself transcend this if I had to. I'm in the thick of this panic and no amount of meditation will lift me out.

I walk deep into the woods, pushing past the brush and briars. Far off the trail, I find an old oak tree and I sit down behind it. I open my backpack and take a drink from my sports bottle. And then my cell phone rings. It almost sends me up the tree. Who the hell is calling? I rip through my backpack and answer it.

"Huh-hullo."

"Get rid of it." The voice on the other end is raspy and hushed.

"Who is this?"

"Get rid of the phone. They're using it to track you." And then whoever this is hangs up.

I look at the phone. Who was that? And more important, what the hell was I thinking? I bash my cell phone into the tree, and then I stomp on it until it's just jagged pieces of plastic and wires. Who was that? Shimmer's fucking with me.

"Take the battery out, dumbass," I hear two voices call out in the distance. I look up and see Sage and Rat, standing arm in arm. Rat is holding a cell phone.

I grab my backpack and scope out every direction to see where I can run.

"Stop!" They say in harmony. "We're here to help."

"Stay the fuck away from me! I've got a gun!"

They know I'm lying or they don't care, because they keep walking up to me. Their movements are completely synchronized.

"Travis. In less than two minutes there will be a police helicopter flying all over this lake. There will be dogs. They will get you. Trust us. We're psychic." They smile the same creepy smile. "Let us help you."

They glide up to me like a fog.

I sling my backpack and hit Rat in the face. But it's like two for the price of one because they both hold their faces. I run away from them as fast as I can. Rat takes after me. He's a fast little fuck. I zigzag between the trees. I try to outsmart him. But I can feel those two muddying up my mind, and with all this vodka in me, it's hard to keep them out. Sage keeps telepathically telling me to freeze. She keeps trying to make me feel like I can trust her. And Rat is right on my heels. I turn around and give him a left uppercut. I knock him on his ass. I'm going to kill the little fucker.

I go for his throat. I'm going to rip his jugular from his neck.

But before I can get my hands on him, he kicks my balls so far up my ass I almost choke on them. I hit the ground and squirm. I'm racked so bad that I heave up vodka and stomach acid out of my nostrils.

Rat grabs me with one of his judo holds and pulls me to my feet. I'm stoned on the pain. He's got me by my good wrist. But it's one of those holds where, if I resist, he'll snap it like he did the other one.

Goddamn! It hurts like almighty fuck.

"Come on, dumbass. You're going to get us busted." He pushes me through the underbrush, back to his albino sister.

SageRat takes me to a black funeral hearse that's parked near the wooded area. They force me into the backseat. Rat holds my wrist with his judo hold and Sage is in the driver's seat. I keep trying to think of ways to break away, but every time I even twitch, Rat twists my arm and I stifle a scream.

"Where's my family?" I glare at Sage through her rearview mirror. Her blue eyes are twitching all over the place.

"Good question," she says. "We don't know."

"What do you mean you don't know? You fucking kidnapped them!"

"We didn't kidnap anyone." Rat squeezes my wrist. "Well, except you, of course."

That's when I see red and blue lights flashing all around us. There's a helicopter circling overhead and a roadblock in front of us. They've got me.

"Looks like trouble, boys." Sage slows the funeral wagon to a stop behind the other cars. "Get him in the box." She points to the pink coffin in the back.

"What? I'm not getting in any fucking coffin."

Rat twists hard and I'm in so much pain I can't stand it. Before I know it, I'm cramming myself into the box.

"Now keep quiet and don't move around a lot." Rat shuts the lid.

I have to cross my arms like a corpse to fit. The coffin's not exactly my size. Rat wrestles with the lid, but he finally gets it to snap shut. My face is just inches from the top. This is some kind of kid-size coffin and I'm growing inside it. Or it's shrinking around me. Whatever is happening, I'm so claustrophobic, I want to scream like a little girl. Wait a second . . . Shit! This is some dead girl's coffin. I'm touching some dead girl's ooze. Her decay is crawling all over me. My eyes are strobing in the dark. I'm about to have a stroke. Or a heart attack. I can feel my pubic hair turning white. I'm about to die of fear. Like those urban myths of teenagers dying in their dark basements from fright.

I try to calm down because I can hear Sage talking to the cops. I try to think good thoughts, but I'm fresh out. All I can see is Shelby and Noah in coffins like mine. And I sob. I try to stifle it, but it just runs out of me like the embalming fluid of the corpse that was in here before me. I can smell it. The fluid is dried in this silk.

God, please, get me through this. I'm about to get us busted. Get me to Shelby. Help me save Noah. Please, I'll never drink again. I promise. I swear this time.

Then I hear Sage and Rat talking in stereo. They must be using their remote control because the cops let us go.

"You kids have a good day." I hear the officer's voice smile and I feel the tug of the hearse driving us away.

No search. No nothing. They did it. But after we get past

the roadblock and down the road a bit, Rat doesn't open the coffin. I knock on the roof and yell, "Okay. Let me out now!"

But the vampire mutherfucker doesn't answer. I throw a panic. I'm sure there are only a few seconds of oxygen left. I completely freak. I tear and claw at the satin lining. I punch and push, but I can't knock the lid off. I imagine them burying me alive. I see the dirt hit the top of the coffin. I can't believe I let them talk me into getting into this thing. Then I feel the car jerk to a stop and the lid slowly comes off. I throw it off me. And sit up all wild and gasping for air and sunlight.

"We're here." Rat grins.

"What the hell's the matter with you? Didn't you hear me? I couldn't breathe!"

"It has air holes in it." He points to both sides of the coffin.

"There were cops all over the place, Travis." Sage turns around and smiles. "We had to keep you hidden."

I look out the window. We're at the Hiltop. It's this run-down old Hilton hotel, and whoever bought it was too cheap to replace the Hilton sign so they just replaced the letter N with a P. Hence the name, Hiltop. The place is covered with smut from the freeway and you can see the drapes falling down in the windows. It's the biggest, weirdest dive in Dallas.

"We're practically five minutes from my house. We can't stay here. Cops drive by here all the time," I say.

"Chill out, yuppieboy. Haven't you ever heard that the best place to hide from the cat is in its ear?" Rat looks at me and then tongues his fangs. "Hell, I was living in your attic for the past week and you never knew it."

"Then where's my family, mutherfucker?" I lunge at him, but he punches me square in the face. It knocks me back onto the coffin. The asshole knows how to fight; I've got to figure out some other way to attack him. So I back off and hold my bloody nose. I run through how many seconds it would take to unlock the back door, open it, and run. But then where would I run? What am I going to do?

"Travis, I'm sorry." Sage gives me her best attempt at sympathy. "But like we told you, we don't have your wife and kid."

"Look, I'll do whatever you people want." I wipe the blood from my nose. "Just let me see them."

"Travis, we're not with Shimmer anymore." Sage's left eye looks at me while her right one wanders all over the place. "We ran away."

"You what? Then who has my family?"

"I'm afraid Ikshu does." She bites her bottom lip and her fangs show a little bit.

"Then what was Rat doing in my attic?"

"He was trying to protect you." She sighs.

"You mean you and Rat aren't doing this for Shimmer?"

"No, dickwad." Rat squints at me. "We're doing this because sister here turned all Good Samaritan on me."

"Shut up, Rat. And help Travis out of the limo." Sage gets out and slams the car door. She catches her gossamer dress in the door and has to reopen it.

"Shhhh-it!" Sage hisses. "The stupid door ripped my dress!"

I feel safe in saying that I'm not in the most stable of hands here.

The Hiltop Inn. The mysterious, *Brady Bunch*–era hotel that looms over Central Expressway and Mockingbird. It even smells like the seventies in here, like moldy shag carpet and strawberry lip gloss. This is one of those places you drive by and wonder: "What kind of jackass would ever stay in a dump like that?" Now I know what kind of jackass. One who's on the lam. One who's taken up with make-believe vampires in a funeral hearse. One who's desperate to find his wife and kid.

Rat and Sage already have a room so we go in the back way and up the service elevator to the fifth floor. The room is all disco wallpaper with two swaying double beds. Rat shoves me as we're walking in.

"Watch it!" I sneer.

"How does that blood taste, yuppieboy?" Rat pushes me again.

I turn around and bow up on him. I'm so pissed I could tear him limb from limb. That is, if I knew karate. We stare each other down and my boiling hate for him is spewing out my ears.

"Both of you! Quit!" Sage yells and the mirror in the bathroom shatters.

"Did you just do that?" I edge closer to the door.

"I'm PMS-ing," Sage announces.

I just look at her. She's crazy. And then I look at Rat. He's crazy. They are both fucking out of their heads.

"Sage, please." Rat puts up his dukes. "Just let me do one roundhouse kick to his head. Just one. He's begging for it."

Sage walks over to Rat and kisses him softly on the lips. He convulses a little. Which is exactly what I would do if she ever did that to me. But then I hear the tinkling of a silver bell. They shut their eyes and the exact same angelic expression falls across their faces. When they open their eyes, they are the same terrible person. They are SageRat.

"Fear no evil, Travis," they say in harmony. "I am more complete when I am together."

"Uh . . ." I back up. There's a breeze blowing through the room, but no windows are open. "More complete?"

"Rat's anger comes from fear. And SageRat knows no fear. I am integrated. I am safe. I am whole."

"So what do you want?"

"I have come to help you." They put their arms out to hug me. But I keep my distance.

"Help me do what?" I back up against the wall.

"I have come to help you get your family back. That is, if you help me."

"Help you do what?"

"Kill Ikshu," they say.

"Why do you need me?" I shake my head. "Why can't Rat just pounce on him?"

"You are Ikshu's nemesis."

"If that's the case, why didn't he kill me when he had the chance?"

"This is how he does it. Slowly."

"So he's doing all this to get rid of me?"

"No, he will leave your body alive and kill your spirit. He wants to control you like he did with the most tender part of me."

"He controlled you two?"

"He possessed the Sage. He knew that part of me needed love. Affection. Sex," Rat and Sage say in unison. "For this, Ikshu must die."

"So how'd you get away from him?"

"The day you broke my Sage heart, you healed the wounds that kept me in bondage."

"But Ikshu told me to do that." I squint at them and try to do the math.

"He underestimated you." They blink together and smile. "He thought my kid fears would drive you mad. He thought they would weaken you so he could take you over, but instead you drove out the misery and freed me of Ikshu's abuse."

"So you need me to kill Ikshu and you'll help me get my family back."

"No flies on you, are there, dumbass?" They both wink at me—Sage with her right eye and Rat with his left.

I am famous.

Travis Anderson is front-page news. "The DOT-COM PSY-CHO" is what they're calling me. The perfect family gone haywire. A soulless maniac murders his wife and child because he doesn't want a divorce. It's the kind of white-bread hubris play that sells newspapers. And since my son is presumed missing or dead, the Amber Alert has been sounded. Which means there's an APB broadcast across Dallas radio and TV stations, asking for leads to my whereabouts. The media are having a field day with this. As well they should be. After all, it looks like I murdered my family and it looks like I got away. To be completely honest, if I saw these newscasts and I didn't know better, I'd say this Dot-Com Psycho needs to fry in the electric chair.

These reporters are selling the drama, and why wouldn't people buy it? You see a blood-splattered marriage bed and we all know how the story goes. It's OJ Part Two. Add a few character assassinations from Supper Club and my asshole neighbors, and you've got yourself an open and closed case: I did it.

On Channel 11, there's an interview with Lisel. The video

title under her reads: LISEL THOMAS–FRIEND OF SHELBY ANDER-SON. It should read: LISEL THOMAS–UNGRATEFUL BEE-YAWTCH.

Lisel tells the cameras that she always knew I was "a little off," but she never thought I would do something like this. The bitch is all tears and makeup. Jim just stands slightly off camera and silent. He's Lisel's pillar of strength. I find this all very sick and ironic. So much so, it gives me a staggering headache. Here are two of the fakest people I know making all this bullshit real.

"Please, Travis, if you're listening. Just turn yourself in!" Lisel screeches.

I flip the channel.

On Channel 4, there's a clip of Reed Bindler covering his face and refusing to comment. It's just a flash of video, but I'm almost positive that I see Reed holding the Shimmer brochure that Debra McFadden gave me. He must have gone through my office before the police did. Typical Reed–always looking to cover his own ass. He wanted to make sure there was noth-ing in our office that would get him in trouble–no drugs or other shit that the cops could come after him for.

But for once, Reed being a self-centered fuck might be a good thing. His blistering narcissism goes hand-in-hand with an uncanny survival instinct. So he's got to know something's up. Hell, if he does have the Shimmer brochure, he knows I've gotten in way over my head. He also knows I got the shit kicked out of me–that I didn't fall down any stairs. I can guar-antee that's why the mutherfucker won't comment; he knows this is all linked to the magic five million dollars. And Reed must figure that if I got that money from a bad source, it's just a matter of time before that source comes after him.

I hate to say this, but Reed Bindler might be my only hope.

18

Homemade Sin

"Look at all the pretty people, doing, oh, so many hideous things." Sage rips open the blinds, revealing a window full of harsh morning light and Dallas traffic.

I sit up from my pillow and shield my eyes.

"Ugh, shut those." I pull the extra pillow over my head, and lie back down.

"How the hell can you sleep when you know those fucks have your wife and kid?" Rat barks. "You're worthless."

He's right. How could I have let myself fall asleep? It's just that things seem so fucking hopeless. Neither I nor SageRat can find Shelby and Noah with remote viewing. Sage says it's because Ikshu is blocking us. What if he's not blocking us? What if he's killed them? But Sage says we would be able to feel something like that. I don't know what to think anymore. I've been held up in this roach motel for two days now, and last night, I just collapsed. I couldn't help it. I just gave out. I'm weak. I admit it.

"You must get up, my darkness," Sage says. "Today, we go to Draco."

"What?" I sit up and inspect my cast. It's still sort of wet from my jump in the lake.

"Today, you become invisible!" She swings her bathrobe around like a vampire cape. "Today, you become one of us!"

"Jesus, Sage, stop acting like Anne Rice and just tell me what you want."

"We're getting your disguise, dumbass, so we can get you out of here." Rat inspects his piercings in the hotel mirror. The hole in his cheek is infected, so he dabs it with a cotton ball of antiseptic.

"Yes! You will be like us! You will be invisible!" Sage flings herself onto my bed, giddy with the idea of it all.

"I hate to burst your bubble, but I can see you."

Sage crawls across my bed and gets close enough to kiss me. I pull my covers up to my chin. She's so ugly it hurts. But I try to be nice, and I look straight into her milky blue eyes. I see an ocean of pain. I have to force myself not to turn away.

"Do you see this face?" she hisses.

"Yeah." I wince.

"It's ugly. And in this world, especially in a world like Dallas, that means people go out of their way not to look at me."

She backs up and I can breathe again.

"When you're ugly, you're invisible." Rat turns away from his mirror with a fresh coat of black lipstick. "And yuppieboy, we're about to ugly your ass up."

"Yes! Yes! Yes! You'll be perfectly hideous!" Sage giggles and rolls around on my bed.

Burned Books is a bookstore down by the Dallas Fairgrounds, where everyone is fugged up and punked out. We drive there in the hearse, with Sage at the wheel, Rat in the backseat, and me in my coffin—just in case we get pulled over. We park in an alley, and Rat rushes me into the back door of the bookstore.

Inside it smells of pot, incense, and old paperbacks. We're greeted in the back room by this big mutherfucker with tattooed arms and a bone through his nose. His name is Draco and on his right arm is the Book of Genesis—Adam fucking Eve while they're wrapped up with a snake. On his left arm is the Book of Revelations—a multiheaded beast, raging horsemen, and a 666 in the middle of a mushroom cloud.

Draco doesn't smile.

Draco is one scary mo-fo.

Draco wants me to strip.

Draco doesn't take no for an answer.

So here I stand in the back room of Burned Books, in my boxers, while Sage, Rat, and Draco conspire and whisper among themselves.

"He needs ink," Draco grunts.

"Yes! Ink!" Sage claps.

"And teeth." Draco squints. "But not fangs."

"How about yellow, gnarly ones?" Rat nudges Draco.

"Good idea. And maybe we dye the hair?" Draco bites his knuckles.

"What about clothes?" Sage asks.

"A grease-monkey jumpsuit." Draco raises his thick eyebrow.

"Brilliant! Draco, you're a genius!" Sage swoons.

"So did you bring it?" He crosses his big, scary biblical arms and looks at Rat.

"Right here." Rat reaches into his trench coat and pulls out a plastic baggie with an old rotting comic book in it. He hands it to Draco.

"First edition Crumb, very nice." Draco kisses the plastic-covered comic book and grins. "Okay, let's get to work."

Draco claims to be the Goth king of Dallas. Draco says he's a warlock. He talks about his coven, and about how he works here at Burned Books during the day, selling weird shit like demonology books and midget porn videos. At night he claims to roll around with nubile lesbian witches, casting spells on Highland Park families and other assorted Republicans.

I think Draco is full of shit.

And I wish he would just shut up and get finished with my disguise. It takes him almost two hours to get me ready with all his talking. I'm worn out from all the peroxide, hair dye, and crazy talk. When Draco's done with me, he shoves me into a dark, nasty bathroom.

"Take a look at yourself, my pretty." Sage turns on the light.

I actually scare myself. There's this hillbilly punk-ass Neanderthal staring back in the mirror at me. I can't believe that's me. The stubble on my head is now blue-green and I've got black thorn tattoos growing up my neck. (They're fake, not enough time for real ones.) Under my mechanic's jumper, I have on a stained T-shirt that says HOUSE OF BAMBOO: LIQUOR IN THE FRONT. POKER IN THE REAR. And to top it all off, I've

got a mouthful of crooked false teeth that make me look retarded.

"Your Goth name shall be Isaiah," Draco says. "Crazy
Dumb Saint of Lakewood."

"Crazy dumb saint?" I slur through my fake teeth. "How'd
you know that?

"The blue god. Last night. In a dream," Draco grumbles.
"He's the only reason I'm doing this . . . well, that and the
comic book you guys gave me."

Sage and Rat were right. When you're ugly, you're invisible. I
walk into the Hiltop in broad daylight; people stare, not because I'm the Dot-Com Psycho, but because I'm uglier than
ass. Everyone turns their heads in disgust, and then I'm invisible to them. Not invisible, like they can't see me. It's a different
kind of invisible, like they don't want to see me. And they definitely don't want to talk to me. At first it kind of stings when
people do this. But then I remind myself that I don't care what
these people think. I've got a wife and kid to find, and if these
assholes want to think they're better than me, let them.

Anyway, Sage, Rat, and I get back to our room and I decide to hold a meeting. We're getting nowhere with all this.
Let's face it, Draco's little makeover is a far cry from finding
my family. It's time I calm the fuck down and get methodical
and cold-blooded about this. It's time to stop being such a
blubbering pussy. It's time I take charge. After all, the longer
Shelby and Noah are gone, the colder their trail gets. And the
lower the odds are that I will ever find them.

"We've got to get moving." I pick up their stuff and throw it
into their suitcase.

"Get moving where? And with what money?" Rat asks.

"I can get us money. Just get your stuff together."

"By now Shimmer's frozen all your assets, Travis. Don't be stupid." Sage stands in the bathroom doorway, brushing her long white hair. "If you call a bank, they'll just use it to find us."

"Reed Bindler." I point at them. "We can get money from Reed."

"Isn't that the bastard who called the cops on you, dumbass?" Rat plays with the ring in his nose.

"Yeah, it is. But I think we can talk to him. If I can't convince him, you two can do your thing on him."

"Travis, you have to understand." Sage puts her hand on my shoulder. "Eclipsing someone's will only works if you're close to them. And they can't have something to hold on to . . . like Reed saw you in the bloody room. It's going to be real hard for us to overcome that."

"Look." I keep throwing stuff in the suitcase. "Reed's all we've got. He knows about Shimmer. I think I can talk to him. We need somebody on the outside to help us."

"And what if he doesn't buy it?" Rat sits on the bed with his arms crossed.

"Then we're fucked." I put in my Bubba teeth and zip up their suitcase. "Let's go."

Reed Bindler lives in a mansion in Highland Park. His daddy built it for him for his thirtieth birthday. He thought it would settle him down. But instead of filling it up with grandkids, Reed fills it up with wet T-shirt contests and coke parties. Reed's place isn't so much a house as it is a space-age bachelor fortress, with its big white walls and sleek aluminum gates.

Shelby always said this place was a rude and vulgar interruption in Highland Park's polite architectural conversation. I'd have to go one further, and say that it's more like flipping the bird to the neighborhood's old money.

Anyway, Sage pulls the hearse up to the call box, but she doesn't roll down the window.

Instead she chants.

"Open the gate. Open the gate. Open the gate." She stares at the gates like she's fucking Carrie or something. "Three by three, so mote it be."

But nothing happens. It doesn't budge. We sit here and wait. She chants again, and still nothing happens. She sighs.

"That's the thing about psychokinesis. Sometimes it works, sometimes it doesn't." She shrugs. "Now what?"

"Why don't we just call Reed and tell him to let us in like normal people." I cross my arms and sit back. "Ever thought of that?"

"You are such an asshole," Rat growls.

I roll down my window, climb out just enough to reach the box, and push the button.

"Hullo," Reed answers.

"Reed. Travis. Let me in."

"Travis? What the hell?"

"Just let me in. Before someone sees me."

The call box clicks off. The fucker hung up on me.

"Way to go, dumbass. He's calling the cops." Rat pulls me back into the car.

Sage throws it into reverse, and as we go racing backward down the driveway, I notice that Reed's gate is slowly swinging open.

"He opened it!" I point. "Go back."

Sage jerks the car into drive and we go barreling into the compound before the gate shuts. As we go inside, a big white Lego-looking building reveals itself. It's Reed's house. I had almost forgotten how cold and modern it was—like a museum or a mall. It's just an enormous white block with big glass panes stuck randomly on it. The front door is a giant rectangle of brushed aluminum. And all the plants around the house have been pathologically groomed into bonsai midget versions of themselves.

This place is so cool and self-important.

This place is so Reed Bindler.

Anyway, all three of us pile out of the hearse and walk to the front door.

"How Dallas," Sage whispers. "Nobody in this town has a Gothic sensibility at all, do they?"

I put my fake teeth in my pocket and push the neon-lit doorbell. Some kind of feng-shui-authorized chime plays. It takes a few minutes and then Reed answers the door.

He's on a Razor Scooter.

He's also on crack.

I guess that's why he let us in.

"Holy shit, boy! Look at you!" Reed greets me with a hard-edged grin.

"We need to talk," I say.

"Talk?" He keeps the same frozen smile as he looks at Rat and Sage. "What are you people?"

"Your worst nightmare." Rat sneers.

"Your loneliest fantasy," Sage sings.

Reed steps back a little. But he's so full of cocaine courage that he gets in Sage's face to inspect her. She hisses at him and spreads her dress like a cobra.

"Jesus!" Reed trips over his scooter and falls on his ass.

Sage and Rat die laughing.

I walk inside and the demonic duo follow. Reed's house has no furniture. He never bought any. It's empty, like his soul. Our footsteps echo across the marble floors and high ceilings. Rat shuts and locks the door behind us as Reed bumbles to his feet, all coked up and confused.

"Rat. Go secure the house," I say, "while Reed and I have a chat."

"Who died and made you Hitler?" Rat fidgets with his lace sleeve.

"Do as he says, brother." Sage keeps one eye on Reed and one on Rat. Literally.

Rat coughs into his fist as he passes me. "Hass-hole!"

"Can you kind people excuse me for a second?" Reed smiles and points to the guest bathroom. "Gotta take a pisser."

"Sure. Whatever," I say. "Just make it quick."

As Reed jumps on his scooter and zips across his football field of marble, Sage tugs at my sleeve.

"Do you think it's safe for him to go by himself?" Sage whispers.

"Reedy's a big boy. He can potty by himself."

"But what if he calls the cops?"

"He wouldn't do—shit!" I run after him. "Reed!"

Sage was right—Reed wasn't going to the bathroom. I find him in the kitchen and the bastard's got a butcher knife in his hand.

"You killed her!" He comes tearing after me, swinging the knife.

"Oh! Fuck!" I turn and run back to the foyer.

Sage just stands there, completely unconcerned that Reed is trying to kill me. And that's when Rat comes sauntering back.

"Make sure you get him in the heart!" Rat grins.

Reed glances at Rat, and then looks back to me. He's breathing hard and full of hate. I can feel it come off him like a busted radiator. There's really nowhere for me to run. He's got me cornered between him and the big aluminum door. He swings that knife at me; I dodge it and fumble for the lock.

"You killed my baby!" Reed holds the knife up. The blade glistens in the halogen light.

"What baby?"

"You know what baby! My baby!" He breaks down into a pile of tears and lowers the knife. "I can't do it." He falls apart. "Why'd you . . . why'd you kill them?"

"I didn't kill anyone." I swallow the lump in my throat and turn around.

I keep my eye on him and slowly slide away.

Shelby's baby isn't mine. It's his.

I can't breathe.

Shelby's carrying Reed's kid.

I just want to disappear. I don't want to know this. I look over at Sage and Rat, and those two psychopaths are just standing there, not even trying to help me.

"Oh, dearest Rat." Sage strolls over to her brother. "Do that trick. You know the one. The one that makes me scream."

"Don't feel like it." He pouts.

"I'll scream so loud if you do it. Please?" she begs. "For Sister-precious."

"Okay, I'll do it." He glares at me and then lowers his gaze at Reed Bindler.

Rat jumps into the air like Jackie Chan, kicking Reed in the head, knocking him to the ground. Reed gets up with his butcher knife, slashing at the air and spitting. But Rat does this jujitsu move and that knife goes sliding across the floor. Sage runs after it.

"Got it!" She raises the blade over her head like the god-damn Statue of Liberty.

Rat proceeds to sling and pound Reed like bread dough. I actually smile. I almost clap. If anybody deserves this, Reed Bindler does. I'm hoping, praying even, that Rat breaks Reed's miserable neck. I want him to die for what he did to me. I want him to pay for fucking my wife. I want him to rot in hell for destroying my family.

"Now, Rat!" Sage jumps up and down. "I want to see it now!"

"Okay." Rat simply lets him go.

Reed Bindler is bloodied and dazed. But he tries to put up his dukes anyway. Rat simply holds his tiny fist less than an inch from Reed's shoulder and just barely punches him. Reed goes soaring across the foyer like a Mac truck hit him.

Sage screams. Loudly, as promised.

Rat takes a flourishing bow. "Thank you, thank you. That, ladies and dumbasses—that is what we call 'the One-Inch Punch.'"

Reed is KO'ed on the black marble. A puddle of piss pools up around him.

"Bravo! Bravo!" Sage claps. "I just love that trick! I want to marry it!"

19

The Other Cheek

My heart is broken. My stomach is cramping. My colon is spastic. I'm torn up inside. And now I'm stuck in Reed's Zen garden bathroom, riding the porcelain motorcycle. They don't make enough Pepto-Bismol to soothe and coat what's wrong with me.

I look around the bathroom. Shelby's probably been in here. Naked. Doing things with Reed Bindler that I don't want to even think about. The big Jacuzzi bathtub. It talks to me. It tells me that Shelby took long baths with Reed in here. It tells me that my wife has committed all sorts of sin in this bathroom. And now I am stuck in here with her adultery and my diarrhea. This is the most disgusted I've ever been with life and all its fluids. All the runny nastiness that rules our lives. The sperm that makes us fuck, the beer that makes us drink, the blood that makes us sick, the shit that makes us spew. These fluids are the problem. And I feel like my life is covered in them.

I really just want to die. The only thing that keeps me from offing myself is Noah. I've got to get him back. I've got to get him away from Ikshu. Just thinking about how that crazy mutherfucker stole my boy makes my stomach twist and burn. Why can't I just shut my eyes and find them like I did the Vancouver girl? But every time I shut my eyes, I see horrible shit. I see Ikshu hurting Noah. I see Reed fucking Shelby. I see the barrel of a gun in my mouth. All I can do is sit on this pot and spew. I'm so full of poison it's coming out my butt. That's how bad Shelby has fucked me up. That's how bad all this has violated me.

"Are you okay in there?" Sage knocks on the door.

"No, I'm not! Go away!"

"Well, you need to hurry up," she yells. "We've got to leave. Rat got a premonition."

"I can't hurry up! I'm sick!"

"Well, my precious, you'd better get un-sick. Rat says he can feel the cops coming."

"Aw, fuck!" I reach over to grab some toilet paper, but the roll is empty.

"What's the matter?" she asks.

"Reed's out of toilet paper." I get up with my pants around my ankles and look under the sink. "The asshole's a goddamn millionaire, and he doesn't have one goddamn roll of mutherfucking toilet paper!"

"Travis! We have to hurry. Please!"

"I'm hurrying already!"

I look everywhere. In the medicine cabinet. In the drawers. Nothing. Not even a cotton ball. So I grab one of Reed's bath towels. The plush black one hanging by his Jacuzzi. I wipe myself with it and then neatly refold it and hang it back up. I don't know why I do this. Obsessive compulsive, I guess. It's not like the cops are going to put my ass-wipe towel in a plastic baggy and use it as evidence against me.

"Travis! Please!" Sage moans.

I bolt out of the bathroom, still fastening my pants.

"Okay, let's roll."

"Oh, thank darkness. Let's hurry. Rat's waiting." She flings her hair and points toward the stairs.

We both rush downstairs, only to find Rat in the kitchen eating a bowl of cereal. Reed's tied up with his Hermès neckties and has a wad of dishrags in his mouth.

"False alarm." Rat slurps on a spoonful of milk. "The cops aren't coming until tomorrow."

"What?" I try to catch my breath.

"Got it mixed up. The premonition was for tomorrow. Not today. The cops'll be coming for us tomorrow. So relax. We have another day to kill."

"Oh, Ratty. You had us so scared." Sage tucks her long cornsilk hair behind her ear. "Where did you get that?"

"Over there." He points to a box of Cocoa Puffs on the counter. "There's milk in the fridge."

"Lovely. I think I'll have some." Sage glides over to the cereal and fixes herself a bowl. "What about you, Travis? You cuckoo for Cocoa Puffs?"

"I'll pass."

Reed looks at me. He's terrified. He's come down from the crack. And his bruises are turning purple and shiny. Rat beat the shit out of him, and I'm glad. Real fucking glad. Reed Bindler has needed an ass-whipping ever since I met him. I'm just sorry I wasn't the one to administer it.

I take the rags out of his mouth.

"Help!" he screams. "Somebody!"

Rat drops his spoon on the table and glares at him.

Reed immediately shuts up.

"Sorry," Reed mumbles.

"So you fucked my wife." I clench my good hand into a fist and my intestines do the same.

"You're going to kill me, aren't you?" His bottom lip quivers. "Just like you did Shelby."

"I didn't kill Shelby." I grit my teeth and do my best not to bitch-slap him. "I've told you that."

"Okay. Okay. Whatever you say. Just don't hurt me," he sobs.

"Jesus, Reed! I was set up!" I stumble over my own thoughts. I can't concentrate. I keep seeing his lips kissing Shelby's tits. I want to knock his head off.

"I'm sorry, man. I promise." He trembles. "I'm sorry I fucked your wife."

"*Sorry?* Dude, you're not sorry. You're just scared. That's what you are. Scared we're going to kill you."

"Please don't kill me!" He loses it. "Oh, God! Please!"

"Reed. Listen to me!" I shake him. "I didn't do it! Shimmer did. The people who gave me the five million dollars. They took Shelby and Noah. They made it look like I killed them!"

I step back and Reed looks at me. He doesn't know what to think.

He sniffles and snorts. "So you didn't kill Shelby and Noah?"

"What did I just tell you, Reed?"

"Then my baby's okay," he mutters.

His baby? His baby, my ass. Since when did Reed Bindler give a shit about anyone but himself? And why the fuck did it take him knocking up my wife to make this happen? What did I do to deserve this? I can feel my blood turn to lava, exploding through me all hot, thick and full of hate. I want to bash the mutherfucker's skull in.

Reed looks up at me with his puffy, bloodshot eyes. I've never hated anyone more in my life. I really do think I could kill him. I could kill the mutherfucker with my bare hands. I could put my thumbs through his eyes and jump up and down on him like a pogo stick. But I don't touch him. I don't even spit on him. Because we need him now. We need his money. So I try to remember my deep breathing exercises. I try to let my hate go. But it's thick and sticky and I'm not sure I want to let it go. Meanwhile, Rat and Sage munch on their cereal, and watch me and Reed bicker, like they would a TV.

I eventually get Reed to understand what happened. Or at least he acts like he understands. And since me finding Shelby and Noah involves Reed finding "his baby," he agrees to help us. Rat takes him to the bank while Sage and I hole up at the house. I wonder what the teller's going to do when Reed, with all his bruises, asks for ten grand in nonsequential, unmarked bills. I don't think there's any law against being beaten up and making hefty withdrawals. Let's just hope Reed's accounts aren't still frozen.

While Rat and Reed are off getting the cashola, Sage and I meditate so we can locate Ikshu and my family. Sage insists on sitting on this king-size futon. It takes me a while to calm down enough to get centered. Sage claims that all this rage and drama is blocking me and that I've got to learn to detach. But I tell her I have detached. The fact that I didn't tear Reed's head off today proves that I'm the fucking king of detachment.

She just rolls her crossed eyes at me.

Anyway. I breathe deep and visualize my chakras lighting up. Red. Orange. Yellow. Green. Blue. And then a purple vision strikes me down like lightning, smack-dab in the middle of my head:

Reed fucking Shelby doggie style on this bed.

"I can't do it in here!" I jump off this futon fuck-pad and try to shake off that filthy vision.

"Detach." Sage looks at me with her twitchy blue eyes.

"I can't detach. Reed fucked her! In this bed!"

"Okay. Okay." She gets up. "I guess you're picking up their vibrations. Let's take this into another room."

We walk across the hall to the empty guest room. Sage closes the blinds and shuts off the lights. We sit cross-legged on the Berber carpet. I breathe deep and before I can even get my chakras lit, I see Shelby and Reed doing kinky things with whips and chains.

"They did it in here, too!" I feel sick to my stomach again.

Sage opens her eyes and squints at me through her long, white eyelashes.

"There's probably not a room in this house that's going to be clean of their sex, Travis. You're just going to have to get over it. That is, if you want to find your spawn."

"Get over it? Do you know what she did to me?"

"My precious, I know exactly what that whore did. Her essence is smeared all over this house."

"Don't call her that."

"What?" Sage's eyes dart around the room. "You still love her? I can feel it. She broke your heart, but you still love her."

"Don't say that, either."

"Ah, you have an aversion to the truth, my dark one." She smiles.

"What truth?" My stomach wrenches.

"The truth that you're in love with a whore."

"You'll have to excuse me, I'm about to be sick." I get up and run to the john. I barely get my pants down before my ass bursts into tears.

While I was in the bathroom, Sage took the time to do some remote viewing on her own. She thinks she found Ikshu and my family. The only problem is she doesn't know if they're in China or if they're in France. She saw them dining at a French café, with the Eiffel tower in the distance, but later she saw them standing at the threshold of a great Chinese palace.

"Well, maybe they're at a Chinese restaurant in Paris," I say.

"No, that's not it. I saw them in China. I saw it." She shakes her head. "There were Chinese people everywhere. I could hear them thinking in Chinese. I could taste the cabbage and ginger on their tongues. But just before that, I saw Ikshu drinking a Merlot, and I could feel the French people speaking French and being snooty."

"Are you sure this is where they are today? Maybe you're picking up the future? Like, maybe they were in France and now they're heading to China."

"Travis, I know when I hit a target in real time."

"But you said yourself, Ikshu is blocking us."

"His guard was down this time. I got through. I don't know how else to explain it."

"Well, which is it? France or China?" I can feel the hope draining out of my heart.

"I suspect, Travis, it'll be nigh impossible to get you out of the country wherever they are."

"Look, you just find them! I'll figure out how to get us there."

"Calm down, my dark prince. When Rat returns, we'll conjure up SageRat and get more precise information. In the meantime, I think I'll braid my hair like a Valkyrie." She gets up and sashays out of the room, swaying and waving her arms.

"Freaky bitch," I whisper under my breath.

"I heard that!" she calls out from down the hall.

Reed got the cash. Ten thousand dollars in small, unmarked, nonsequential bills. But Rat says that he could feel remote viewers from Shimmer watching them at the bank. He says the Feds will be here in less than five hours. So we have to hurry. I'm not quite sure what to do with Reed. I mean I can't fucking stand to look at the wife-stealing son of a bitch. Much less ride in a hearse across the country with him. Perhaps we'll have to put him in the coffin, since he doesn't have a disguise. Or better yet, I can use him as a human shield when the cops open fire on us.

You know, I can just see it now. I risk life and limb. I kick Ikshu's Holy Vishnu ass. I save Shelby from being sliced up by that Helter Skelter wannabe. And Reed will take all the credit. Just like he did with our company. I fucking hate Reed Bindler.

What the hell am I saying? How screwed in the head can I get? I'm sick. Sick. Sick. Sick. Here my family is in mortal danger, and I'm obsessing over who's going to get the credit for saving them. How pathetic can I get? And get this, when I was in Reed's bathroom looking for toilet paper, I found a bottle of Percodan. And I stole it.

I know this is terrible of me. Beyond terrible. But it's just that those pills seemed so lonesome in that medicine cabinet all by themselves. I had to put them in my pocket. Besides, I've decided that they're just for emergencies. Kind of like a cyanide tooth cap. Of course, I don't plan on killing myself if things go south. But I might need to take a few for a rainy day, like when Shelby tells me herself that she's not carrying my child. Maybe I should just take one now. Maybe just one Percodan would help me calm down and think straight. After all I've been through, I do deserve at least one itsy-bitsy painkiller.

What am I saying? Taking one will lead to taking two, which will fuck me like rabbits and multiply into taking six or seven. My mouth is watering just thinking about the warm fuzziness. I take the bottle out of my pocket, shake it, and stare through the amber plastic. But for the first time in about a week I feel the pink-haired ghost hovering around me. She shows me what warm fuzziness did to her. She shows me the heroin needles that stabbed her to death.

I put the bottle back in my pocket.

Sage kisses Rat and they do their SageRat thing. They go under and this time they both swear that they see Shelby and Noah in Mexico, riding a boat on the Mayan River of Time. (Whatever that means.) SageRat also claims that Ikshu and Debra McFadden appear to be in Germany at a biergarten watching people in lederhosen dance happy little jigs to oompah-pah. This is bullshit. Why are they seeing them all over the world like this?

So I go under myself. It takes a while to get into a groove, but I jump into the ethers and I concentrate on Noah. I find him; I can feel it in my heart. But things are foggy. The images are abstract and random. I see murky images of what looks like the Hotel Del Coronado in San Diego. But something's not right. It's hot. Too hot for San Diego. I try harder to zero in, but that pops me right out of my groove and I lose Noah's vibration.

"I can't get a definite impression." I shake my head. "Why can't I?"

"I don't know. I've never had this happen before." Sage's eyes creep and twitch.

"I think Ikshu must be blocking us." I stare at the fat red zit growing on her cheek.

"No, this is different than blocking," she says. "Besides, Travis, you should be able to overcome Ikshu's blocking. You're his ordained nemesis."

"Okay, then it's settled," I say. "We're heading for San Diego. That's where I saw them."

"The hell it's settled," Rat snaps. "I saw them in Mexico."

"You also saw them in Germany," I counter.

"Look, let's not fight." Sage touches her brother's shoulder. "We'll go to San Diego, and then we'll go to Mexico. And if we don't find them there, we'll try Germany."

"Fuck that." I can feel my face turning red. "I'm not chasing that asshole all over the world. He's screwing with us."

"Oh, okay, yuppieboy," Rat sneers. "I suppose you have a better plan."

"As a matter of fact, I do."

"And what, pray tell, is it?" Sage clasps her hands at her chest.

"I say we go to Shimmer. I think we should kidnap

Solomon and make him tell us where Ikshu is."

"Are you fucking stupid?" Rat scoffs. "Do you know how much security they have? They'll annihilate us!"

"You said it yourself, Rat. The best place to hide is in the cat's ear."

"I said the cat's ear, not the lion's mouth, asshole." He gets in my face. "Do you know what they do to viewers who escape? Do you?"

"Perhaps Travis does have a point, brother dear," Sage interrupts. "Perhaps we should slay the beast at its heart. Perhaps we should take over Solomon."

"Perhaps! Perhaps! Perhaps! I'm not going back to Shimmer!" Rat's black eyes flash and he sniffs the air like a dog. "What is that? It smells like the cops."

"What are you talking about?"

"It's another premonition. We need to leave. Like now!" he says.

"Where's Reed?" I look around the room.

"Upstairs, taking a bath." Sage points to the ceiling.

"Well, let's get the fucker and go!" Rat panics. "We've got less than thirty minutes and they'll be knocking at the door."

That's when we hear Reed scream. A blood-curdling scream. The kind of scream one lets out when one finds a corpse or witnesses a murder. All three of us run up the stairs to see what's the matter. We find Reed, dripping wet and naked, with his head under the shower nozzle, frantically washing his hair and scrubbing his face.

"What happened?" Sage asks.

"Someone wiped their ass with my towel!" he cries out. "One of you sick fucks wiped your ass with my towel!"

20

Going to Hell in a Boxster

Once again, Rat's premonitions are off. Way off. It wasn't the cops he smelled. It was Shimmer. Dr. Jude Solomon to be exact. He called Reed's house just minutes after Rat started smelling things. Some remote viewer in San Jose found us, and Solomon was ready to make like Monty Hall. He was ready to make a deal. I told him sure. I'm up for a deal. Where do you want to meet?

He said he would come to Dallas. And that he would meet us on the thirty-yard line of Texas Stadium. He warned me about being armed. And I warned him that I didn't need a gun. That I have super brain powers now, and that if worse came to worst, I would just explode his fucking head with my mind. He said he didn't think that was funny. And I told him, I didn't think Shimmer kidnapping my wife and kid was all that funny, either. So I guess we're even. He said don't be late. I told him roger wilco; I'd be there with mutherfucking bells on.

So I drive to Texas Stadium by myself in Reed's Boxster. Rat and Sage are behind me in the hearse while Reed stays back at the ranch, compulsively washing the shit out of his hair-replacement system. Solomon must think I'm fucking stupid. I know that this is some kind of setup. I know that Solomon doesn't have Shelby and Noah; Ikshu does. And I know they're nowhere near Dallas. But I go anyway. Because I can only run so far. I can only hide for so long. It's time to face the fuckers and let them know who they're dealing with. They're dealing with a dangerous man. A man who has nothing else to lose. A man with fake hillbilly teeth and blue hair.

Here's what we're going to do. SageRat is going to sit in the parking lot and concentrate on taking over Solomon. Sage says Ikshu has had his fangs in Solomon for the past few months and that they should be able to step right in. They say it should only take a few minutes and Solomon will be their meat puppet. Let's just hope their remote influencing works. Those two aren't the most reliable of psychic freaks.

I have visions of guns, lots of guns around Solomon. And if things go south today, I could end up sleeping with the fishes in the Trinity River. I know that as well as I know my own name.

But I go almost without fear. I stand hand in hand with Jesus and Courage. Because something nameless pushes me to go. Maybe it's Fate, or maybe it's the Angel of Death leading me here. But I know that I have no choice. I have a date with Destiny, or at least her in-bred cousin, Circumstance. And it's time for once in my life to take a stand. It's time to take back what was mine. It's time to fix what went wrong and bring things back to good. And if that means facing down Solomon and his toadies, I'm going to do it.

So I park Reed's car, tie an old red bandanna on my head, spit out my fake teeth, and I enter at the North Gate. It's propped open, just like Solomon said it would be. I look around and go in. The field looks smaller than it looks on TV. I walk past the seats to the field. I jump the rail and walk to the thirty-yard line and wait. I look up at the giant skylight and I remember my dream, the one I had before I ever talked to Shimmer. The one where the scoreboard flashed: LAUGHTER IS GOD'S MUSIC. The puzzle pieces are all falling together. The gears click and then grind to a halt inside my head.

The vampires that I killed in that dream were Sage and Rat.

I get chills. I'm all static electricity. Lightning is about to strike. And that's when I hear the whap-whap noise of a chopper overhead. I look up and see a helicopter descend through the stadium skylight. I hold on to my do-rag and shield my eyes from the windstorm. The chopper bounces down on the Astroturf. Solomon and his squadron of Shimmer Nazis file out of the craft with their guns and surround me. And then my dog, Max, jumps out. The fuckers *stole* my dog! Max lowers his doggy head, puts his ears back, and trots across the windblown field to my side.

"Put your blah-blah-wish-wish-blah!" Solomon shouts over the whap-whap noise.

"Max!" I reach down and pet him; he licks my hand and jumps up on me. "Good boy, Max. Good boy."

"I thed! Put your blah-blah wish-wish!" Solomon yells.

"What?" I yell back as I scratch Max's neck. "I can't hear you!"

The goons cock their rifles and aim. I put my hands up and Solomon approaches me. The helicopter blades slow down and the winds die. Max barks at the goons.

"Good boy, Max! Sic 'em!" Max runs crazy in and out of the Shimmer goons, growling and nipping at their heels.

I shut my eyes and listen to their thoughts. They've been told not to kill me. But this doesn't keep my heart from beating like a pan of Jiffy Pop.

"If you harm me with your mind, Travis, they've been ordered to thoot," Solomon says.

"I'm not going to hurt you," I say. "Tell them to put their guns down."

"You promise?" He looks at me all worried and sweaty. "I mean, if you kill me, or-or-or do something to me like explode my head, or something, then I can't help you."

"I said, I promised."

He waves to his toadies to lower their guns. And they do. But the guns clacking pisses Max off even more, and he runs in and out of their legs, trying to herd them away from me.

"Call your dog off!" Solomon orders.

"Max, come here, boy!" I give him a two-finger whistle. Max comes running with his tongue hanging and his tail wagging, all proud that he showed those fuckers who's boss.

"Sit, boy!" I say.

Max obeys, and takes his place right next to me.

"Good boy." I scratch him under the chin.

"Now, let's talk." Solomon grabs me by the arm and walks me across the field; Max heels behind us.

I want to rip the gray hair out of Solomon's head. I want to
pummel the fucker's face into hamburger meat, like Brad Pitt
did to that kid in *Fight Club*. I want to kill him for taking my
family. But I have to keep my cool. I have to get him to talk
and then I can whip his ass.

"So where're my wife and son?" I try to control my sneer.

"Ikshu has them." Solomon takes a deep breath and looks
at me from behind the bags under his eyes. "We didn't mean
for this to happen."

"You didn't mean for this to happen? You fuckers kidnapped my family, and then you set my ass up!"

"We didn't do that, Travis. Ikshu did. He's a rogue influencer."

"Don't fucking lie to me Solomon. I'm psychic."

"Obviously not, Travis. Because you would know right now
I'm telling you the gospel truth. Ikshu's been able to use his in-
fluencing to control a number of very powerful people in
Shimmer, as well as the CIA . . . me included."

"So how do I know that Ikshu's not making you say all this
now?"

"Because he's let me go. He had to; he's focusing on Agent
McFadden, and, we believe, some very key personnel at the
Pentagon."

"The Pentagon?"

"Yes, he used Shimmer as a means to infiltrate the United
States Clandestine Services, and from there, he has broadened
his influence."

"How do you know all this?"

"The girl." He looks away. "The one we had you find in
Vancouver. She was a Shimmer employee. Her name was

Annie. She was a viewer. A former disciple of Ikshu's."

"The pink-haired girl? The one you guys killed?"

Solomon looks down at the ground. He's crying. I can feel the guilt well up in him like vomit in a drunkard's throat.

"I was under Ikshu's influence," he whispers.

"But why did Ikshu want her dead?"

"She got too close. She knew too much."

"And you guys killed her."

"She was my fiancée! Goddamn it!" Solomon's face is pinched and red. "He made me do it!"

"Shit." That's all that I can say. I'm stunned. I'm looking at a guy who had his own girlfriend murdered. A man who claims some Holy Vishnu wackjob got into his head and made him do it. This just keeps getting fucked up and more fucked up the deeper I get.

He doesn't even try to stop his boo-hooing. I almost wonder if he's going for theatrics. But I don't think he could stop crying if he wanted to. I think he's for real. And then the pink-haired girl, Annie, I guess, starts pressing on me, weighing down on my shoulders. She's needy and urgent. She wants to say something, but I can't make out what it is. It's like a tape in fast forward. But before I know what I'm saying, three small words just spill out of me.

"I forgive you."

He looks at me, deep in the eyes. "Annie?"

I'm looking back at him. But it's not me. I feel like I'm watching this happen outside of me. And then I stumble and fall back into myself. I shake my head; I feel nauseated.

"You-you were channeling my Annie." He smiles at me.

I feel uneasy—interrupted and used.

"Just don't touch me, okay?" I step back.

"Annie," he whispers. He stares up at the big Texas sky through the stadium skylight. He's off in Never Never Land— crazy from his guilt and elated with memories of this pink-haired ghost.

"Earth to Solomon!" I cup my hands and shout. "Earth to Solomon!"

I grab Solomon by the shoulders and shake him. "What the hell are we doing here?"

The Shimmer goons cock their rifles at me. Max barks and growls at them. So I let Solomon go.

"Sorry." He rattles his head and rubs his temples. "All of this has really messed with my head . . . Uh, what was I saying . . . oh, yeah, we have viewers back at Shimmer looking for Ikshu, but he's been off the radar."

"What about Shelby and Noah?" I feel panicked just saying their names to this idiot.

"We're trying. But so far, no luck." He purses his lips.

"How the fuck can that be?"

"If we knew that, Travis, we would have found Ikshu by now. He's obviously gotten very good at blocking us. That's why we need you."

"Need me for what?"

"Bait."

Obviously, SageRat wasn't able to take over Solomon. Those two are so fucking unreliable. Solomon says he thinks they're still controlled by Ikshu. And I explain to him that Sage is a woman scorned. And that I don't think Ikshu, no matter how fucking powerful his brain may be, could outmaneuver that kind of fury. Then Solomon proceeds to tell me that Ikshu was quite the Casanova. He was doing Annie and Sage and Debra. That's how he sunk his hooks so deeply into them. Solomon says that sexual seduction is the ultimate in mind control. That it allows the influencer to control the person without having to keep constant concentration on them. After you fuck someone, you basically have their soul. That is, if you're an influencer. And then you can keep your target on autopilot after that. Ikshu learned that trick from Rasputin, Solomon says.

Anyway, Solomon sends the Shimmer goons back into the helicopter, and he stays behind with Max and me. The three of us walk out to the parking lot to find Sage and Rat, but the hearse is gone. There's nothing out here but acres of blacktop and yellow lines.

"They were right here. I swear." I point to their empty parking spot and look all around.

"I'm afraid I was right, Travis." He scans the lot. "Those two are still with Ikshu. We need to get you out of here."

So we run across the parking lot to Reed's Boxster. I get in the driver's seat and Max sits in Solomon's lap. It's a tight fit, but he somehow makes it work. I start the car and we roar out of the stadium lot.

"We have to get out of Dallas. I've been compromised." Solomon moves Max's panting snout out of his face.

"So?"

"*So.* Agent McFadden will have a termination squad deployed to kill me. If she hasn't done so already."

"I'm not so sure SageRat is still controlled by Ikshu. I have a feeling they got scared and went back to Reed's."

"Why would they do that?" He stares at me.

"I don't know. I just have a hunch that's what they did." I look at Solomon and Max licks my face. I push the pup away and laugh. "Stop it, Max."

"Forgive me if I don't want to risk my life on some random feeling you may have, Travis. In the lab you were only fifty/fifty, remember? I think you need to get us out of Dallas. Now."

"No. I don't think we should do that." I downshift the tiptronic transmission and the engine growls.

"Why not?" He tries to keep Max from gnawing on his hand, and then licking his nose.

"Because I'm the one driving. That's why." I punch it and weave in and out of the I-35 traffic. Solomon just shakes his head and keeps his pie-hole shut as we pass and cut off various BMWs, Lexuses, and Audis on our way to Highland Park.

We get to Reed's house in record time. His front gates are busted open. I see visions of Sage driving the big black hearse through it. I look at the gate and then at Solomon.

"Do you have a gun?" I ask.

"Yes."

"Do you know how to use it?"

"Uh, yeah, good enough," he says.

"Give it to me."

"Why?"

"Because you're lying. You shoot like a girl."

"I'm a psychiatrist. Not a spy, Travis," he sighs as he pulls his gun out of his calf holster. He hands the piece to me. It's a .44 Magnum. I check the chamber. It's loaded.

"Damn. Mighty big gun for a man who's not a spook."

"I just think we need to go." Solomon pushes Max to sit down. Max whimpers.

"Listen, Solomon. You were all fine and dandy with using me as bait. Now when it comes to putting your ass on the line, you're wanting to run and hide. Doesn't work that way. Least not with me."

"Well, I don't think walking into an ambush is how to do this. I think we should explore other options!" He sweats.

"Grow some balls. I'm through exploring options! And if this is an ambush, they're going to be real sorry they ever fucked with Travis Anderson!"

"Travis, you're not thinking straight. Let's just leave. You can't fight them by yourself."

"Watch me!" I get out of the car and slam the door.

Max barks as I walk up the long driveway, gripping the .44. I'm ready. If SageRat has been fucking me over, they'll pay. And if there's a house full of agents, let them take me. I'll let them take me right to Ikshu. And then I'll kill the mutherfucker with my bare hands or with my mind or however the hell a nemesis takes down his appointed victim.

As I walk up to Reed's big white Rubik's Cube of a house, I notice that the front door is busted wide open. I feel my stomach fill up with lead. My tongue turns to rusty iron. I take the safety off the gun and slowly walk inside. I hold my gun up, close to my face, like cops do in the movies. I look around the empty marble foyer and yell, "Here I am, mutherfuckers! Come and get me!"

I jump back behind the open door to miss any open fire. But my echo is the only thing that greets me. So I shut my eyes and scan the house with my mind. But I don't feel a single heartbeat in here. Nobody's home. So I walk around the first floor of the mansion. And it's in the kitchen where I find Reed Bindler.

Dead.

Visions of Rat snapping Reed's neck explode all around me. I look over my shoulder and then reach down to touch Reed's throat. There's no pulse. He's deader than a bag of hammers. And there's a fake lottery ticket next to his corpse. Rat's calling card. There's a note scribbled on the back of the ticket. All it says is: TRAVIS, *YOU FUCKED UP!*

21

Static in My Attic

"Reed is dead," I mumble to myself as I stagger back to the car. I'm so stunned I can't even blink. I'm dizzy and my heart feels tight and swollen, like a rotten tooth. I think I'm having a panic attack. I think it was seeing Reed's body lying there like that. I can't get that image out of my head. I feel my frayed nerves unravel and snap. My whole body goes numb.

The weight of what I just saw drops me to my knees and blood-hot tears stream down my cheeks. And it's not that I'm sad, really. I think I'm just shocked. Shocked that he's dead. How could I be sad? He fucked my wife. He knocked her up.

What's really freaking me out is I know for a fact that these people will kill at the drop of a hat. Which means they could do the same to Noah and Shelby if I fuck up. Their deaths are no longer just a possibility; they're a probability. And that scares the ever living shit out of me.

I shut my eyes and try to regroup. But images of Shelby and Noah's future murders flood my head and pour out of my eyes. I can't let myself think like this. I have to shake this off. But what did Rat's message mean? How did I fuck up?

I hear the gongs of madness banging for my arrival. I cover my ears. And pray that all this just goes away. What's really evil is that all this has left me jagged and broken—terrified for my family's life. Fear isn't a luxury I can afford right now. I have to pull it together. I have to be able to outthink, outmaneuver those psycho fucks. Somehow I've got to take a rain check on this nervous breakdown.

I breathe deep and I stand up. I square my shoulders and force myself to think straight. I squeeze the remaining tears out of my eyes and swallow the salt in the back of my throat.

That's when I feel the Percodan bottle throbbing in my pocket. It's pressing against my leg as if to say that it would like to help. So I pull it out, collect some spit in my mouth, and take one. And then another. I almost immediately feel better. I know that at this point it's only psychological, but, hell, I'll take whatever crutch I can get.

I wipe the sweat from my forehead with my arm. That's when I catch a whiff of myself. I smell like onions and shit. I can't even remember the last time I took a shower. Bathing was something I did back in another lifetime, in some galaxy far, far away, where supper clubs and golf scrambles were as brutal as things ever got.

I can already feel the Percs humming in my stomach. Whistling their song of impending numbness. They let me exhale. Now I can deal with what's happening again. I walk down the driveway to Solomon, who's still sitting in the Boxster, biting his fingernails.

Solomon drives while I ride shotgun and hold Max. Who, by the way, keeps breathing his doggy breath in my face and stepping and re-stepping on my lap. We've got to get another car. Solomon seems to find all this very amusing.

"Sorry. I don't know why I'm laughing," he chuckles.

"We need to get another car. This isn't going to work with the dog."

"I can't rent a car."

"Why not?"

"I gave my people strict instructions: if I didn't bring you back within one hour, it would be assumed that you had taken me over. The moment my credit card hits a scanner, the CIA, FBI, and the local police would be all over us."

"Well, fucking call your people and tell them I didn't take you over."

This really cracks him up; he giggles uncontrollably.

"I can't," he says in between laughs. "They won't believe me. There's no way for them to know you're not making me call."

"Why didn't you tell me this?"

"Hey, I thought you had a plan." He cracks up. "Ba-ha-ha-ha!"

"No, I didn't! I told you I thought I knew where SageRat was. That is not a fucking plan!"

"It's just as well." He holds his nose to stifle his laughter. "It seems from this recent hit that SageRat and Ikshu are still together. So I'm sure that Agent McFadden has already deployed a termination squad to take us out."

I hear what he's saying, but nothing's making sense. The Percodan has coated my brain in Teflon. Nothing sticks. Instead, I'm fascinated with all the big houses we pass down Preston Road. These painkillers make everything look bigger—all blown up like circus balloons. Swollen and diffused. Every house is Super-Grande and manicured like Disney World. *Or Alice in Wonderland.* Or better yet, Never Never Land. Highland Park is Never Never Land.

"This pill makes you small," I sing to myself as I put in my hillbilly teeth.

And then I hear Solomon say, "We can trust no one. Not even my people."

He looks at me, completely puzzled by my protruding brown teeth.

"What are you doing?"

"My disguise," I slur.

Solomon busts up laughing and turns on the blinker.

He turns into Highland Park Village—the Rodeo Drive of Dallas. People are dashing in and out of the fancy stores. It reminds me of Shelby and the way she used to spend my money. Everyone here is so well dressed, so well thought out and together. Maybe it's just the pills, but all these people seem sort of soft and overbred, like veals. They look happy and untroubled. I wish I was one of these veal people again. But I'm not. I'm like Rat and Sage now. A sinewy mess with a shattered soul and crooked teeth.

Solomon parks the Boxster.

"Stay in the car," he snickers as he gets out. Max begs and whines. He wants out, too. Then he barks at some good-looking blonde on her way to work out at Larry North's. She glares at me with my blue hair and rotting teeth. Shame peppers my cheeks and I have to look away.

"When you're ugly, you're invisible." I repeat Rat's mantra to myself.

I catch a glimpse of Solomon in my sideview mirror. He's frantically searching the trunk. He walks around the front with some kind of Sharper Image screwdriver and a smile. He's still laughing. He nervously looks around and bends down. He quickly takes the license plates off the Mercedes parked next to us and exchanges them with our car's. He jumps back in, all out of breath, shaky and still giggling.

He starts the car, jerks us out of our parking spot, and peels out down Mockingbird. He lets out a heavy sigh. And I just sit here.

"What's the matter with you?" Solomon glances over at me. "Are you on something? You're on something."

"Huh?"

"You took something," he chuckles.

I try my hardest to say something—anything, but all I can do is nod my head, yes.

"You're a real piece of work," Solomon laughs. "That's why I've been laughing like this."

I try to string together a quick comeback, but I feel too good right now to put forth that kind of effort. I just hold my tongue in my mouth and keep all these fuzzy thoughts to myself.

Solomon drives down Mockingbird, east toward I-30. His herky-jerky driving is making my dog nervous and me nauseous. I put my arms around Max and try to calm both of us down with my mind. And it kind of works. I feel better and Max stops fretting.

I have no idea where we're headed and, thanks to these magic little pills I took, I really don't care. I do, however, still have this burning need to connect with my family. Since I'm relaxed now, I shut my eyes and call out to them in my mind. I try to light up my chakras, but all I get are weird Salvador Dali images. Melting watches and shit like that. I see Technicolor visions of the veal people wandering in and out of the Gucci store with Mouseketeer hats on their heads. Meanwhile, Solomon keeps laughing and singing, "M-I-C-K-E-Y-M-O-U-S-E."

I must be fucking with his morphic resonance. Either that, or Solomon's gone mad.

When I wake up, we're crossing the mighty Mississippi, from Louisiana into Vicksburg. Max is pawing at my chest and whining. He needs to piss.

"We gotta stop." I roll my neck and smack my mouth.

Max is going crazy, trying to stand up in my lap and putting his tail in my face.

Solomon doesn't say a word. He pulls off onto the first exit after the bridge. I open the door and Max runs off to a tree and just stands there with his leg up. If dogs could glare, he would be glaring at me.

"Have a good nap?" Solomon gets out of the tiny car and I do the same.

"Yeah, I guess." I hold out my arms and stretch. My mouth is dry and tastes like dogshit. My legs are sort of asleep and tingling.

"I guess we can spend the night here." Solomon looks around. "There's a Holiday Inn across the street. We can get a couple of rooms away from the highway."

"What are we doing here?"

"I dunno. It was a straight shot down I-20."

"Exactly. Don't you think they'll be looking for us here?"

"Well, I'm sorry, Travis. This isn't exactly my area of exper-
tise."

"It's called *common sense*, Solomon. You don't take major
highways when you're on the run."

"Oh, so thorry! What do you suggest, then?"

"Fuck, I dunno. I don't know where to go." I can feel my
blood pressure rising, and my heart feels like Jiffy Pop again.

"Well, haven't you tried any remote viewing?" He gives me
a puzzled look.

"Yeah, I have, but I just get a bunch of weird shit."

"Like what? Maybe I can help interpret it."

"I see rich people wearing Mickey Mouse ears."

"Mickey Mouse ears?" He raises an eyebrow. "That's
why . . ."

"Yeah, I took a Percodan. Probably fucked with your morphic whatever."

"Whoa." He shakes his head. "Talk about anomalous cognition. Ikshu used to work at Disney World."

"Disney World? Wait a second. Wait one fucking second.
Don't they have some kind of international thing?"

"Yeah, Epcot." He nods.

"Do they have France and China?"

"Yeah, I think so."

"What about Mexico and Germany?"

"Probably."

"Then that's it! That's fucking it!"

"What's it?" He peers at me.

"Just get back in the car."

"Why?" he asks.

"We're going to Disney World."

We blaze through Mississippi. We blast through Alabama. I drive most of the way while Solomon sleeps, and poor Max rests his head on the dashboard. I juggle a banana Moon Pie, a Coke, and the steering wheel. I try to figure out why Ikshu would be at Disney World. And then, as mile marker after mile marker zooms by, and rusted barns and piles of kudzu flash past me, Ikshu's motivations become clear to me. In fact, it becomes painfully obvious as to why he would be at Disney World. So much so, I feel stupid for not having figured this out before.

It's the rats.

The ones that left the horrible scars around his ankles. He wants revenge on the rats. And the biggest rat in the world is Mickey Mouse. In Ikshu's twisted mind, he's avenging his childhood. I don't know what he's got planned, but I'm pretty sure it will be catastrophic. I pray—no, I beg God for Noah and Shelby's safety. I pray that I get there in time to keep him from hurting anybody. The gravity of this thought pushes my foot down hard on the accelerator, throwing my neck against the car seat.

Solomon wakes up with a start and Max groans.

"Why are you driving so fast?" He braces himself against the dashboard.

"I figured out why Ikshu is at Disney World."

"And that's why you're going a hundred and twenty? So we can be pulled over?"

As much as I hate to admit it, Solomon's right. I put on the brakes and slow it back down to seventy.

"Jesus, you're going to kill us," he bitches.

"So do you want to know why Ikshu is at Disney World or not?" I feed Max the rest of my Moon Pie.

"Well, I would hypothesize that he was at Epcot to throw remote viewers off his trail. You know, with all the faux architecture and foreigners."

"Yeah, but I think that's only part of it. I think it goes deeper than that."

"Really?" Solomon raises an eyebrow.

"I think he went there to relive his childhood."

"Oh, okay," Solomon rolls his eyes. "Now I guess you're a psychiatrist."

"Well, at least that makes one of us." I check the rearview mirror and change lanes to pass a semi.

"What is that supposed to mean?" he sneers.

"I'll tell you what that means. It's obvious that Ikshu was mental. Yet you were so desperate for talent, you went ahead and took him anyway. You basically created this monster."

"That's hardly fair, Travis."

"You're telling me you didn't know Ikshu was wacko? You had no fucking idea that he thinks he's a Hindu god sent to destroy the goddamn world?"

"He concealed that from us. He's very duplicitous."

"Hello! He keeps a shrine to Charles Manson in his room!"

"Let me explain something, Travis. Often subjects who exhibit aberrant behaviors score the highest in the skill sets that we're looking for. Basically, people with some sort of cracked view of reality make the best psychics."

"And you don't see this as a problem? You're basically teaching psychopaths how to control people with their minds and you're all surprised when it blows up in your face?"

"Look, Travis. If we didn't find Ikshu, someone else would have. The Russians or the Japanese. Remote influencing is only dangerous if it gets in the wrong hands."

"You just made my point for me," I say. "Ikshu is obviously dangerous. So what does that make Shimmer?"

"I wish I could be as smug as you, Travis." His heavy eyebrows meet, like two hairy caterpillars kissing. "I wish I could have all the answers. I wish I could let my wife fuck my best friend and fool me into raising someone else's kid."

"Huh?" I have to swerve to miss a car that slowed down in front of me. "How did you know about that?"

My heart is beating in my throat from both the car and that comment that came out of nowhere.

"Travis, you're about the only one who didn't know." He smirks at me like Ikshu used to.

I put both hands on the wheel and squeeze. My stomach twists and I think about Rat's lottery ticket and what he wrote on it. *YOU FUCKED UP!* Why would he write that if he was still controlled by Ikshu? But then again, why would he kill Reed? I look over at Solomon; he's turned away from me, looking out the window. I touched a nerve when I questioned Shimmer's role in this debacle. Maybe that's why he said that to me. Or maybe Ikshu's still got a hold on him.

"Tell me this, Solomon. How did Ikshu get his fangs into you?"

"I'm sorry, what?" He shakes off whatever he was daydreaming about.

"How did Ikshu take you over? Did he, you know . . .?'"

"No . . . God, no. Of course not." He looks at me wide-eyed and shocked that I would even ask such a thing.

"Then, how?" I try to get a good look at his eyes. "How did he take you over?"

"It was a very slow erosion of my will." He pets Max. "I was his therapist. Over time, you can develop a sort of empathy with your patients. Ikshu manipulated that."

"And that's all it took for him to get you to kill Annie?

"I don't want to talk about this."

"Okay. Fine. Suit yourself. Just trying to figure out how to take him down . . . Guess I'll just make my plans without you."

"Yeah, I guess you will." He turns and looks out his window again.

"Ever heard the phrase 'Physician, heal thyself'?" I jab.

He doesn't respond. He keeps his face turned to the passenger window.

I actually feel bad for making that last remark. I really can be an asshole sometimes. So I keep my trap shut and drive down this long stretch of Florida highway, thinking about what it must have been like for Solomon to be force-fed the murder of his own fiancée.

I don't know what to think anymore. I just know I need some fresh air, so I roll down the window. I've got this taste in my mouth. It's a cross between garlic and capers. I think it's the tang of suspicion.

We stop outside of Tallahassee for the night. We have trouble getting a room, since we can't use a credit card. The only place where we can get in with cash is a dark Motel 6 right off the highway. Max and I share a room. Solomon and his guilt share another, two doors down. I double bolt the door and prop a chair against it.

I collapse onto the bed. But it's hard to get to sleep. Images of people who've used this bed keep running through my head. I see a guy with a hairy backside pounding on this cauliflower woman. I see a toothless carny getting it on with a pockmarked hooker. Then I see Ikshu going over and under, under and over Debra McFadden, Sage, and the pink-haired girl. I could count these nasty-ass visions like sheep—there're so many of them.

Jeez, these people have done it all over this thin mattress. It's giving me the heebs. These sheets are crawling with weird hairs. I have to get up and call the front desk. I ask them for some new sheets. The motel dude basically tells me to go fuck myself. *The sheets are clean,* he says and hangs up on me.

I get back in bed with all my clothes on. I put a towel on the pillow and I try to shut my eyes. Now I keep seeing this montage of Shelby and Reed doing it. Then I see Reed's corpse—the rats nibbling at his rotting face. And then, I see the rats crawling all over Ikshu. I am haunted. I can't stop thinking. I feel the bottle of pills quivering in my pocket. They whisper me promises of sleep. So I take one. Okay, I take three. Then all my worries and visions drift into the night and I can get some rest. For the first time in weeks, I dream. And it's a good dream.

I see blue skies and a green, green golf course. There's a black and white cow in the distance with a bell around her neck. Shelby and Noah are here with me. Shelby's got the new baby on her hip, and she tells me that this little girl is actually mine. I kiss both of them. And then Noah tugs at me. He wants to play airplane. I pick him up and zoom him around as he holds out his arms and sputters.

Then all of a sudden we're sitting at a big picnic of fried chicken and potato salad. Shelby tells me that it's from heaven. I look in the wicker basket and pull out what looks like a wedding invitation. I munch on a drumstick and read it.

Dear Travis,
Heartfelt laughter is a sign that I am with you.

And remember: Thou shalt not kill.

Your Pal,
The Blue Mutherfucker

(P.S. Sometimes I feel like a comedian playing to a crowd who's too afraid to laugh.)

Shelby takes the letter from me. She folds it into a paper airplane and throws it into the wind. Noah claps as the plane does loopty-loops. The new baby giggles and scrunches up her little nose. The cow moos in the distance.

Then I pick up my golf bag and play nine of the most amazing holes of golf anyone could ever imagine. I'm talking water hazards the size of the Pacific. Putting greens on the cliffs of Dover. The third hole is the entire island of Maui.

I am Tiger Woods. I am a golf god. I can do anything. I hit that dimpled white ball and it explodes into the air. The little mo-fo does exactly what I will it to do.

After making a hole-in-one on the moon, I pick up my clubs and fly back to earth, to the ninth hole in Florida. I'm a little disappointed; it's just a normal golf course with palm trees and bunkers built for mortals. It does, however, have a Mickey Mouse sand trap. So I pull out my favorite wood and swing.

I choke.

"Fuck me!"

The easiest hole of the course and I shank it. The ball flies into the sand. I shake my head and lumber over to the trap. I pull out my nine iron and swing. I hack and hack. I'm a one-man sandstorm. I suck. Then Shelby walks over to me. She's dressed like a harem girl—all purple scarves and veils.

"Stop fighting. It's only a trap if you let it be. Just schwing!" Her voice rings like a tuning fork. She lifts her veil and kisses me. I wake up with her taste on my lips.

I try to go back to sleep. I want to keep dreaming. But the best I can do is linger between remembering this dream and waking up. I'm lying in this motel bed—happier than I've ever been. I'm not sure I've ever been this happy.

And this scares me. Bad.

I try to remember how I felt when I married Shelby. When we bought our house. When Noah was born. Was I this happy? I can't remember. I can barely remember Shelby's or Noah's face. I'm going crazy here. I can't remember what color Shelby's eyes are. I think they're blue. I think Noah's are blue, too. But I can't remember for sure. What the fuck is happening to me? I'm freaking out. I hear jungle drums beating wild and fast. And then this big, black dread eclipses my room. I get real still and hold my breath.

I feel something wet and sharp poking me. I pull off the covers and there are mounds of cold, muddy crawfish all over me—flipping and flicking. They're pinching at the flesh on my stomach. They're trying to burrow into my belly button!

"FUCK!"

I bolt out of bed and slap the mudbugs off me. Then they just disappear. Just like that. The whole crawling, swampy mess of them. Gone. But the room still smells like dirty water.

I'm all sorts of fucked up. I look around the room for some-place to hide. The only place that seems safe is the corner. But I'm too scared to move. It feels like I'm walking on the ledge of a skyscraper. Max is barking. He's freaking out, too. He knows I've gone nuts.

I run for the corner, hit the wall, and slide down onto the floor. I curl up into a ball. Perhaps if I can make myself small enough, this Angel of Death feeling will pass over me.

22

Crash Boom Bam

Solomon says he didn't get any sleep last night. He started laughing at about midnight and couldn't stop. But I didn't tell him that it was my fault. We both know I took the pills. And we're both too tired to fight about it. So we load up Max in the Boxster, and we head south to Orlando. Solomon drives. I hold Max and drink a soured McDonald's coffee. Max helps himself to my Egg McMuffin.

I can't get the crawfish out of my head. I hate shellfish. I especially hate waking up with them crawling all over me. And what was that dream supposed to mean, anyway? Why was I playing golf? And what did Shelby say to me just before I woke up? I should have written it down. But I was too busy going insane.

I shut my eyes. I'm overflowing with visions and equations of all this yin-yang crap. I see that life is just one big cosmic golf fuck—a nonlinear humping of opposites. Fission and fusion. Golf and sex are the keys to life. But I already knew that.

What did Shelby say when I was standing in the Mickey Mouse ears? She said something about a trap . . . wait . . . fuck me: Disney World is a trap. But what did the crawfish mean?

"They meant *back up*." The pink-haired girl tickles my ear.

"Huh?"

"Crawfish," she seethes. "Back up."

"What?" I shut my eyes and listen hard.

"Ikshu is with you. Get away."

"How?" I move my lips.

"Solomon," she groans.

"Stop the car!" I shout.

"We're almost there." Solomon gives me a cockeyed look.

"Stop, goddamn it!"

"Why?"

"Because I said so. Pull over. I have to take a leak."

"Can't you just hold it?" Solomon's teeth look evil and gray.

That's when I think about clocking him. I look at the speedometer; we're going ninety. If I knock him out now, we're both dead. I've got to talk him into pulling over and then I can clock him. Or can I? He's a pretty big guy.

"Come on, Solomon. My bladder is screaming over here."

"Oh, Travis Anderson." Solomon sounds like Ikshu. "Are you lying to me?"

"Ik-Ikshu?" I can barely spit out his name.

Solomon doesn't answer. Max growls. I hold the pup by the collar and shut my eyes. I try to influence Solomon into pulling the car over. But I'm so freaked out, I can't think straight, much less take someone over. Then I remember how

I reached into Sage's heart and pulled out her kid fears. Maybe if I do that to Solomon, I can free him. So I visualize and chant. I see myself reaching into Solomon's heart and pulling out his kid fears, but nothing happens. I hear Ikshu's thoughts ringing inside Solomon's head.

"I can hear you knocking. But you can't come in," Ikshu mocks me.

Max is growling even louder now. He's tense and ready to attack. So I let him and he goes straight for Solomon's face.

Solomon tries to push him off. But Max is pissed. Solomon weaves all over the road, punching and wrestling my dog. Max shakes Solomon's ear like a chew toy and our little car swerves and jerks in rhythm to their fighting. Max takes a hard blow to the side and yelps. He retreats to my lap and whimpers. Solomon's ear looks like bloody bubble gum, but Ikshu still has a hold on him. Solomon keeps driving like nothing happened. Just when I think it's over, Max lunges at Solomon's face again. This time Solomon screams. I hear horrible wet tearing sounds coming from this bloody mingling of dog and man. I glance at the speedometer. Solomon's slowed us down to forty miles per hour. Fuck, that's slow enough. I say a silent prayer and pull up on the parking brake.

The tires scream.

Rubber burns.

And we spin like a pinwheel in a hurricane.

Solomon jerks the steering wheel to the right, throwing us off the road. We go crashing into a ditch. Max rubber bands against the shattering windshield. And everything just freezes in midair. Glass. Fake Bubba teeth. Max. Empty Coke cans. It's like a fruit cocktail suspended in Jell-O. Then air bags and steam explode all around me, knocking my head against the leather seat.

When the airbags deflate and I open my eyes, I see diamonds everywhere. And for just a split second I think I see the blue mutherfucker standing outside my window. I look over at Solomon; he's knocked out and missing half of his right ear. Max is somehow back in my lap. He's covered in glass and shivering. I'm not sure how badly he's hurt. I think I'm okay. I am, however, bleeding somewhere on my head. Either that, or some of Solomon's or Max's blood got in my mouth during the crash, because I can taste it.

I try to open my door, but it's smashed shut. I look up. There's a rip in the canvas top. I tear the hole bigger and pull myself out. I crawl over the mangled steel and fiberglass. I reach in and pull Max out. I stand here with my dog and look at what used to be a Boxster. It's a total fucking wreck—the kind that you don't walk away from. I can hear Solomon groaning from the driver's side. I put Max down and look through the hole in the ragtop. Solomon's bloodied from his chewed-up ear, but other than that, he looks okay. I mean, the way we crashed, he should have been killed. What the hell kind of airbags are they putting in Porsches these days, anyway? There's no way I should be walking away from this.

I wonder if maybe I'm really dead and just don't realize it. But as soon as I think that, I know I'm not dead because my neck is stiff, my arm is still in a cast, and I feel a small gash on my scalp. I'm obviously still in a body. I reach down and check Max. He doesn't seem to be hurt. Not a cut. He's got to have some kind of internal injuries. I saw him break the windshield and bounce back into my lap. But the pup's panting and happy. He shakes himself and bits of glass go flying every-where. It's crazy; we both seem fairly unscathed. If I didn't have whiplash and this cut on my head, I'd say we just experi-enced a miracle.

I deliberate whether or not to help Solomon out of the wreckage, but then a VW Microbus pulls over to gawk or help. As much as this seems heartless, I decide to leave the muther-fucker to the kind folks in the van. I don't know if Ikshu still has a hold on him or not, but at this stage, I can't afford to be a nice guy. Besides, that fucker helped steal my family. He needs to sit in broken glass for a few hours. Maybe that will teach him a lesson about destroying people's lives.

Anyway, I walk down the shoulder of the highway and Max trots behind me, wagging his tail. He's very proud of him-self. He knows he saved my life.

"You're a good boy, Max." I roll my neck; I hear it snap, crackle, and pop. I wonder if I don't have one of those spinal cord injuries that you can walk away from only later to calm down and realize that you're really paralyzed. Thinking about this makes me want a big handful of Percodan. But I'm scared that if I take them, I'll calm down and discover that I really broke my neck. Then Noah and Shelby would be dead for sure. So I just keep walking to Disney World, figuring out my plan of attack, rubbing my neck, and trying not to think about impending wheelchairs and breathing machines.

Max and I follow the mouse-eared highway signs to Disney World. According to the signs we're about five miles outside of the Magic Kingdom. The giant Epcot golf ball floats in the dis-tance. I try to zero in on Noah and Shelby. But I keep seeing

SageRat waltzing around. I also keep smelling sunscreen. The piña colada kind. Cars zoom past us and I try to keep my head down. But one car, a blue Ford Contour, pulls over onto the shoulder and starts to back up toward us. I reach for my gun but realize I must have left it in the car.

There's no place to run. To my right is a swamp of palmetto. To my left, I've got speeding traffic. I stand frozen in place, not sure what to do. The car's brake lights glow red and it jerks to a stop. Then a small hand with black fingernails and silver rings shoots out of the driver's side and waves us to come over. It's Rat. Then Sage crawls out of the passenger side window, covered in a black shawl and movie star sunglasses.

"Hurry, my precious! Before someone sees us!"

Max barks, but he doesn't growl. I close my eyes and scan their minds. They're clean. Or at least I think they are. I walk over and get in the backseat with Max.

"Are you stupid or what?" Rat turns around and bares his fangs.

"Just shut up and drive," I say.

Rat puts the rental car in gear and floors it. The economy engine strains as he weaves us in and out of lane after lane of overpacked Ford Explorers and minivans.

"How's that for driving, muthafucka!" he shouts.

"Rat, please, behave." Sage touches his arm.

"Tell fuckface to behave!" he snaps.

"Should we invoke SageRat?" She takes off her sunglasses and eyeballs her brother.

"Okay, I'll play nice." He glares at me in the rearview mirror.

"We thought Ikshu had gotten you." Sage turns around. Max starts sniffing and licking her arm. She's coated in some kind of goopy piña colada–flavored sunscreen.

"Is this your dog?" she asks as she scratches Max behind the ear.

"Yep."

"He's very cute. I like him." She smiles her kooky fanged smile. "And I usually don't like cute things."

"So why did you kill Reed?" I look into her crossed eyes.

"Really, dumbass, it should be obvious by now," Rat says.

"Reed attacked me with a butcher knife and Brother-lovely snapped his neck. It was all very traumatic. I suspect Ikshu had infested him." Sage turns back around and checks her look in the rearview mirror. "Travis, do you have any idea why Ikshu is doing all this?"

"Yeah, I think so."

"Pray tell, illuminate us," she says.

"Well, I think it's the rats."

"The what?" Rat scoffs.

"You know, Mickey Mouse. He's like some kind of cartoon version of the rats that attacked Ikshu as a child. He's come to Disney World to take revenge on the rats."

"Travis, my darkness, I think you might be on to something." Sage puts on her purple lipstick: she puckers and smacks. "But I don't think that's exactly it."

"Yeah? No shit," Rat grunts.

"But what I just said makes perfect sense," I argue. "The dude's emotionally disturbed."

"Who isn't?" Rat glances back at me.

"Who gives a fuck as to why he's doing this?" I lean forward. *"He's doing it.* That's all that matters."

"Actually, Ikshu's motivations do matter, my blue pretty." Sage turns back around. Her lips look like an ink pen exploded in her mouth. "I think Ikshu has been using Disney World to get his hands on top government officials."

"Yeah," Rat adds. "All sorts of senators, CIA fucks. Pentagon big daddies. He entices all these power mongers to come down, he gets inside their brains, and they become his meat puppets."

"I still don't see what this has to do with me." I squint.

"It has everything to do with you. Everything." Sage smoothes back her long white hair. "Ikshu has orchestrated all of this so you will have no other choice but to come after him."

"Why me?" I shake my head.

"Normally, they just terminate viewers who escape, but for some reason, Ikshu thinks you are fated for something greater," Sage says.

"Me? Why me?"

"As far as I can divinate," Sage sighs. "You are Ikshu's nemesis and he knows that. I think he wants to drive you mad, then you won't be able to fulfill your destiny."

"Come join the dark side, Luke," Rat does his best Darth Vader.

"What is my destiny, exactly?" I look out the window at all the passing minivans.

"I'm still trying to figure that one out, but it's obviously tied to Ikshu's."

"This just doesn't make any sense," I say.

"Prophecy seldom does." Rat smirks. "Prophecy seldom does."

Max looks at me with his weepy eyes, and barks like he agrees with Rat.

*   *   *

The Walt Disney World Dolphin and its sister hotel, The Swan,
loom over the man-made shores of Epcot. These hotels are
mind-blowing feats of architectural crapola. Imagine a green
Babylonian pyramid flanked by five-story spitting fish and its
cotton candy twin, buttressed by giant green swans. This is
what they call a "themed resort experience." The Dolphin's
theme being Bozo the Clown swallowed some gold fish and
then puked them all over the place. It's a circus tent swirl of
underwater hell in here. However, Rat insists on staying. He
thinks that he can feel Debra McFadden's vibrations. I can't really argue with him. The Dolphin is just the sort of place that
she would get all moist about.

Anyway. Sage acts like she's blind and that Max is her
seeing-eye dog. That's how we get a room with a Border Collie, but without a reservation. In fact, the front desk people trip
all over themselves to welcome us. Let me tell you this: these
people scare me. Their hollow eyes make me think that maybe
Ikshu or somebody has eaten their brains. Despite their gracious hospitality, I can tell they aren't used to dealing with
freaks like us. Especially freaks who have fangs and no credit
cards. But since Sage is "disabled," they go overboard to ac-
commodate us. They even upgrade our room to a handicapped suite. And they smile extra hard when Sage fumbles
for her money and asks them to count it for her.

"You know you can go to the front of the lines at all the
parks with this handicapped pass." The front desk girl slides
Sage a card with a wheelchair logo on it.

"What's the use." Sage takes it. "I still won't be able to see
anything."

Then there's this pregnant pause. The desk girl doesn't have a scripted response. She just shrugs and tries her best to stay cheerful.

"Well, have a Disney Day," she says.

"Yeah, fuck you, too." Sage snatches her room key off the counter. She then turns around and makes herself trip over Max's leash. She falls in a thud on the floor.

"Omigosh," the girl gasps. "Are you okay, ma'am?"

Rat helps his sister get up, and Max barks. I just stand here looking at my feet.

"No, I'm not okay!" Sage spews. "I'm blind!"

The desk girl flinches. "Sorry. I, uh, we can, uh, help you to your room if you like."

"No, that's okay." Sage gropes for the counter's ledge. "Brother-lovely will help me." She gives Rat a rather unsisterly kiss. The cute girl gasps and tries her best to muster up a smile.

I look at all the families checking in next to us; they're trying not to stare. I can feel their disgust, like we're spoiling their view. Part of me doesn't blame them. Sage has no business acting like this, especially in front of kids. But these people's glib normality and easy happiness taunts her. And to be honest, it taunts me, too.

I should be checking in with Shelby and Noah. Not scaring small children with this blue-haired rockabilly getup. I reckon this is how Sage must feel every day. Rat was right about the ugly thing. When people stare at you long enough you become this invisible creature that nobody wants near them. You're someone that nobody wants to see. And it makes you feel pretty fucking miserable.

Being at the "happiest place on earth" without my family

only makes things worse. All this sun and fun doesn't cheer me up; it makes me suicidal. It's like watching lovers cuddle and flirt when your heart has been ripped from your chest.

When we get up to our room, I wrap my cast in a garbage bag and take a shower. It's the first time I've taken a bath since Dallas. It feels good to wash all the miles and dirt off me. It helps clean my mind of all the nightmares—the real ones and the ones in my head. Steam and soap have always helped me think. I close my eyes and let the hot water run down my face. It opens my sinuses and relaxes the tiny muscles in my face. I have a vision of Noah. He's riding the Dumbo ride with Debra McFadden. Goddamn it—that bitch has my son. I get out of the shower, towel off, and sling on my dirty clothes. I run out to the other room.

"They're at the Dumbo ride! I saw them! Let's go!"

"Not just yet, my darkness." Sage looks up from her park map.

"Yeah, can't you see we're working here?" Rat turns back to Sage. "Now, if I take MGM, you can take Epcot and yuppiefuck can take the Magic Kingdom."

"I've seen Noah! I know where he is!"

They just sit there, poring over their stupid maps.

"Travis, Ikshu knows we're here . . . Hello." Sage looks at me sideways and cross-eyed. "Besides, Brother-lovely and I are concocting the most delicious plan."

"Fuck that! I'm not waiting for that bastard to hurt my kid!"

"But Travis, this is a dance with the devil." She smiles a wicked smile. "And it must be choreographed."

"Screw that! I'm not wasting any more time!" I slam the door and run down the hallway to the elevator. This is just some kind of spy game to those two. Fuck them. This is my life. This is my family hanging in the balance here. Waiting for a goddamn delicious plan is not a fucking option.

I concentrate on Noah as I ride down the elevator. My vision is clear and full of sweet smells. He's riding a fiberglass Dumbo and laughing. He gets off the ride and takes Debra McFadden's hand. I think he's okay. He looks okay. I have to get to him before Ikshu has a chance to hurt him. Fuck Sage and Rat, I have to get to my little boy.

23

Toronto Blessings via Orlando

M-O-N-E-Y. That's what it takes to get into the Magic Fucking Kingdom. Forty-eight dollars to be exact. And I don't have it. I left all of Reed's cash back at the hotel with Rat. My son is somewhere beyond those turnstiles and I forget to bring the money to get in. Fuck me.

I scope out the concourse for someone who looks like an easy mark—someone uncomplicated and weak willed. I see this chubby couple standing in line. A freckled wife and lumpy husband. They look like simple folk with simple minds that will be easy to pick. They've got on matching Donald Duck T-shirts, and they've both crammed themselves into bike shorts. The man has a red fanny pack resting just under his gut. There's got to be money in there.

Maybe I can take the high road here. Maybe I can awaken their goodwill and they'll just give me the fifty dollars. I concentrate on lighting up my chakras. I send my will out to the husband. I concentrate on his compassion, which normally rests in the green glow of the heart. I imagine striking flint-stones together to start the warmth of human kindness. But it's so cold inside this bastard's heart that I actually get chills.

There's no way to kindle goodwill with this dude; he has none. Fuck it. The guy's a prick. The asshole actually stole the money for this trip from his till as the assistant manager at some movieplex. He beats his wife and kids. I see him harassing his teenage employees. He's a bastard ruled by hate and pain. So I concentrate on the cold blue reason of his head. I commandeer his brain. I muddy it up. I blow clouds of dusty sleep into his eyes. I imagine icicles all around his gray matter. I freeze him.

I stare at the dude. I push my way through the well-scrubbed masses and sidle up to my target. When his wife looks away at some bush trimmed into a dancing bear, I unsnap his fanny pack and put it into my jumpsuit. I carefully step away and zigzag through the throngs of people. By the time I get away, I'm about to pass out. Remote influencing a total stranger is torture. It's sort of like treading water while holding two fifty-pound weights in your hands. I feel like I'm about to drown, but I have to keep paddling and straining.

And then I just have to let go.

I collapse on the pavement. No matter how hard I try, I can't open my eyes and get back up. I'm not unconscious, because I can hear people shuffling and gathering around me. My brain is just overheated and I hurt. Bad. I fell on my broken arm.

The sunshine hurts my brain when I open my eyes. I stumble to my feet and there's a small crowd staring at me.

"You okay?" someone asks.

I don't answer. I just wave them off, and go take a seat on a nearby park bench. My arm is killing me. So I find the Percodan in my pocket and swallow a heaping handful. I choke on them, but manage to gag and swallow them down. It takes a few minutes and their black magic hits my head with a swoon of milk and honey. I feel wavy and boneless. I feel better than good. I take the stolen fanny pack out of my jumpsuit and tear into it. There's a big roll of hundreds wrapped in rubber bands. And a pack of flavored condoms? Eww. I put the Benjamins in my pocket with my pills and leave the fanny pack and rubbers under the park bench. I get up and hobble over to the ticket counter.

That's when it starts. People start falling out, roaring and weeping like they're being tickled to death. We're talking mass hysteria. As I walk up to the counter, the crowd parts for me like this big Red Sea of laughter.

"One three-day pass." I slam a wad of cash down on the barrelhead.

The Disney ticket dude can barely stop goofing and snorting long enough to take my money. He holds his sides and bends over red faced, straining. He struggles to punch in my transaction in the computer, and then cracks up. He gives me my pass and drops to the floor, rolling and howling.

I lurch over to the gates and hand my pass to this ticket-taker girl. She drops to her knees giggling and gulping for air as I trip past the turnstiles. It's the morphic whatever and the Perc. I don't know how to make it stop. So I just keep stum-

bling down Main Street USA, through the belly-laughing kids
and overjoyed parents, looking for Noah and Shelby or some
Shimmer fuck who can lead me to them.

Being hit with a stun gun doesn't feel like you think it would.
It's not some gentle easy way to take someone down. You
don't just pass out. You rattle around and cramp up, and *then*
you pass out. A stun gun sends this evil buzz into your body
that spasms every one of your muscles, and just when you
think your heart is going to burst into flames, your brain short-
circuits and you pass out. When you wake up, you have this
weird coppery taste in your mouth and a really bad headache.
And I should know. Because I have that weird coppery taste in
my mouth and my brain feels swollen and sore. I also have a
slight burn on my neck from the damn thing.

The last thing I remember before getting zapped was
going to the Dumbo ride and Noah not being there. So I
wandered around the park all day, doped up and desperate.
Eventually, the Percodan and laughter wore off, and I was
searching the crowds in Frontierland. That's when someone
got me from behind. I don't know who did it. A Shimmer op-
erative, most likely. But whoever it was shot me full of electricity, hog-tied me, and locked me in this room. Now I've
got this bad metal taste in my mouth and no way of getting
out of here. I am completely screwed, and now so are Shelby
and Noah.

The door opens and Debra McFadden appears with duct
tape over her mouth and her arms behind her back. Rat and
Sage are standing behind her, pushing through the doorway.

"What the fuck?" I stare.

"Look who we found!" Rat grabs a handful of Debra's hair and lifts her up on her tiptoes.

"You would make such a lovely corpse." Sage caresses Debra's cheek. Debra screams and moans through her taped mouth.

Sage breezes over to me and starts to untie my hands and feet.

"What the hell happened?" I yell.

"We couldn't very well have you ruining our scrumptious little plan." She jerks at the knotted cord around my ankles and loosens it. "Sorry about the stun gun. That was Brother-lovely's idea."

"Yeah, I bet it was." I sneer at Rat, but he's busy trying to mesmerize Debra.

"You don't understand, my precious." Sage gets my hands undone and helps me to my feet. "You were falling right into Ikshu's trap. I think he wants you to find him. I had a vision that he wants you to witness the murder of your family."

My head is spinning. I push the visions of Shelby and Noah in coffins out of my head.

"He wants to drive you mad," Sage continues. "Like I said before, I think he knows you are his nemesis, and if you are fated to defeat him, he's going to take your sanity and your family with him."

I try my best to process what Sage is telling me while at the same time keeping myself from hyperventilating.

"Are you ready to talk?" Rat growls in Debra's ear. "Or do I have to beat the truth out of you?"

She answers him with a series of rapid nods and whimpers. So Rat rips the tape off her mouth.

"Travis!" she cries out. "Don't believe them! Ikshu faked Shelby and Noah's deaths because Rat was in your attic! These two think they're vampires, for God's sake! Ikshu is your friend!"

"Shut up!" Rat grabs Debra by the neck.

"She's brainwashed." Sage puts her hand on my shoulder; I step away.

"Let her talk." I walk over to Rat and Debra.

Sage looks at Rat and then he glares at me.

"Look, dumbass, she's being influenced, okay?" he says.

"Like I said, let her talk."

Rat nudges Debra. "Go ahead, keep talking, Debs."

"Travis, please! Ikshu would never hurt a fly, I promise!" Debra's eyes are wild and earnest. "The plan was to take you into custody and bring you here to be with your family. We were trying to enroll you and your family in an identity protection program, to protect you from terrorists like these two. I swear on the Holy Bible! Please, for Shelby and Noah's sake! Travis, you have to believe me!"

"What. Ever." Rat rolls his black eyes, and pushes Debra out of his way.

"What about Dr. Solomon, Debra?" I ask.

"That was SageRat controlling him!" she pleads. "You have to believe me!"

I look at Sage and then at Rat. Both of them gaze at me with cold, hard eyes. Then I look at Debra again. She glances away.

"Tell me about Ikshu's shrine to Charlie Manson." I cross my arms. "Explain that one."

"This whole fiasco is that albino's fault!" Debra sneers at

Sage. "She's the evil one. She wants revenge on Ikshu because he didn't want her!"

That's when Rat shocks Debra in the back of the neck with his stun gun. There's a series of loud clicks, Debra jerks around, then drops to her knees and passes out.

I look up at Sage and Rat. She's bawling. He's scowling.

"Why'd you do that?" I step back against the wall.

"I'm not evil." Sage sniffles. "I'm not."

"Debra McFadden is a mutherfucking liar." Rat looks down at his stun gun and then at me.

I'm stuck against this cold wall, trying to swallow the lump that's swelling in my throat. Then this cloud of India ink washes over me. I have visions of Sage on the playground, being pummeled by her classmates. They leave her bloodied and nearly dead. Her little brother finds her and cradles her thrashed body in his arms. She's not breathing, so he gives her mouth to mouth. It was at that moment that SageRat was born. That injured little girl reached out to her brother, and their minds have been mixed together ever since.

I touch Sage's arm and she looks up at me with her crazy, blue eyes.

"It's okay," I say. "It's okay."

Rat wants to kill Debra McFadden, but I won't let him. Instead, we settle on shaving her head, tying her up, and force-feeding her some Percodan. We leave Debra gagged, bound, and locked away in this room. A room, which by the way, is in the tunnels below the Magic Kingdom. There's a whole underground city down here, with hordes of Disney employees rushing to their jobs. They get dressed for work down here, walk through this maze of tunnels, and then pop up at their locations like trained prairie dogs—all smiley and creature cute. There are miles and miles of offices, break rooms, and bathrooms down here. These underground walkways are teeming with shiny happy people and golf carts.

Anyway, Rat dragged me down here after he shocked me. He'd stolen a set of skeleton keys from the custodial staff, and found this empty training room, which is perfect for locking people in. It's at the end of a tunnel that nobody goes down anymore because the ride that it goes to is closed. Even if Debra does manage to take off her gag to scream, nobody will hear her. I've got to hand it to those two freakers; discovering this tunnel was pretty damn ingenious.

I guess Sage and Rat really do have a "delicious little plan." So I might as well go along with them. They've obviously done their homework. And I figure the more people I have looking for my family, the faster I'll find them.

Sage kisses Rat and they invoke SageRat. The two of them smile at me and tell me to follow them through the tunnels. The employees stare and gawk at us. I guess blue-haired bums and albino vampires aren't covered under their dress code. But SageRat turns their remote influencing on full blast, and nobody stops us. Then SageRat whammies the tunnel security goons into letting us into the "Character Factory."

This is the place where they keep all the big suits for the characters like Goofy and Snow White. We go through a series of checkpoints, and then we're standing in row after row of cartoon heads and costumes. They're hanging on hooks—like slabs of beef in a meat locker. It looks like a cloning lab for cartoon body parts in here.

A college girl, all dolled up like Cinderella, dashes past us. She's cussing herself for being late and sucking down the last few drags from her cigarette. She squirts some Binaca in her mouth, steps on her cigarette, hikes up her skirt, and dashes up the stairs. Somebody dressed like Donald Duck goes waddling after her.

SageRat leads us through the walls of costumes. We pass half-dressed men and women fighting zippers and big fat character heads. Some of the employees are taking off the heavy suits. They're all red faced and sweaty.

At the end of the rows is a rack of Mickey Mouse heads. SageRat outfits me in one of these rigs. The black tights. The red shorts. The bubbly yellow shoes. The four-fingered gloves and the enormous rat head and exoskeleton harness to hold it on. The heavy suit hurts my arm a bit, but I can live with it.

SageRat says this is all part of their plan. That since the parks are teeming with Shimmer operatives, this is our only choice. This way we can roam the parks freely and no one will think twice about us. Besides, these Disney characters draw children to them like blinking slot machines sucker in old ladies, and that should help me find Noah and Shelby even faster. Plus, Sage and Rat have to stay together and the Chip and Dale suits facilitate that.

After we're all geared up, the three of us put on our cartoon heads and wobble up the stairs into the Orlando heat. As soon as my fat yellow feet hit the cobblestones of Fantasyland, I'm mobbed. Little hands pull and tug at me. Shrill laughter echoes in my helmet. Kids shriek and jump up and down while their parents snap pictures. Top all this off with the fact that it's 101 degrees in the shade, and that I have no peripheral vision, and

I think this might be the dumbest thing I've ever agreed to do.

I used to think that these costumes were made like NASA space suits—all air-conditioned and shit. Well, they're not; I'm sweating to death in this thing. I can feel a heatstroke coming on.

I look over at Chip and Dale. They're hamming it up, acting all slapstick and chipmunky. Their movements are completely synchronized and the tourists seem to think this is some kind of gag. Then Chip and Dale hold hands and skip off down the way, waving and blowing kisses to the adoring crowd. Meanwhile, I just stand here with these screaming kids hugging and clinging to me like socks just out of the dryer.

I guess SageRat has the right idea. So I wave my puffy white gloves and put my hand over my mouth like I'm laughing. And it works. The kids slowly climb off and step back to watch me act like an idiot. I don't know what to do, really. I try these break dance moves that I learned in the eighth grade. All the little kids crack up and point. A Will Smith song comes on over the park's PA system.

And I bust a move.

I don't think these people have ever seen Mickey shake his thing like this before. I mean, I'm going full blown spastic. My break dancing has turned into something of this clumsy ass-shaking dirty-dancing grind.

And people are loving it. They're falling out, laughing and pointing.

I see this little rhinestone granny in tears with laughter. I bust a move over to her and get my groove on. To my complete surprise, she ups the ante and starts to bump and grind like she's some kind of rump-shaker in a rap video. I'm talking, granny puts her hands on her knees and does the bumpty-bump.

The crowd is roaring. This little old lady shakes that butt in front of this uptight dad. I try to do the Running Man and back away from the crowd. That's when I spot Valya, my fucking housekeeper. She's standing by the spinning Tea Cups. What the hell is she doing here? Shimmer must have snatched her up with Shelby and Noah. Leave it to Shelby to go into government protection and take the help with her.

While the crowd is busy watching dirty granny get it on with the uptight white guy, I break dance over to the Tea Cups.

Valya's just outside some gift shop, looking in the window at the glass figurines. I tap her on the shoulder, and she turns around and startles.

"Da, Mickey," she chuckles. "You bad, bad boy. You scare me."

I take her by the hand. She turns her cheek and blushes. I step back and bow like I'm asking her to dance. She covers her mouth and shakes her head no. But some of the crowd has followed me over here, and they're cheering Valya on. So she shrugs her thick shoulders with a girlish smile and agrees to waltz with Mickey.

Everyone goes wild, clapping and cheering for us. Valya buries her face in my shoulder. Then I dip her and she beams like a child. I dizzy her up real good, twirling and spinning her around. Then I waltz her past the Tea Cups, past this Old World facade, to the hidden employee entrance. She starts to panic and pulls away.

"Yah pa-za-VOO po-LEET-suh!" she shouts.

I grab her around the waist and I drag her heavy ass, kicking and screaming down the stairwell.

"Shhh. Valya. Calm down. It's me," I try to tell her. "Just listen."

But she will have none of that. She slaps and beats upside my big mouse head. She claws and spits, and even tries to bite me. When I finally wrestle her to the bottom of the stairs, she rears back and clobbers me in the stomach. I double over and then I get her big fat Russian knee in the nuts.

"Ugh!" I grab my package and drop to my knees.

Valya shakes her chubby fists and spits on both sides of me. Then rattles off some kind of Russian pox and double-times it back up the stairs.

"Help! Duh Mickey Rat!" she howls. "It try to have its vay vit me!"

I hear the door upstairs slam behind her. I lean against the cinder block wall and try to catch my breath. I'm in so much pain I can barely see straight, but I manage to take this clunky head thing off.

I hear Valya bellowing at people in Russian all the way down here. It'll be just a matter of seconds before security comes looking for me. But who are they going to believe? Mickey Mouse, or some babbling Russian lady.

The more I think about it, I better get my ass back up those stairs. Disney security would never arrest me in front of people. So I put the heavy-as-fuck head back on my sore-as-hell neck, and I pull myself up the stairs. I go back out into Fantasyland, back out into the murderous heat, and this galaxy of sticky little hands, looking for my hysterical Russian maid and my family.

24

Magic Kingdom Come

I see Shelby. Or I think I see Shelby. I've been walking for the past hour in this rat suit, tripping through the bamboo-lined streets of Adventureland, so I'm a little punch drunk. Actually, I'm not even sure that it is her. She's got her back to me, and won't turn around. But her hair is crazy with curls. Her ass—tight. Her arms—full of shopping bags.

That's got to be Shelby.

Wait, if that's Shelby, then where's Noah? Where's my boy? I try to follow her, but all these kids and their parents keep getting in my way. Finally, I just say fuck it; I push past them and take off after Shelby.

Trying to run in these cartoon feet makes all these Brazilian kids point and laugh. They chase after me. There are thousands of them, all running like Carl Lewis on a sugar rush. They glom onto me like Velcro. I get up and try to push them away, but they think I'm playing tag or something. The more I knock them off, the more they keep coming back.

Shelby's backside walks farther and farther away, into the wet green leaves and artificial mists near the Jungle Cruise. She disappears into the crowd and my sweaty heart goes with her. I feel myself swooning on the edge of a blackout with all these little kids pulling me under.

"Shelby!" I call after her.

She doesn't turn around. My yelling only makes the Brazilian kids grow wilder and they start tearing me apart. Meanwhile, their parents just smile and take pictures. I try my best to throw the kids off me, but they're everywhere. One brown-eyed boy tugs at my gloves. Another pops my suspenders and laughs like the goddamn Lord of the Flies. Then they all dog-pile me until my knees give way. I fall onto the hot concrete with kids crawling all over me like ants. I can't breathe so well, and the Milky Way spins and pulses in my right eye.

"Winkin', Blinkin', and Nod," Rat and Sage say in telepathic stereo.

Chip and Dale are holding hands and skipping up to me. They bow their heads and everything gets thick and slow.

"Winkin', Blinkin', and Nod. Winkin', Blinkin', and Nod," SageRat sings.

The Brazilian kids fall off me and then twirl around like savage little ballerinas. SageRat holds up their hands, and the kids drop to the ground and curl up at my feet. Their parents drop their cameras and diaper bags and do the same. Adventureland is now full of tourists sleeping like bums in the middle of its pristine streets. I step over the bodies and flatfoot it into the Jungle Cruise mists, yelling Shelby's name.

However, it is not Shelby that I find. It's Ikshu. He's standing under a fig tree with his hands clasped around his prayer beads. He looks up at me and smiles his weird gray smile.

This was a trap, and I have bitten. Hard.

"I'll trade you a vodka bottle for your family." His Holy Vishnu head shines in the sun.

I just stand here frozen as the kids from the Jungle Cruise come up to me and expect me to put on a show, to dance or goof around. But I can't move. I can't even think.

"Your wife is ripe with Reed's child," he whispers in my mind.

I push all the kids behind me with my big white hands. I lower my mouse head and charge Ikshu like a bull. I knock his Holy Vishnu, Kalki the destroyer, psycho-killer, riddle-spewing ass on the ground. I land right on his chest and proceed to beat the ever living shit out of him. I can't stop hitting him even though my broken arm is killing me. I'm stoned on hate. Numb with anger. Ecstatic with rage. His nose cracks and black blood goes everywhere. I keep working him over and one of his creepy gray teeth goes flying and lands on the concrete.

I get my hate off. But Ikshu doesn't even act like I'm hurting him. In fact, this weird smile creeps across his face.

The sick fuck's enjoying this.

He spits out some blood and a couple of broken teeth.

"Not yet," he gasps.

I rear back to hit him. That's when the crazy mutherfucker pulls out this knife, and before I can stop him, he drives it into my back, just above my waist, into one of my love handles.

I don't really feel it go in. I just feel this uncomfortable pressure, and then this strange cramping. Something hot and wet drips down my side.

It's blood.

My blood.

I stand up. The crowd pixelates and blurs into this ugly Monet painting, and I hear Ikshu's mind echoing in my mouse head.

"Betrayal is a fierce initiation, my wayward son." He smirks.

"You stabbed me." I try to suck in as much air as possible. "You fucking bastard! You stabbed me!"

I'm bleeding. I'm hyperventilating. I'm dying.

I look over my shoulder, and see the handle of his knife sticking out of me. In a dizzy, this-is-not-happening sort of way, the knife reminds me of the pushpins in my corkboard at the office. Like it's stuck in something that belongs to me, but it's not me. I can't get my lungs to expand. I can't breathe. I look down at where Ikshu was. Only his dark blood is left. He's vanished.

The kids and their parents come back into focus. One dude is all in my face with his video camera. But the rest of the crowd is keeping their distance with their hands over their mouths and their kids' eyes. I can smell their disbelief. It smells like old bananas and cat food. They can't believe this is happening any more than I can. A wave of nausea hits me. I feel all twisted inside. I reach over to pull the knife out of me, but the pink-haired girl blisters out of nowhere.

"Don't. That would only make it worse." She glows like an angel.

She takes me by the cartoon hand, and leads me back underground, back to the abandoned room where Debra McFadden is tied up and sleeping off the Percodan. Sage and Rat are here, waiting for me. They take this Mickey Mouse contraption off my shoulders and cut me out of this suit. I'm drenched in sweat and smeared in blood.

"I think," my teeth chatter, "I'm going into shock."

"Don't be such a pussy. It's just a flesh wound." Rat does a bad Monty Python accent.

"Look the other way," he tells me.

"Huh? Why?"

Rat rips the knife out of my side.

"Shit! Fucker! Jeez! Fuckfuckfuck-fuck!"

Rat holds up the bloody dagger. It's got jagged teeth on it that tear you up when it's pulled out. Blood pours out of me and Sage presses a Roger Rabbit beach towel against the hole in my side.

"Where'd you get that?" I ask.

"Stole it," she says matter-of-factly. "From a gift shop."

"I'm too messed up," I slur, "to even ask why an albino would need to steal a beach towel."

"Like I didn't see this coming?" Sage rolls her eyes and pours hydrogen peroxide onto my bleeding love handle, and I scream for God to take me. Now.

"Good thing he got you in the side like that." Rat bends over and inspects my wound. "Looks like you had enough yuppie fat to keep it from hitting any of the good stuff."

"Get the Percodan out of my pocket!" I tell him.

"Can't, dumbass." He steps back and puts re-wetting solution into his black eyes. "It'll make us laugh."

He blinks the saline out. It almost looks like he's crying for me.

"Please!" I beg.

"How do you expect me to sew you up if I'm laughing?" Sage holds up this giant hooked needle. Rat strikes a match and Sage puts the tip of the needle into the flame. The red-hot metal sizzles when she pours hydrogen peroxide on it.

"Where the fuck did you get that?"

"Stole it from wardrobe."

"Like sister said." Rat tongues his fang. "We saw this coming."

"Then why the fuck did you let this happen?"

"Oh, my precious. No one can stop the future. The best you can do is prepare for it." She threads the needle. "And that's what we did."

"Now this is gonna hurt like hell," she says right before she squeezes my torn love handle together with one hand and drives the needle into my skin with the other. Rat holds me down with one of his judo holds. I yell and squeal and carry on as this needle the size of the fucking Empire State Building sews my flesh together. I feel a few tugs and twitches and she's done.

"Good as new." She licks my blood off her fingers.

I pass out. Cold.

In the blackness, there's this long hallway and a bright light at the end. Holy shit. I think it's the bright light that people on *Sally Jesse* talk about when their stomach stapling surgeries go south. It's the cliché of death that I'm barreling toward. I slam right into it. The white light scatters me like the colored bits in a kaleidoscope, making me feel all swirly and clean.

Fuck! I can't believe this shit. I just kicked the mutherfucking bucket.

I wake up with a sneeze. Feathers run across my face and tickle my nose.

I sneeze again. I open my eyes. There's a peacock dragging its heavy feathers past my face. I sit up and shake off my haze. I'm in a room full of silk tapestry and mountains of pillows, like an opium den or the inside of a genie bottle. The pink-haired girl is kneeling next to me. She's dressed like a belly dancer. I look up and see the blue mutherfucker, sitting quietly, blissfully, on a golden throne flanked by two real-life lions. It smells like lemon pies and honeysuckle in here.

"Wait a second, you're supposed to be dead." I touch the pink-haired girl's arm. It's warm and soft. Kind of sweaty.

I look over at the blue dude; he nods his head with a smile.

"I can't be dead." I look around at all the silk and fancy pillows everywhere. "I've got a wife and kid to save. I can't be."

"Calm down. You're not dead. Or at least you won't stay dead." She wipes the sweat from my forehead.

I study her face. It's pink and alive. "Is this some kind of near-death experience?"

"No," she smirks. "I'd say it's more like a near-life one."

I look over at the blue guy. He shoots me the peace sign and his lions roar and lick their chops.

I shudder. "What's he doing here?"

"He's God," she says.

"But he's the blue dude. He can't be."

"Oh, but He is."

"He can't be." I gulp. "Ikshu and the Holy Vishnus have

done all sorts of really sick shit. You can't tell me their blue dude is God."

"Look, Travis, Ikshu and the Holy Vishnus are no different than the Holy Roman Empire, or the Ku Klux Klan. Or even the Puritans. Or anyone who has ever waged a holy war. They fear. And, unfortunately, they fear God."

"What are you talking about?" I can't stop looking at the blue dude. "Ikshu doesn't fear God. He thinks he *is* God."

"I hate to break this to you, but he's halfway right," she says.

"What do you mean he's halfway right? Are you telling me that God is a wackjob serial killer?"

"No, Travis. That's not what I'm saying." She shakes her pink head. "But we are all children of God. Sort of like the cells in a body. Ikshu is also a cell in that infinite body."

"Well, if that's the case, Ikshu's a fucking cancer cell."

"Not a bad analogy."

"Then why doesn't God stop Ikshu?" I point at the blue guy.

"He is stopping Ikshu." She touches my cheek. "He just needs your hands to do it."

"God wants me to kill him?" I lean back from her intense stare.

"I never said that." She tilts her head and gives me a slow smile.

"Jesus, don't do this to me. Just talk to me in plain English. Just give me some straight answers."

"The answer is this, Travis. There is power and there is force." She widens her eyes. "Power overcomes force. Killing Ikshu would be force, not power."

"I just asked you not to do that. Don't give me some fuck-ing Bazooka Joe riddle and then expect me to act all Zen about it."

I clear my throat. For some reason I'm choking up. I think I'm about to cry. I have to bite my bottom lip to keep from los-ing my shit. I don't know why I'm doing this. It's like that time I saw Blythe's soul at Supper Club. Everything is so beautiful here. I can't stand it.

I glance over at the blue dude again. I feel bad for cussing in front of him. But he doesn't seem to care. He just looks at me with a smile as warm and penetrating as the sun.

"I can't tell you what to do, Travis." The pink-haired girl turns my face back to her. "I can only tell you how things are."

"What about this knife cut? Can you at least get God over there to heal it?" I reach around my side and feel the wet stitches. "It hurts."

"The question is, Travis, can you heal it?" she says. "Are you strong enough to apply the balm of forgiveness?"

"What the hell are you talking about?"

"I'm talking about Shelby." She looks at me sideways and sad-like. "Shelby and Reed."

"Look, Annie, I've had it with the goddamn Sunday School lessons! I've got a wife and kid to save!"

"No, Travis, I'm afraid you have an entire world to save." She reaches over and puts her finger on my lips. The wind blows the silk into my face. I feel heavy as lead, like a raindrop forming in a cloud. Then I fall through the pillows, through the sky, back to Orlando, back to the artificial beauty of the Magic Kingdom, through the limestone and dirt, down deep into the underground arteries of Disney World.

*　　*　　*

I wake up with Sage kissing me full on the lips. I throw her off me.

"Ugh!" I wipe my mouth. "Jesus! What are you doing?"

"Mouth to mouth." She smooths her tongue across her teeth. "You went into shock. You stopped breathing."

"She's coming to." Rat points at Debra McFadden, gagged and bound next to me on the concrete floor.

"Oh, she's such a nuisance." Sage twists a strand of her white hair. "Let's just kill her and be done with it already."

"My pleasure." Rat raises his foot over Debra's neck.

"No!" I shout. "Don't!"

He holds his foot in midair.

"No, don't, what?" His black eyes glisten.

"Don't kill her," I say.

"Look, Travis." He puts his foot back down on the ground. "I can appreciate the bleeding heart shit. Really, I can. But this ain't no day at the country club. This bitch is serious. She's ex-CIA. She can kill you with her hands."

"She's tied up."

"Not really, dumbass." Rat points at Debra. "As long as she's alive she's a loose end. One that could come back and bite us in the ass."

"We can't kill anyone." I feel tears welling up in my eyes, but I don't know why.

"Travis, are you fucking crazy?" Rat throws up his hands. "The whole purpose of your existence is to whack Ikshu."

"I'm afraid Brother-lovely is right." Sage puts her hand on my shoulder. "Everything augurs that you are the nemesis. You're supposed to kill Ikshu. It's your destiny."

"But the pink-haired girl said I shouldn't." I look back at

Sage. "She gave me some riddle about right and wrong."

"Are you talking about Annie?" Sage asks.

"Yeah, Annie. Her ghost speaks to me. I just saw her when I passed out."

"Look, dumbass, I knew Annie." Rat looks at his boots and then at Debra's neck. "Sweet chick, but she didn't know shit about being a spy. She was a free-love hippie chick. And that's why she's dead."

"Like it or not, Travis," Sage lets out a heavy sigh, "this is war. There will either be casualties on our side or their side. You pick."

"I don't want to pick. I just want my family back."

"Then I suggest you start by removing the obstacles that stand between you and your family." Rat raises his foot. "We can start with this one, squirming right here on the floor."

"I said don't!" I jerk him away from Debra. "We need her. Maybe she'll talk."

"Good luck." Rat pushes me off him. "Ikshu has locked her head up."

"I'll take my chances." I lean down and rip the tape off Debra's mouth.

"Fire!" she screams. "Fire!"

"Oh, shut the fuck up." Rat kicks her in the stomach.

Debra doubles over and groans. I look at Rat like he's a psycho.

"It worked, didn't it?" He toys with the frilly lace around his sleeves and inspects his black fingernails.

I kneel back down and touch Debra's shoulder.

She spits a loogy in my eye. I wipe her snot away and try my best to stay calm.

"You're all gonna die!" she shouts. "You're all gonna roast like pig-pig-piggy pigs!"

I stand up and step away from her. She's thrashing and struggling against her bindings. She looks like a caterpillar wiggling on the ground after someone sprayed it with Raid.

"Let me handle this," Sage breathes in my ear.

"Don't kill her." I grab Sage by the wrist.

"Okay." She looks at me and tries to jerk away. "No kill."

I let her go and hold my fists, ready to step in if things get out of hand.

"Like pigs, huh?" Sage leans over Debra. "I've never seen an albino pig before. Perhaps you mean I'm going to roast like a rabbit. You know, an albino rabbit. I'm sure you've seen one. They've got marvelous ruby eyes. Quite the lovelies, really. In fact, most albinos are beautiful. Don't you agree, Debra?"

"No! They're frigging hideous!" Debra's eyes sparkle with hate. "Like you! You ugly twat!"

"Nice mouth, McFadden." Rat walks over to Sage and ribs her. "You kiss Ikshu with that mouth?"

Debra doesn't answer, she just spits and cusses and writhes on the cement floor.

Rat and Sage hold hands and kiss. When they are done, they open their eyes and they are one. They are SageRat.

"Your evil cannot pollute me." Debra squeezes her eyes shut. "I am Kalki's handmaiden. I am pure."

"Tell it. Tell it. Tell it," SageRat chatters. "Tell it. Tell it. Tell it. Tell it."

This causes Debra to have a fit. A big one. We're talking a grand mal extra grande. Foaming mouth, banging head, rolling eyes, piss-your-pants kind of seizure. But it's in between the spazzing about and the gnashing of teeth that we learn why Ikshu is really here.

"H-bombs!" she gags. "Mushroom clouds! Fireworks! Shattering this illusion created by the rat to be fed on by pigs!"

"What the hell is she talking about? H-bombs? Pigs feeding off rats?" I look at SageRat. "What the fuck?"

"Is it not obvious? Ikshu's meat puppets have planted nuclear bombs all over Disney. He's going to destroy the capitalistic dream that Americans feed off."

"Ikshu has the bomb? That's fucking crazy."

"Indeed it is." SageRat glares at Debra.

Debra's eyes tick back and forth. Slow, and then fast like a rattlesnake's tail. She hacks and chokes for a couple of seconds.

Then her head drops dead to the floor.

"I told you not to kill her!" I look at SageRat in disgust.

"I didn't kill her," they say. "The truth did."

25

When You Wish Upon a Bomb

I watch Rat cram Debra's body into my bloody Mickey Mouse suit.

"Someone just died here. Shouldn't we do something? A last rite, or at least say a prayer, or an 'I'm sorry'?"

"No." Rat doesn't turn around; he keeps dressing the body.

"Why are you doing that to her?"

"Well, dumbass." He struggles to put the puffy gloves on Debra's hands. "If someone does come in here—say, security or someone like that—they'll find Mickey taking a nap, not some dead lady lying in her own shit."

"Oh, look!" Sage picks up a plastic card off the floor "This must have fallen off her."

I grab the card from Sage and read it.

"It's a key card for the Grand Floridian." I have visions of the Hotel Del Coronado in San Diego—all red roofed and turn-of-the-century white. That's what I was seeing back in Dallas. That's why I thought they were in California. The Grand Floridian is a knockoff of the Del Coronado. That's where Ikshu's keeping my family.

"Where is this?" I hold up the card to Sage.

"Just outside the Magic Kingdom. Why?" She takes it from me and inspects it.

"How do we get there?" I ask.

"The Monorail, I guess." She looks at Rat.

Rat glances back at her and readjusts Debra's head against the wall.

"Then let's go!" I throw open the door and motion them to hurry their asses up.

The three of us run through the tunnels and pop up on Main Street. But there's a wall of people between us and the exit.

It's a parade.

Everyone is stoned on calliope music and goofball floats. We push and shove our way through. Sweaty parents cuss us. Babies cry at the sight of us. Meanwhile, Rat starts lifting people's wallets and replacing them with his phony-baloney lottery tickets.

"Would you stop that!" I grab his wrist in mid-snatch.

"We need money." He pulls away from me.

"No, we don't!" I grab him by the wrist again, and drag him through the parade-goers. He doesn't resist. He knows I'm right. Plus in just those few seconds the little judo freak stole more wallets than he can carry.

We finally make it to the Monorail station. Most everybody is back watching the parade, so the lines are short. But they still aren't moving fast enough. So I cut us to the front of the line. People bitch and moan. Then they get a good look at us— me with my blue hair, Sage with her albino skin, and Rat with his black eyeballs—and they get over it pretty fast.

When the Monorail finally does arrive, people get off on the other side, and then the doors swoosh open on our side. The three of us rush to the front. I look around, ready to commandeer some kind of controls, but there aren't any to commandeer. The cockpit is in another cabin. It's like a subway in here. Just a bunch of public seating and rails to hold on to. All I can do is stand and wait. After what seems like hours, days, weeks, months, years, decades, the doors slide shut and this electric train hushes over the topiaries and everglades.

Sage and Rat sit down and count their stolen loot. They start trading the credit cards like baseball cards.

"I'll give you two Visa Golds for that Platinum Master-Card." Sage passes the cards to Rat. He shakes his head and pushes them back to her.

"I can't believe you two!" I throw up my hands. "Ikshu could be doing something to my family right now. Right fucking now! And you guys are fucking around!"

They both ignore me, and go about pilfering the stolen wallets.

I take a deep breath and look out the window. I try to get a grip. Then out of nowhere, Debra McFadden forces herself into my head. She sits heavy on my shoulders and makes me feel sad for her. I tell her to go into the light. But she'll have none of that. She's crying and confused and won't listen.

I tell her that there's a room full of pillows and silk. I tell her it smells good in the light, like lemon pies. That it makes you feel swirly inside. But she just screams and bolts out of my head, leaving me chilled and confused myself.

I feel sorry for her. She was Ikshu's meat puppet and now she's dead. She died for what she believed, or rather what Ikshu made her believe. I guess if your own beliefs don't get you, someone else's will. Hell, it's not H-bombs that are the problem here; it's the crazy beliefs that incite people to set them off.

What the hell? My wife and kid are hanging in the balance, and here I am obsessing about Debra McFadden. Screw that. God, or the blue dude, or whoever, picked the wrong guy to play the martyred saint. I am not holy dead guy material. The pink-haired girl meant well, but I don't know who she's kidding. There's got to be a time to kill.

It's called survival of the fittest.

I can't just sit back and play Buddha while Ikshu slaughters millions of innocent people. That fucker's got to die. I don't care what made Ikshu this way. If the blue dude wants to use my hands to stop Ikshu, he's going to have to understand that my hands come attached to this brain. And this brain says Ikshu's going down.

Anyway, the Monorail glides into the Grand Floridian. The air brakes jerk and hiss, and the sliding doors wish themselves open. I run out of here and into the big white hotel, leaving Sage and Rat behind gathering up their stolen cash and credit cards.

Inside the lobby, bellhops run around with brass trolleys full of expensive luggage. Everyone here is tan and beautiful.

Well, at least I know I'm at the right place. *These are definitely Shelby's people.* It's like the return of the Highland Park veal people. And they make the memories of my life in Dallas sting me. I miss my family. I miss my golf clubs. I miss my beer. I miss being one of these charmed-lifers.

I shake off feeling sorry for myself and pull the key card out of my pocket. I take a good look at it and the damn thing doesn't have a room number. This place is huge. How the hell am I going to find them? Then I feel the card vibrate and pulse between my fingers. It talks to me in this Morse code. It tells me that it belongs to room 4 dash 3 dash 5.

I run to the elevators. I push the button, over and over like this will somehow prime the elevator through the shaft. The happy families keep their distance from me and my considerable BO. I am a stinky blue-haired bum and I scare them. I am everything that these people have come here to get away from. I am riddled with the tragic contagion, and these kind folks are smart. They stay away so that they don't get any on them.

When the elevator does finally arrive, everyone stands back and lets me get on by myself. It's a long ride for just four floors. The doors slide open and I run down the hall to 435. I don't knock. I jam the key card in and out of the slot. The tiny light blinks green and I bust in.

"Holy shit." I freeze.

Ikshu has a knife to Shelby's throat. I see this, but I don't. This isn't—can't be happening. I'm numb and crazy and wired. And then my heart stops. Where's Noah? I scan the room, but he's not in here. I immediately think the worst. *He's dead.* My knees go rubbery.

"Welcome to end of Kalyuga." Ikshu talks through Shelby's mouth. "Welcome to Armageddon."

"Where's Noah?" I'm shaking so hard that my vision is blurry. I try to imagine ice water running through my veins. I try to force-feed myself to be brave. Now is not the time to be freaked. Now is the time for courage and ice water calm. But unfortunately, I'm just seconds away from shitting my pants.

"I have eaten him with some fava beans and a nice dry Chianti." Shelby's eyes roll back in her head. She twitches, like she's trying to resist Ikshu's control.

"He's lying," the pink-haired ghost murmurs. "Noah. Safe. Valya. Dumbo ride."

The pink-haired girl pulls back this veil in my mind, and for a split second I have a vision of my boy riding the floppy-eared elephant. I hope I didn't just imagine that.

God, please let that be true.

"Ikshu, let her go. I'll do whatever you want. Just let her go."

"Oh, no, Travis Anderson, it is I who serve you. I, who bring to you what you want." It's Shelby's voice, but Ikshu's words.

The bastard is showing off.

Shelby whimpers. Ikshu's psychic boa constrictor uncoils from around her brain.

"Every fear that you wallowed in, every jealousy you delighted in, I brought to you," he says with his own mouth.

"What?"

"You were suspicious. I made your suspicions real. You were insecure. I brought you insecurity. You didn't trust anyone. I gave you no one to trust. You wanted to be the hero. I became your villain."

"Let her go, Ikshu!" I try to light up my chakras, but can't. "Please, you can take me. Just let her go."

"But Shelby is a slut, Travis." Ikshu licks Shelby's cheek. "I have heard you think it many times."

Shelby weeps. She's scared shitless. Tears pour down her cheeks as Ikshu presses the knife against her throat.

"I'll come back to Shimmer," I stammer. "I'll remote view. I'll do whatever you want me to. Just don't do this."

"There is no bargaining with me, Travis Anderson. I am God." His eyes flicker and burn. "You have sent me your prayers of hate and destruction and I am going to answer them."

"What do you want from me?" I stare at him. I pray for his head to explode. But nothing happens. That's when Sage just all of a sudden accumulates behind me.

I turn around, and she's so white she's almost glowing.

"So my precious Ikshu has a new play pretty, I see." Sage puts her hands on her hips.

"You!" Ikshu points his knife at her. "You will be next!"

"I think not, my dark lord." She bows her head and her white hair swings forward.

And then CRASH!

Rat explodes through the French doors. In this flurry of glass and drapes, Rat's foot connects with Ikshu's head. Before I can even think, Sage grabs Shelby's arm and twirls her away from Ikshu's knife. Meanwhile, Ikshu is thrown to the floor. Rat lands on top and opens his can of aikido-brand whup-ass on Ikshu. Sage passes Shelby off to me. She's shaking and crying and out of her head with fear. So I whisper to her that everything will be okay. But she can't hear me over her own sobs and Rat's battle cries.

I grab Shelby by the arm and pull her out of the room. We run down the hall and leave Sage and Rat to their business with Ikshu. Once we get to the elevators, Shelby's shaking so hard I'm afraid she's going into shock.

"It's okay. It's okay." I try to hug the shivering out of her. "We're going to get Noah and Valya and get out of here."

"What's happening?" she sobs. "Where am I?"

She grabs on to me. She cries hard into my neck. I just hold her and stroke her hair.

"Shhh, everything's going to be okay," I lie.

I hear Rat scream bloody murder. Then Sage comes running out of the room, down the hall after us.

"He's getting away!" she yells. "He's getting away!"

"How?"

"He sprayed brother with Mace!" Sage is all out of breath. "And then he went out the window!"

"I don't give a fuck about Ikshu, I'm going to get Noah!"

"Focus, Travis, focus." Sage shakes me. "You have to find Ikshu first!"

"No! I've got to find Noah!"

"I'll find him. You are the nemesis. You must stop Ikshu!"

"What the fuck? Why? Why me?"

"You have to. I've seen it!" she pleads. "Otherwise he's going to kill us all!"

"Fuck! Fuck! Fuck!" I throw up my hands.

"Look, I'll take Shelby back to the Dolphin. Then I'll find Noah."

"He's with Valya at the Dumbo ride." My stomach drops to the floor just thinking about not being able to go after Noah.

"Shelby." I shake her lightly to get her to stop freaking. "This is Sage. She's going to take you back to the hotel."

Shelby tries to suck it up, but then she takes one good look at Sage and faints. I check her breathing. She's okay, but she's out cold.

I pass her over to Sage. I kiss Shelby on the cheek, and then I run back to the room.

I hear the shower running.

"Which way did he go?" I run into the bathroom. Rat has his face under the shower.

"Fuck if I know! The bastard sprayed me!" he says.

I notice Ikshu's wooden prayer beads on the floor. I pick them up and try to get them to talk.

They start to hum and pulse. They're speaking to me in Hindi. I can't make out what they're saying. And just as I'm about to throw the beads back on the ground, they begin to pull me like they're magnetized to something.

"Rat! Come on! I know where he went!"

"I'm not going anywhere!" he yells back. "I think the Mace melted these contacts to my eyes!"

I feel bad for Rat, but I can either help him or I can save the world.

So I go solo.

I let the wooden beads pull me out of the Grand Floridian, to the Monorail, all the way to Epcot, to the giant golf ball called Space Ship Earth.

Ikshu's prayer beads pull me inside, through the maintenance doors, past security, and up a thin ladder that leads to the roof. As I'm climbing, my hands sweat and I'm overcome by the height. I look down and then wish I hadn't. I start to shiver. I drop Ikshu's beads into the blackness. I'm hanging here from this ladder that's hanging from the ceiling. A ceiling that's a good seven stories up. Just thinking about how high up I am makes me want to scamper my ass back down, and forget about all this. Let Ikshu blow this place up. I'm not climbing outside and crawling around the top of this golf ball thing. I don't do heights. I have vertigo so bad that I feel like I'm falling, over and over.

And over and over.

It's really hard to get a sure grip with this cast on. The dizziness overtakes me, and my cast slips off the rung.

"FUCK!" I scramble to grab back on before my other hand slips away and I fall. My heart goes diving after those lost beads, but I manage to grab back on to the thin metal ladder. I cling to it like it was my own skeleton.

I just have to crawl up ten more feet. Then I can kill the psycho mutherfucker and be done with this. If I don't climb up this ladder that psychopath is going to nuke us all. No seeing Noah go to kindergarten. No pulling his first tooth. No reading him to bed. No Little League. No nothing. Ikshu has the power to stop me from living my life. And that's something I won't give him no matter how much of a pussy I am about high places. He's taken enough of my life. Now it's time for me to take his.

So I take it rung by rung.

Rung by mutherfucking rung.

It's a long, shaky ascent, but I get to the top and open the hatch. I pull myself up and through to the roof. The wind

blows all around me and I grip the hot white tiles with everything I've got. The top of this ball slopes off pretty fast. One
wrong move and I go splat. I'm so high up I can see all the
Magic Kingdom's lights twinkling as the day turns orange.

At the sloping edge of this giant globe, I find Ikshu, sitting
cross-legged and chanting.

"Okay, pig fucker." I try to crawl over to him on my hands
and knees. But I start to slide off the dome. I scramble to re-
gain my hold. My heart is beating in my head, ballooning out
of my ears. I keep seeing myself go splat on the concrete
below. I'm sweating so bad, it's dripping in my eyes and fucking up my vision.

"You shouldn't fear death, Travis Anderson. You, like all
these people, are mired in the carnality of this world. This car-
nival of pain. This festival of materialism."

"Oh, shut your cakehole, Ikshu." I find some piping and
hold on to it for dear life. "I've had it with the fucking
proverbs, okay."

"Oh, Travis my son, you think too much. Your mind is the
monster, not me."

"Ikshu, come on, man. Let's just get down from here."

Ikshu ignores me and starts chanting his humma-humma
bullshit. So I crawl out away from the roof hatch. I put one
hand in front of the other. The wind blows dust in my eyes and
I have to shut them for a second. It takes a while, but I very
carefully make it over to where Ikshu is sitting. I try my best
not to look down.

Then my sweaty palms slip and I start to slide. I freak so
bad I almost spit out my heart. I try to scramble back up, but I
can't get my footing again. I'm sliding over the edge!

Without even thinking I grab onto Ikshu's bedsheet. He's anchored to a metal rod and he grabs me by my good wrist. He keeps me from going over. My muscles feel like they're ripping off the bone. Ikshu lets out a big groan and begins to slowly pull me up. I kick and struggle to get back to safety.

"I am your savior." He smiles at me and his hollow eyes reflect the Disney lights.

I want to pull away, but if I do, I'm history.

I hold on to Ikshu for dear life and he heaves and hoes me back up.

After I get situated, we both just sit here. Ikshu starts chanting again while I try to stop shaking. I'm so rattled I can barely breathe. I try to look at anything except the swirling ground below.

"Ikshu, please. Let's just get down and talk about this." I fold my arms in an effort to stop shivering.

He smirks. "I made your wife betray you."

"What?" I feel like he just hit me in the head with a two by four.

"I was the tiny voices in your dreams. I was the alligator in the pool. I am the betrayal swelling in her womb."

"Shut up!" The gongs of madness clang and echo. The jungle drums beat faster and faster like machine guns.

The Jiffy Pop explodes.

I lose it.

What little remains of my sanity—of my contact with reality—goes flapping out of my head like bats chasing after moths.

The fucker used his remote influencing bullshit to rape my wife. He made Reed rape my wife!

Rage boils all around me and everything else just falls

away. I keep seeing everything Ikshu has taken away from me. My wife. My boy. My life. This horrible vision keeps looping over and over in my head.

"I have tasted your wife many times, Travis Anderson."

Everything burns red and bloody.

I lunge at the bastard-fucker-son-of-a-bitch.

I go for his throat. If the asshole wants to die, I'll be more than glad to oblige.

I squeeze my hands around his neck and he chokes and gags. I actually am enjoying this. I'm actually getting off on killing this bastard. Then I notice a small scar on Ikshu's chest, right over his heart. And then everything stops, like someone just slammed on the brakes. I get visions of Draco's left arm with all its mushroom clouds and apocalyptic shit.

This buzz of psychic knowledge courses through me.

And that's when it hits me.

This is how Ikshu's going to do it. This is why he wants me to kill him. He's gotten someone to surgically implant some kind of heart monitor in his chest. And when his heart stops, it will send a radio signal to detonate the bombs all over the park. This is his twisted way of playing Jesus or Kalki or whoever he thinks he is.

Ikshu is the bomb and I'm supposed to be the fuse.

A very short fuse.

26

Apocalypse Maybe

"No!" I yell. "No! I won't!" I roll off Ikshu, and just lie here on my back. Meanwhile, he sits up and looks at me. He's choking, gasping for air. Tears are running down his face. He's obviously a little confused.

"What are you doing?" he growls at me. "It is karma!"

"Just give me a second, okay?" I'm trying to make sense of all this crazy shit. Did I just see what I think I saw? Ikshu's heart is wired to set the bombs off? Maybe I'm just crazy? Maybe I should just off the bastard and be done with this?

"We don't have a second!" He starts coughing. "You must kill me, Travis Anderson, it is destiny."

All I can do is sit here and hold my shaking hands. I look over at this Holy Vishnu dude. I almost killed him. I wanted to kill him. I wanted to choke the fuck out of him. I was getting off on seeing his eyes bulge and his tongue swell. For those few hot seconds I was a murderer.

What am I saying, *wanted to*. I still want to kill the fucker. But I can't. He's fixed it to where I can't.

"Goddamn it!" I shout.

I sit up and start to slowly rock back and forth and I watch the sun drop into the horizon while the Florida sky rolls black and blue. I take a couple of deep breaths and look at Ikshu again. He's still trying to catch his breath. So I figure if I keep looking at the sky maybe this will all disappear like the sun just did.

Or maybe it won't.

Then all of a sudden these big-ass spotlights flash on. They shine all over Space Ship Earth, causing sheets of June bugs, moths, and mosquitoes to swarm. Meanwhile, people are gathering down below, hooting and hollering at us. The assholes must think we're up here to put on a show or something.

"Do you hear the voices calling?" Ikshu looks up at the bruised sky and then at me.

"Who?" I cling to the white tiles.

"The Fates. They are calling you to your destiny, Travis Anderson."

"No. No, they're not."

"But they are. For you are the Judas who would betray me, the Pontius Pilate who would martyr me." He covers his mouth and snickers. "You even have blue hair, just as my teachers said you would."

"Look, Ikshu." I look over the edge, and then immediately wish I hadn't. "I'm just some guy who wants his family back. So let's just get down from here and we can play *Jesus Christ Superstar* on the ground if you want."

"No, I do not want."

"Then what? What the fuck *do* you want?"

"What do I want?" He lowers his gaze like he's trying to re-mote control me. "I want to free this world from its prison of meat and sex. That is what I want, Travis Anderson. And you are going to help me do it. You are my nemesis."

"No, I'm not." I stare back at him.

"It is your dharma. You are the mortal hubris that will ig-nite chaos incarnate."

"Where do you get this shit?"

Ikshu pauses.

"It is karmic law," he says. "From my devastation, purity will be reborn."

"Says who?"

"It has been prophesied." He puffs up his chest.

"By who?" I ask. "The fuckheads who put a three year-old in a closet with a bunch of starved rats? Is that who told you this shit?"

He doesn't answer. I think I hit a nerve.

"Have you ever considered the fact that you might not be God? That maybe somebody got their hands on you and really messed you up? Have you?"

"You know, Travis Anderson, the relationship between Krishna and Radha was an adulterous one." He looks at me with cold snaky eyes. "Not unlike the one I had with your wife this lifetime. Adulterous, yet divine."

"Alright, Ikshu!" I feel the hate surge into my hands. "I know what you're doing."

"Debra and I taught your wife the most intricate of con-gresses. Perhaps when you get down from here, your wife can show them to you."

The fury churns and blows in me like a hurricane. I want to kill the mutherfucker. I want to kill him so bad it hurts, but instead I sit on my hands and try to think how I can get out of this.

"I am God. I do not need you." Ikshu stands up and stretches his arms out. It makes me dizzy just watching him. "I will simply jump."

"No!" I reach out for the air around him.

He keeps taking steps forward.

The pills in my pocket rattle and shake. They scream for me to take them. They tell me the only way for me to fix this is to take them.

All.

The stupid little pills tell me I have to OD. It's the only way, they say. They tell me I'm the one who gets to play Jesus here. Not Ikshu. I'm the crazy dumb saint who gets to die.

That's just my mutherfucking luck. The only way to save Noah and Shelby is die for a bunch of candy-ass bastards at Disney World.

Great.

So I take out the ugly amber bottle, rip off the childproof cap, and chugalug the little fuckers. I start to choke on them, but manage to swallow them all down.

"One way or another, Travis Anderson. It is destined." He stands there on the sloping edge.

"No! Don't!" I plead.

"That is the divine plan." He looks back at me. "But if you will not cooperate, then you leave me no other choice but to jump."

"No, my lord!" I do my best cult member impersonation. "I am Vishnu's humble servant!"

"Do not lie to me, Travis Anderson." He puts his hand over his scarred chest. "I am Ikshu. I am become Death, Shatterer of worlds."

"I would not lie. I am your proud servant." I bow my head.

I'm obviously speaking his language, because he's smiling like he's got a woody.

"I'll be glad to kill you." I try to make my eyes look empty and spooky like his.

"Do you understand? Do you really understand, Travis Anderson?" He steps away from the edge and I can breathe again. This is almost too easy. The psycho starts to giggle as he sits down next to me. He's sweating out cumin and curry. Jesus, please don't let this be the last thing I smell.

And then, POW!

A spiderweb of white fire rains down in front of us. Pop-pop-pop! A blue umbrella of shooting stars sprinkles the sky. Green lasers dance and cherry fireballs supernova.

It's Epcot's IllumiNations.

POP-POP-WHISTLE-POP!

"Ah, yes." Ikshu's face shines in the glow. "It is time. The universe is saying it is time, Travis Anderson."

The Percodan is making my eyes roll back in my head. I took at least twenty of those fuckers and still Ikshu is just barely smiling.

"Just wait. Just wait until the finale." I beg. "Just wait."

"Yes, it will be a most beautiful finale. A grand finale indeed." He smiles, but doesn't laugh. "What a wonderful synchronicity Brahma has gifted me with."

I try my hardest not to pass out. I fight sleep, but I'm getting the shit beat out of me by the sandman. My eyes flutter;

my head nods. So I pray. I pray for laughter. I pray for a plague of it.

But nothing comes.

Not even a smirk.

The Percodan pulls me under, and the fireworks slap me awake. I think I hear laughter. I look over at Ikshu and he covers his mouth. He giggles just a little, and then a lot. He falls back cackling, and begins to slide down the slope. I have visions of him falling to the ground, and then this vaporizing flash burning the flesh off a theme park full of skeletons.

I grab his bedsheet and do my best to hold on. But he's heavy for a vegetarian fucker. And I'm drugged and out of shape. My hands and arms feel like they're about to snap. Ikshu laughs his ass off as the Disney fireworks burst and sparkle all around us. I can hardly keep my head up, much less keep Ikshu from falling. I pray for a burst of superhuman strength, the kind you hear about mothers getting when they have to push a car or boulder off their babies. But it doesn't come. God doesn't seem to be in the mood for any fancy parlor tricks tonight. No angels sent to catch me. I just have these two weak hands and this Percodan buzz, and that's it.

So I reach over and grab Ikshu's wrist. He jolts and gasps like I hit him with a car battery. Which causes me to almost lose my hold on him. I struggle to pull him next to me, onto a more level spot. I think about Noah and Shelby. I let my love for them be my anchor. But love is simply not enough.

I've got to get Ikshu to help.

"Ikshu, you can't die like this. You have to let me kill you. It's our destiny!" I strain and struggle to pull him back up the roof.

He looks up from his laughter and nods his head. He starts trying to crawl back up.

Somehow every nerve and sinew I have holds on. My weak spaghetti arms inch Ikshu up the slope. It's not a miracle by any stretch. But it's good enough to keep him from blowing this place to kingdom come. And that's all I'm asking for right now.

As I pull Ikshu back up, I hear this hiccupy roar from below. I look down and see all of Epcot busting a gut. People are hysterical, pointing and laughing at us. And I remember the blue dude's letter, the letter from the golf dream. Something about being present when there's laughter. That's why he told me not to kill. This freaky laughter was the only way to stop Ikshu.

Ikshu struggles back up to where I am. He's gets back to where it's safe. So I keep holding on to him while he howls. I let the Percodan sing its dopey song while my morphic resonance does its thing. I lie here dying as Ikshu laughs and convulses so hard that he passes out.

And then I do the same.

The last thing I remember before everything went black is a big fat rainbow explosion, and the whap-whap noise of helicopters. I also halfway remember thinking about a random passage from *On the Road*. Something about only wanting to be around people who were like Roman candles. *What the hell was Kerouac thinking?* Fuck hanging out with people who are like Roman candles. They'll just blow up in your face. From here on out, if I somehow don't die, I only want to know boring middle-of-the-road mutherfuckers. No more vampires. No more CIA fucks. No more Kalki the destroyer wannabes.

Then everything went fuzzy and disappeared.

*   *   *

I wake up and find myself strapped to this bed. I'm alone in a white room. A hospital room. I hope it's a hospital room. But there's no TV and there are no nurses around.

What if I've died and gone to hell?

I hurt. Bad. My stitches are torn, my wrist is broken, and my brain is swollen. I also have this chemical taste–sort of like bitter cherries–in my mouth. I have never felt so bad in my life.

This is hell. Or the outer rings of purgatory.

"Where am I?" I try to yell, but all that passes across my cracked lips is a painful hiss. My throat is shredded and dry.

The pink-haired ghost doesn't answer. The blue dude doesn't appear. The bed remains silent and still, and so do the walls. Nothing wants to talk to me. I should have never sent that bogus email to Shelby. This is my punishment for being psycho-jealous. This all started when I sent that goddamn email. None of this would have happened if I had just trusted her. If I had just ignored those bad dreams, I never would have screwed up my company. Then Reed would still be alive; Noah would still be in swimming lessons; Shelby would be at Neiman's; and I would be on the golf course with an iced-down twelve-pack.

"But then who would have saved the world?" Sage floats into the room, wearing a geisha girl robe.

"Sage?" I try to whisper, but it feels like I swallowed a handful of razor blades.

"Don't speak. Your throat's scratched up." She puts her long white finger on my lips. "They pumped your stomach. You OD'd."

I just look at her. She's bright pink. I think she's got a sun-
burn.

"Where's Noah and Shelby?" I panic.

"Relax. They're fine." Sage pushes me into my pillow.
"They're back at the hotel with Max and Rat."

"The bombs!" I strain. "What happened?"

"Tut-tut." She shakes her head and puts her finger over my
mouth again. "Solomon had the military come and get them.
Everything's fine. Nobody got hurt. The bombs are gone."

"Solomon?"

"Yeah, your car wreck knocked some sense into him. He
put a call in to the Pentagon. Talk about some panties in a
wad."

"What happened?"

"Shimmer deployed their helicopters. They put harnesses
on you and Ikshu and lifted you off the globe. Just barely got
you down, the pilot was laughing so hard."

"Where's Ikshu?" I mouth.

"Oh, the almighty asshole's in the room next to you." She
smiles a mean smile and points at the wall. "Your morphic resonance completely kicked his ass. The surgeons ripped that
heart monitor out of his chest and he's still in a coma."

I squint my eyes and shake my head.

"I guess being that close to you when you OD'd did something to his brain." She twists her long white hair. "He's a
drooling vegetable now . . . Looks like you were Ikshu's nemesis after all."

She sits down on my bed, and blots the sweat off my forehead with her silky sleeve. She smiles her kooky-fanged smile,
and for a split second, I think I see her soul because I don't see

a freaky albino Goth girl; I see someone beautiful in the most peculiar way. But then I start to focus on her zits, and my saintly feelings go out the window.

"So, Travis Anderson," she smirks, "you just saved the world, where are you going now?"

"I'm going home," I rasp. "Fucking home."

27
The End Is Near

You should have seen the looks on Jim and Lisel's faces when Noah, Shelby, and I walked into the dining room at the Lakewood Country Club, and sat down for lunch. It was priceless. I went out of my way to wave at them and smile. I even winked and gave them the ol' bang-bang with the fingers. But they wouldn't come over and say hello. They acted as if they'd seen ghosts. In fact, they scooped up their newborn baby girl and left.

I think they're a little embarrassed.

After our disappearance, Lisel tied these stupid plastic yellow ribbons around all the oak trees in our front yard. Then she looted our house. I'm not kidding. The crazy bitch took our dining room set, our wedding crystal, our silver, our bread maker, and my wide-screen plasma TV. Of course, Shelby's grieving mother let her. (Don't even get me started about the in-laws and the "estate sale" they had planned.)

I guess it's got to be sort of awkward for Jim and Lisel to have stolen from the dead, only to have the dead come back, and not be dead. But they better believe I'm going to ask for my shit back.

Fuckers.

Anyway. Shelby's due any day now. And we can't decide on a name. She likes the name Carmen. I think it sounds too much like karma, and I've had enough of that shit to last a couple of lifetimes. So we're still up in the air on that. As far as who's the daddy, that's still up in the air as well. She fucked Reed. So it could be his, but then again it could be mine.

Shelby's all sorts of torn up about it. I tell her that it's okay, that Ikshu was in her head. But she still cries about it. A lot. Which in a sick way sort of makes me feel better. Anyhow, this whole experience has completely fucked her up. Her therapist will be a very rich man after this is all said and done.

I tell her, listen, it doesn't matter what happened in the past. What matters is that a little girl is coming into this world to be our daughter, and I'll be damned if Ikshu is going to hurt her with things that he made us do in the past. I tell Shelby what's done is done is done. And Shelby kind of sucks it up and smiles a little.

Today is what's important, I tell her. And today we have it all. We have Noah's big smiley eyes to stare into. We have his hugs and kisses at bedtime. We have his funny, and not-so-funny, fits that he pitches in the middle of restaurants and stores. And soon we'll have our little girl. We have it all, I tell Shelby. We have our lives back. And that is worth so much more than what we think life should have been.

Not to get all mushy, but when you face down something as

crazy as Ikshu, like I did, something breaks inside of you. Something hard and brittle gives way and you get tender and mushed up. You do weird shit. You get weepy over sunsets, or your heart breaks every time you see your son sleeping. You get your kicks from little things like eating a watermelon with your hands, or taking a leak in your own bathroom. You just get sort of calm and find your happiness wherever you can grab it. It sounds stupid as shit, I know. But that's what happens, I swear.

As far as Shimmer goes, they bought out Anderson-Bindler.com at a hundred dollars a share. Which means they own my company now. But I let them do it. I've decided to work for them. I figure it's the best way to watch Solomon and the rest of those stupid fuckers. That way I can make sure they don't create another Ikshu.

The weird thing is the poison that Ikshu spread didn't just go away when he went into a coma. The CIA and Pentagon bigwigs that he influenced are still programmed with his Kalki the destroyer bullshit. I'm working with Solomon to find these guys and try to deprogram them. So far we've found a five-star general and two Pentagon officials with Ikshu shrines in their closets.

Solomon is pretty much clear of Ikshu's infestation. I think the wreck did it for him. But he does every now and again crave curry, and that kind of worries me. As far as Sage and Rat go, well, they stayed at Disney World. They got jobs wearing those stupid suits. They dress up as Chip and Dale and go around the park all day, hugging and playing with all the veal families. Sage told me wearing that chipmunk suit is as close to normal as she's ever felt. She says she wants to do it for the rest of her life. And Rat's right there with her. So that's kind of a happy ending, I guess.

Personally, I've given up on happy endings. Waiting for things to be perfect is dangerous. You'll miss life if you wait too long. Yeah, I've given up the Perc, but I still want a beer or two or maybe twelve. And I have to fight that urge every hour of every day. Truth be told, I still find myself driving by liquor stores when things get too big to handle. But somehow I've remained sober. At least so far.

And if things weren't crazy enough, Noah got dropped from all his waiting lists for private schools. The assholes in the admissions office said they thought he was dead and if we do sign him up again, we get bumped to the bottom. Bastards. However, I think they just might change their minds once they meet me in person—if you know what I mean.

Actually, Noah's waiting lists are really the least of my worries. The DA is going to bring charges against me for Reed's murder. I've already seen it in a dream: the arrest, the fingerprinting, and the trial. Talk about a major pain in the ass. Between paying for my defense and Shelby's credit cards, we won't have a pot to piss in. But Solomon promises me that Shimmer will get me out of this.

I told him, they better. Or somebody's ass is calling *60 Minutes*.

Oh yeah, and Valya quit last week; she went back to Russia. She told Shelby that she had had enough of America. So I spend a lot of my time helping out with Noah, which means I don't have time to build Web sites for extra cash. But it's not like Shelby's going to have to get a job giving pedicures to her friends at Highland Park Village or anything. We're strapped, but not that strapped. At least not yet.

But you know what? That's good enough. I don't need a

happy ending. I just need my wife and kids. I'm not even worried about going to trial for Reed's murder. I'm sure Solomon or some CIA bigwig will help me get out of it. And if not, there's always my morphic resonance.

So no worries. That's my new motto. I mean, after you've fought evil bare-fisted and broken-armed on top of the Epcot ball, everything else is kind of anticlimactic.

And I mean that in a good way.

Acknowledgments

This book would not exist in this beautiful hardcover incarnation without my bilocating editor Denise Roy; super-ninja agent Jenny Bent and her wonder assistant Michelle Blackley; über-lawyer Elaine English; the astonishing Ann Asprodite; the soulful Grant Morris; the unstoppable Bob Bookman; the rain dancing David List; the eternally gracious Sylvie Rabineau; the magical Jane Garnett; the preternatural David Gordon Green; and the mysterious Michael London.

Unmitigated gratitude goes to Meredith Butler and H.O. for building and hosting PsychicCow.com. May Vishnu flood your web design firm with oceans of clients and may He send them directly to www.emby.org.

My eternal appreciation to my Wednesday Night Writers' Group: Christine and Barry Phillips, David Norman, Harry Hunsicker, Victoria Calder, Amy Bourrett, Brooke Malouf, Ashwinee Bhatt, Rick Silvestre, Jack Ewing, Jan Blankenship, Alan Duff, Erika Barr, Fanchon Knott, Sandy Sadler, and Doris Elaine Sauter.

Special thanks: Leslie Murphy at Legal Grounds in Dallas for pimping my books and for inventing The Suzanne Special; Neal Pollack and Ben Brown for their hospitality at BookPunk; Mary Jo McCabe, you said this would happen; Perry and Michele Tongate for the hookup; Matt Spett, Murad Kalam,

Lisa Berg, Ann Pearson, Olga Arseniev, and Hal Dantzler for enduring years of me talking about this novel and myself.

My unabashed thanks to Southern Methodist University's Continuing Education Creative Writing Program, and Bread Loaf Writers' Conference.

Mad props to my family for putting up with my bullshit. Thanks Grant and Heidi, Dan and Karen, Josh and Denise, Mom and Dad.

Finally and most importantly, thank you Michelle for being so good to me.

Oh yeah, let's not forget God. Thanks, God.

About the Author

Will Clarke doesn't want you to know where he lives or what he's doing next.